Cursed be Atli
King of evil
of glory naked,
gold-bereaved;
gold-bereaved,
gold-tormented,
murder-tainted,
murder-haunted!"

Fires of madness
flamed and started
from eyes of Atli;
anguish gnawed him:
'Serpents seize him!
snakes shall sting him.
Naked cast him
in the noisome pit!'"

There gleaming-eyed
Gudrún waited;
the heart within her
hardened darkly.
Grimmood took her,
Grimhild's daughter,
ruthless hatred,
wrath consuming.

There grimly waited
Gunnar naked;
Snakes were creeping
silent round him.
Teeth were poisoned,
tongues were darting;
in lidless eyes
light was shining.

A harp she sent him;
his hands seized it,
strong he smote it;
strings were ringing.
Wondering heard men
words of triumph,
song up-soaring
from the serpents' pit.

There coldly creeping
coiling serpents
as stones were staring
stilled, enchanted.
There slowly swayed they,
slumber whelmed them,
as Gunnar sang
of Gunnar's pride.

As voice in Valhöll
valiant ringing
the golden Gods
he glorious named;
of Odin sang he,
Odin's chosen,
of Earth's most mighty,
of ancient kings.

A huge adder
hideous gleaming
from stony hiding
was stealing slow.
Huns still heard him
his harp thrilling,
and doom of Hunland
dreadly chanting.

An ancient adder
evil-swollen,
to breast it bent
and bitter stung him.
Loud cried Gunnar
life forsaking;
harp fell silent,
his heart was still.

To the queen that cry came
clear and piercing;
aghast she sat
in guarded bower.
Erp and Eitill
eager called she:
dark their locks were,
dark their glances.

Stanzas 131–140 in the manuscript of the New Lay of Gudrún

THE LEGEND OF
SIGURD AND GUDRÚN

WORKS BY J.R.R. TOLKIEN

THE HOBBIT
LEAF BY NIGGLE
ON FAIRY-STORIES
FARMER GILES OF HAM
THE HOMECOMING OF BEORHTNOTH
THE LORD OF THE RINGS
THE ADVENTURES OF TOM BOMBADIL
THE ROAD GOES EVER ON (WITH DONALD SWANN)
SMITH OF WOOTTON MAJOR

WORKS PUBLISHED POSTHUMOUSLY

SIR GAWAIN AND THE GREEN KNIGHT, PEARL,
     AND SIR ORFEO
THE FATHER CHRISTMAS LETTERS
THE SILMARILLION
PICTURES BY J.R.R. TOLKIEN
UNFINISHED TALES
THE LETTERS OF J.R.R. TOLKIEN
FINN AND HENGEST
MR BLISS
THE MONSTERS AND THE CRITICS & OTHER ESSAYS
ROVERANDOM
THE CHILDREN OF HÚRIN
THE LEGEND OF SIGURD AND GUDRÚN

THE HISTORY OF MIDDLE-EARTH
BY CHRISTOPHER TOLKIEN

I · THE BOOK OF LOST TALES, PART ONE
II · THE BOOK OF LOST TALES, PART TWO
III · THE LAYS OF BELERIAND
IV · THE SHAPING OF MIDDLE-EARTH
V · THE LOST ROAD AND OTHER WRITINGS
VI · THE RETURN OF THE SHADOW
VII · THE TREASON OF ISENGARD
VIII · THE WAR OF THE RING
IX · SAURON DEFEATED
X · MORGOTH'S RING
XI · THE WAR OF THE JEWELS
XII · THE PEOPLES OF MIDDLE-EARTH

THE LEGEND OF
SIGURD AND GUDRÚN

J.R.R. Tolkien

Edited by Christopher Tolkien

HOUGHTON MIFFLIN HARCOURT
BOSTON • NEW YORK
2009

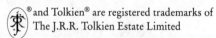
Library of Congress Cataloging-in-Publication Data
Tolkien, J. R. R. (John Ronald Reuel), 1892–1973.
The legend of Sigurd and Gudrún / by J.R.R. Tolkien ; edited by Christopher Tolkien.
p. cm.
"First published in Great Britain by HarperCollins Publishers, 2009."
ISBN 978-0-547-27342-6
I. Tolkien, Christopher. II. Title.
PR6039.032L44 2009   821'.912—dc22   2009007552

Printed in the United States of America

DOC 10 9 8 7 6 5 4 3 2 1

CONTENTS

FOREWORD

FOREWORD

In his essay *On Fairy-Stories* (1947) my father wrote of books that he read in his childhood, and in the course of this he said:

> I had very little desire to look for buried treasure or fight pirates, and *Treasure Island* left me cool. Red Indians were better: there were bows and arrows (I had and have a wholly unsatisfied desire to shoot well with a bow), and strange languages, and glimpses of an archaic mode of life, and above all, forests in such stories. But the land of Merlin and Arthur were better than these, and best of all the nameless North of Sigurd and the Völsungs, and the prince of all dragons. Such lands were pre-eminently desirable.

That the ancient poetry in the Old Norse language known by the names of the *Elder Edda* or the *Poetic Edda* remained a deep if submerged force in his later life's work is no doubt recognised. It is at any rate well-known that he derived the names of the dwarves in *The Hobbit* from the first of the poems in the Edda, the *Völuspá*, 'the Prophecy of the Sibyl' – remarking in a lightly sardonic but not uncharacteristic tone to a friend in December 1937:

3

I don't much approve of *The Hobbit* myself, preferring my
own mythology (which is just touched on) with its consistent
nomenclature . . . to this rabble of Eddaic-named dwarves out
of *Völuspá*, newfangled hobbits and gollums (invented in an
idle hour) and Anglo-Saxon runes.

But it is certainly not well-known, indeed scarcely known at
all (though it can be discovered from existing publications), that
he wrote two closely associated poems treating of the Völsung
and Niflung (or Nibelung) legend, using modern English fitted
to the Old Norse metre, amounting to more than five hundred
stanzas: poems that have never been published until now, nor
has any line been quoted from them. These poems bear the
titles *Völsungakviða en nýja*, the New Lay of the Völsungs, and
Guðrúnarkviða en nýja, the New Lay of Gudrún.

My father's erudition was by no means confined to 'Anglo-
Saxon', but extended to an expert knowledge of the poems of
the Elder Edda and the Old Norse language (a term that in
general use is largely equivalent to Old Icelandic, since by far
the greater part of Norse literature that survives is written in
Icelandic). In fact, for many years after he became the professor of Anglo-Saxon at Oxford in 1925 he was the professor of
Old Norse, though no such title existed; he gave lectures and
classes on Norse language and literature in every year from
1926 until at least 1939. But despite his accomplishment in this
field, which was recognized in Iceland, he never wrote anything specifically on a Norse subject for publication – except
perhaps the 'New Lays', and for this, so far as I know, there

is no evidence one way or the other, unless the existence of an amanuensis typescript, of unknown date and without other interest, suggests it. But there survive many pages of notes and draftings for his lectures, although these were for the most part written very rapidly and often on the brink of illegibility or beyond.

The 'New Lays' arose from those studies and belong to that time. My inclination is to date them later rather than earlier in his years at Oxford before the Second War, perhaps to the earlier 1930s; but this is scarcely more than an unarguable intuition. The two poems, which I believe to have been closely related in time of composition, constitute a very substantial work, and it seems possible, as a mere guess, since there is no evidence whatsoever to confirm it, that my father turned to the Norse poems as a new poetic enterprise after he abandoned the Lay of Leithian (the legend of Beren and Lúthien) near the end of 1931 (*The Lays of Beleriand*, p.304).

These poems stand in a complex relation to their ancient sources; they are in no sense translations. Those sources themselves, various in their nature, present obscurities, contradictions, and enigmas: and the existence of these problems underlay my father's avowed purpose in writing the 'New Lays'.

He scarcely ever (to my knowledge) referred to them. For my part, I cannot recollect any conversation with him on the subject until very near the end of his life, when he spoke of them to me, and tried unsuccessfully to find them. But he briefly mentioned the work in two letters to W.H. Auden. In that of 29 March 1967 (*The Letters of J.R.R. Tolkien*, edited by Humphrey Carpenter, no.295), thanking Auden for sending his translation of the *Völuspá*, he said that he hoped to send him in return 'if I can lay my hands on it (I hope it isn't lost), a thing I did many years ago when trying to learn the art of writing alliterative poetry: an attempt to unify the lays about the Völsungs from the Elder Edda, written in the old eight-line fornyrðislag stanza' (that being the name given to the Norse alliterative stanzaic metre used in the greater number of the 'Eddaic' poems, the 'Old Lore Metre'). And in the following year, on 29 January 1968, he wrote: 'I believe I have lying about somewhere a long unpublished poem called *Völsungakviða en nýja* written in fornyrðislag 8-line stanzas in English: an attempt to organise the Edda material dealing with Sigurd and Gunnar.'

To 'unify', to 'organise', the material of the lays of the Elder Edda: that was how he put it some forty years later. To speak only of *Völsungakviða en nýja*, his poem, as narrative, is essentially an *ordering* and *clarification*, a bringing out of comprehensible design or structure. But always to be borne in mind are these words of his: 'The people who wrote each of these poems [of the Edda] – not the collectors who copied and excerpted them later – *wrote them as distinct individual things to be heard isolated with only the general knowledge of the story in mind.*'

It may be said, as it seems to me, that he presented his interpretation of the sources in a mode that can be received independently of the doubts and debates of 'Eddaic' and 'Nibelung' scholarship. The 'New Lays' themselves, elaborate poems closely modelled in manner as in metre on the 'Eddaic' lays, are therefore paramount; and they are presented here in plain texts without any editorial interference; all else in the book is ancillary.

That there should be, nonetheless, so much else in the book requires some explanation. It may be felt that some account should be given of the actual nature of my father's distinctive treatment of the legend. To provide a comprehensive account of the much discussed problems that he sought to resolve would lead all too easily to the first appearance of the 'New Lays' after some eighty years with a great weight of scholarly discussion hung about their necks. This is not to be thought of. But it seems to me that the publication of his poems provides an opportunity to hear the author himself, through the medium of the notes with which he prepared for his lectures, speaking (as it were) in characteristic tones on those very elements of doubt and difficulty that are found in the old narratives.

It must also be said that his poems are not at all points easy to follow, and this arises especially from the nature of the old poems that were his models. In one of his lectures he said: 'In Old English breadth, fullness, reflection, elegiac effect, were aimed at. Old Norse poetry aims at *seizing a situation*, striking a blow that will be remembered, illuminating a moment with a flash of lightning – and tends to concision, weighty packing of the language in sense and form . . .' That 'seizing a situation', 'illuminating a moment', without clear unfolding of narrative sequence or other matters with a bearing on the 'moment', will be found to be a marked characteristic of the 'New Lays'; and here some guidance may be looked for in addition to the brief prose statements that he added to some of the sections of the *Völsungakviða en nýja*.

After much deliberation I have therefore provided, at the end of each poem, a commentary, which is intended to clarify references, and passages that may seem obscure; and also to point out significant departures made by my father from the Old Norse sources or between variant narratives, in such cases indicating his views, where possible, by reference to what he said in his lectures. It must be emphasized that nothing in those notes suggests that he had written, or had it in mind to write, poems on the subject himself; on the other hand, as one might expect, congruence between the views expressed in his lecture notes and the treatment of the Norse sources in his poems can often be observed.

As a general introduction in this book to the Elder Edda I have cited at length a more finished lecture with that title; and following this I have contributed brief statements on the text of the poems, the verse-form, and some other topics. At the end of the book I have given a brief account of the origins of the legend and cited some other related verses of my father's.

In thus making much use of my father's notes and draft discussions on 'the Matter of Old Norse', and the tragedy of the Völsungs and the Niflungs, hastily set down and unfinished as they are, I have chosen to try to make this book, as a whole, as much his work as I could achieve. Of its nature it is not to be judged by views prevailing in contemporary scholarship. It is intended rather as a presentation and record of his perceptions, in his own day, of a literature that he greatly admired.

In the commentaries I refer to the two poems as 'the Lay of the Völsungs' (*Völsungakviða*) and 'the Lay of Gudrún' (*Guðrúnarkviða*). But in the title of the book, *The Legend of Sigurd and Gudrún*, I have taken up the subordinate title that my father gave to the *Völsungakviða* on the opening page of the manuscript, *Sigurðarkviða en mesta*, 'the Longest Lay of Sigurd', on which see p.234.

The sections of this book are each preceded by drawings made by Mr Bill Sanderson. These are derived closely from wood carvings that adorn the wide door-posts of the twelfth century church of Hylestad in the south of Norway, which are now preserved in the Oldsaksamlingen of the University of Oslo.

The scenes depict in continuous vertical series on each side of the doorway the story of Sigurd's most famous deed, which in the Lay of the Völsungs is told in section V, *Regin*: the slaying of the dragon Fáfnir, which gave him the name *Fáfnisbani*. The carvings begin with the forging of swords by Regin the smith and their testing. Then follow the slaying of Fáfnir; Sigurd tasting his blood with his finger, which enabled him to understand the voices of the birds (stanza 41 in the Lay); the slaying of Regin (stanza 45); and Sigurd's horse Grani, famous in legend, foal of Sleipnir, the mythical horse that Ódin rode: he is shown here laden with the treasure of the dragon, although not portrayed by that artist as so huge a burden as it is in the Völsunga Saga and in the Lay (stanza 48). The continuous carving ends with a different scene: Gunnar playing the harp in Atli's snake-pit (the Lay of

Gudrún, stanza 135): in this version playing it with his feet, his hands being bound (see p.330).

⬥

It will be seen that there is no reference in this book to the operas of Richard Wagner that are known by the general title of *Der Ring des Nibelungen,* or *The Ring.* For his work Wagner drew primarily on Old Norse literature. His chief sources, known to him in translation, were the lays of the Poetic Edda and the Saga of the Völsungs, as they were my father's also. The great epic poem *Das Nibelungenlied,* written about the beginning of the thirteenth century in Middle High German, was not a source for Wagner's libretti in at all the same sense as were the Norse works, though this may be superficially disguised by his use of German name-forms (Siegfried, Siegmund, Gunther, Hagen, Brünnhilde).

But Wagner's treatment of the Old Norse forms of the legend was less an 'interpretation' of the ancient literature than a new and transformative impulse, taking up elements of the old Northern conception and placing them in new relations, adapting, altering and inventing on a grand scale, according to his own taste and creative intentions. Thus the libretti of *Der Ring des Nibelungen,* though raised indeed on old foundations, must be seen less as a continuation or development of the long-enduring heroic legend than as a new and independent work of art, to which in spirit and purpose *Völsungakviða en nýja* and *Guðrúnarkviða en nýja* bear little relation.

⬥

INTRODUCTION

INTRODUCTION

Many years ago my father referred to the words of William Morris concerning what he called 'the Great Story of the North', which, he insisted, should be to us 'what the Tale of Troy was to the Greeks', and which far in the future 'should be to those that come after us no less than the Tale of Troy has been to us.' On this my father observed: 'How far off and remote sound now the words of William Morris! The Tale of Troy has been falling into oblivion since that time with surprising rapidity. But the Völsungs have not taken its place.'

It is obviously desirable that a theme and a mode become so exotic should be 'introduced' in some fashion; and for this first publication of my father's 'Norse' poems I have thought that it would be both interesting and suitable if such an introduction could be provided by the author rather than the editor.

Nowhere in his Norse papers is there any reference whatsoever to the New Lays, except for a collection of four small slips of paper of unknown date on which my father hastily wrote interpretative remarks about them (they are given on pages 51–55). While of great interest in themselves they do not constitute any large view of the mode and matter of his Norse lays in an historical context; and in the absence of any such writing I have ventured to include here a substantial part of the opening lecture (with the heading *General Introduction*) of a series in the English Faculty at Oxford titled *The 'Elder Edda'*.

It is to be borne in mind that this is the draft and record of a spoken lecture to a small audience. No thought of publication could be remotely present. His purpose was to communicate his vision in broad clear strokes. He set the Edda forcibly within a large temporal context, and eloquently conveyed his own conception of this poetry and its place in the history of the North. In other lectures, on particular poems or specific topics, he expressed himself, of course, with caution; but here he could be bold, or even extravagant, not hedging every statement with qualifications in a subject where disagreement over doubtful evidence dogs the steps. Indeed, 'perhaps' and 'probably', 'some hold' and 'it may be thought', are notably absent from this account as he wrote it.

My impression is that this was a relatively early writing; and he added later a number of qualifications to his original statements. There survives also an earlier and much rougher draft lecture with the title *Elder Edda*. This was expressly delivered to a 'club', unnamed; but it was the basis of the much developed lecture of which a part is given here. My father treated that first text in a characteristic manner, retaining phrases amid much rewriting and addition, and produced a new manuscript. It can hardly be doubted that the lecture in its earlier form was what he read, with that title, to the Exeter College Essay Society on 17 November 1926. But how long a time elapsed between the two texts it is impossible to say.

It is primarily in order to hear the voice of the author of the poems presented in this book, writing (in order to speak) personally and vitally of the Poetic Edda, on which he has never been heard since he last lectured on Old Norse at Oxford some seventy years ago, that I print it here, in its later form.

The text is rapidly written and not at all points perfectly legible, and it is here slightly edited and somewhat shortened, with a few explanations added in square brackets and a few footnotes.

INTRODUCTION TO
THE 'ELDER EDDA'

The poetry that goes by this misleading and unfortunate title attracts occasionally from afar people of various sort – philologists, historians, folklorists, and others of that kidney, but also poets, critics, and connoisseurs of new literary sensations. The philologists (in a wide sense) have as usual done most of the work, and their ardour has not more than usual (probably less than in *Beowulf*) been diverted from at least intelligent appreciation of the literary value of these documents.

It is unusually true here that a real judgement and appreciation of these poems – whose obscurity and difficulty is such that only the devoted labour of many philologists has made them available – is dependent on personal possession of a knowledge of the critical, metrical, and linguistic problems. Without the philologist, of course, we should not know what many of the words meant, how the lines ran, or what the words sounded like: this last is in old Scandinavian verse of possibly more importance even than usual. The poets expended an unusual share of their ingenuity in securing at any rate that the noise of the verse should be fine.

It remains true, all the same, that even robbed of their peculiar and excellent form, and their own tongue whose shape and peculiarities are intimately connected with the atmosphere and ideas of the poems themselves, they have a power: moving many even in school or pre-school days in filtered forms of translation and childish adaptation to a desire for more acquaintance.

There remains too the impact of the first hearing of these things after the preliminary struggle with Old Norse is over and one first reads an Eddaic poem getting enough of the sense to go on with. Few who have been through this process can have missed the sudden recognition that they had unawares met something of tremendous force, something that in parts (for it has various parts) is still endowed with an almost demonic energy, in spite of the ruin of its form. The feeling of this impact is one of the greatest gifts that reading of the Elder Edda gives. If not felt early in the process it is unlikely to be captured by years of scholarly thraldom; once felt it can never be buried by mountains or molehills of research, and sustains long and weary labour.

This is unlike Old English, whose surviving fragments (*Beowulf* especially) – such at any rate has been my experience – only reveal their mastery and excellence slowly and long after the first labour with the tongue and the first acquaintance with the verse are over. There is truth in this generalization. It must not be pressed. Detailed study will enhance one's feeling for the Elder Edda, of course. Old English verse has an attraction in places that is immediate. But Old English verse does not attempt to hit you in the eye.

To hit you in the eye was the deliberate intention of the Norse poet.

And so it is that the best (especially the most forcible of the *heroic* Eddaic poems) seem to leap across the barrier of the difficult language, and grip one in the very act of deciphering line by line.

Let none who listen to the poets of the Elder Edda go away imagining that he has listened to voices of the Primitive Germanic forest, or that in the heroic figures he has looked upon the lineaments of his noble if savage ancestors – such as fought by, with, or against the Romans. I say this with all possible emphasis – and yet so powerful is the notion of hoary and primeval antiquity which clings to the name (quite recent) *Elder Edda* in popular fancy (so far as popular fancy may be said to play with so remote and unprofitable a theme at all) that, though the tale ought to begin with the seventeenth century and a learned bishop, insensibly I find myself leading off with the Stone Age.

The Scandinavian lands, archaeology says, have been inhabited since the Stone Age (not to go into niceties of *palaeo* and *neo*). The cultural continuity has never been broken: it has been several times modified and renewed, from the South and East in the main. One seems more justified in Scandinavia – more justified than usual – in saying that most of the people now living there have always been there.

About 400 A.D. or earlier, our inscriptional (Runic) glimpses of the Northern tongue begin. But these people, though speaking a Germanic language – it would seem in a somewhat archaic form – did not take part in the great Germanic heroic age, except by ceasing to be Scandinavian. That is: the peoples whom later we call Swedes, Gautar, Danes, etc., are descendants of people who did not go off, as a whole, into the adventure, turmoil, and disasters of that period. Many of the peoples who did go came ultimately out of Scandinavia, but they lost all connexion with it: Burgundians, Goths, Lombards.

Echoes in the form of 'tidings', of strange news, and new songs imported ready-made, or made at home from the raw material of news, these peoples did receive from those now obscured and confused events. The material of tale and verse came to them – and found very different conditions in Scandinavian lands to those which produced them: above all they found no wealthy courts in the Southern sense, nor headquarters of powerful warlike forces, no great captains of hosts or kings to encourage and pay for poetic composition. And more, they found a different local store of mythology and stories of local heroes and sea-captains. The local legends and the local myths were modified, but they remained Scandinavian, and they could not if we had them, and still less can the tattered fragments of later disjointed memories of them, be taken as a compensation for the loss of nearly all that belonged to more southerly Germania, least of all as the virtual equivalent of those vanished things. Related they were, but they were different.

Then the matter became confused further by the development of a private Scandinavian heroic age – the so-called Viking age, after 700 A.D. The stay-at-homes took to ranging all over the earth – but without losing hold on their ancient lands and seas.

Though courtly conditions then arose, *epic poetry* never developed in those lands. The reasons are little understood – the answers to most really pertinent questions are seldom given – and at any rate we must here rest content with the fact. The causes may be sought in the temper of the times and of the people, and of their language which was the reflexion of them. It was not until relatively late that 'kings' in the North were rich enough or powerful enough to hold splendid court, and when this did come about the development was different – verse developed its local brief, pithy, strophic [i.e. stanzaic], often dramatic form not into *epic*, but into the astonishing and euphonious but formal elaborations of Skaldic verse [see pp.34–37]. In the Eddaic verse it is seen 'undeveloped' (if 'strophic' verse could ever anywhere at any time 'develop' into epic by insensible gradations, without a break, a leap, a deliberate effort) – undeveloped that is on the formal side, though strengthened and pruned. But even here the 'strophic' form – the selection of the dramatic and forcible moment – is what we find, not the slow unfolding of an epic theme.

The latter, so far as represented, was accomplished in prose. In Iceland, a Norwegian colony, there grew up the unique technique of the *saga*, the prose tale. This was chiefly a tale of everyday life; it was frequently the last word in sophisticated polish, and its natural field was not legend. This of course is due to the temper and taste of the audience rather than the actual meaning of the word – merely something said or told and not sung, and so 'saga' was also naturally applied to such things as the partly romanticized *Völsunga Saga*, which is quite unlike a typical Icelandic saga. To Norse use the Gospels or Acts of the Apostles are a 'saga'.

But in Norway at the time we are looking at Iceland was not founded, and there was no great king's court at all. Then Harald Fairhair arose and subdued that proud land of many stubborn chiefs and independent householders – only to lose many of the best and proudest in the process, in war or in the exodus to Iceland. In the first sixty years or so of that colonization some 50,000 came to that island from Norway, either direct or from Ireland and the British Isles. Nonetheless in Harald Fairhair's court began the flourishing time of Norse verse to which Eddaic poetry belongs.

This Norwegian poetry, then, is founded on ancient indigenous mythology and religious beliefs, going back heaven knows how far, or where; legends and folk-tales and heroic stories of many centuries telescoped together, some local and prehistoric, some echoes of movements in the South, some local and of the Viking age or later – but the disentanglement of the various strata in it would require for success an understanding of the mystery of the North, so long hidden from view, and a knowledge of the history of its populations and culture, that we are never likely to possess.

In form – and therefore probably also in some of its older content – it is related to other Germanic things. Of course it is in a Germanic language; but its older metres are closely connected with, say, Old English metre; more – it has formulas, half-lines, not to speak of names, and allusions to places and persons and legends, actually current independently in Old English: that is, it is a descendant of a common Germanic verse and tradition of verse which now escapes us: of neither the themes of this old Baltic verse nor its style have we anything left save the suggestions afforded by the comparison of Norse and English.

But this form in the Edda remained simpler, more direct (compensating for length, fullness, richness by force), than that developed, say, in England. Of course, it is true that however much we emphasize the Norwegian character and atmosphere of these poems it is not free from importation. Actually imported themes – such as pre-eminently the Völsung and Burgundian and Hun stories – not only acquired a leading place in the Edda, but may even be said to have received in exile their finest treatment. But this is because they were so thoroughly naturalized and Norwegianized: the very uprooting had set the tales free for artistic handling unhampered by history or antiquarianism, for recolouring by Northern imagination, and association with the looming figures of the Northern gods.

The only really important modification one must make is in favour of the Goths – difficult as it is to decipher the hints that survive the ages, it is clear that these people of Scandinavian origin but whom fate had marked out for a special history and tragedy were followed step by step by the people of the North, and became with their enemies the Huns the chief themes of poets – so much so that in later days *gotar* remained as a poetic word for 'warriors', when the old tales were overlaid and mingled with other matters. From the Goths came the runes, and from the Goths came (it would appear) Óðinn (Gautr), the god of runic wisdom, of kings, of sacrifice. And he is really important – for the astonishing fact that he is clearly un-Scandinavian in origin cannot alter the fact that he became the greatest of the Northern gods.

This is a sort of picture of the development. This popular local verse of intricate origin was then suddenly lifted up by the tide of Viking wealth and glory to adorn the houses of kings and jarls. It was pruned and improved, doubtless, in style and manners, made more dignified (usually), but it retained in a unique fashion the simpler pithier temper, a nearness to the soil and to ordinary life, which are seldom found in so close a connexion with the graces of 'court' – that is the mastery of the deliberate and leisured artist, even occasionally the pedantry of the genealogist and philologist. But this is in keeping with what we know of the kings of that court and their men.

It must be remembered that the time was a heathen one – still in possession of special, local pagan traditions which had long been isolated; of organized temples and priesthoods. But 'belief' was already failing, mythology and still more anything that could be more properly called 'religion' were already disintegrating without direct attack from outside – or perhaps better put, without conquest or conversion and without destruction of temples and pagan organization, for the influence of foreign ideas, and of the sudden rending of the veil over the North (rent by men from within) cannot be dismissed. This was a special transition-period – one of poise between old and new, and one inevitably brief and not long to be maintained.

To a large extent the spirit of these poems which has been regarded as (a branch of) the common 'Germanic spirit' – in which there is some truth: Byrhtwold at Maldon would do well enough in Edda or Saga – is really the spirit of a special time. It might be called *Godlessness* – reliance upon self and upon indomitable will. Not without significance is the epithet applied to actual characters living at this moment of history – the epithet *goðlauss*, with the explanation that their creed was *at trúa á mátt sín ok megin* ['to trust in one's own might and main']. [*Author's note, added later:* Yet on the reverse it must be remembered that this was applied only to certain commanding and ruthless characters, and would not in any case have been worth saying if many (indeed the bulk of) men had not remained believers and practitioners of pagan worship.]

This applies more to the *heroic*, of course, than the *mythological*. But it is not untrue of the mythological. Such tales of gods are of a kind that can well survive to a time when they are rather the themes of tales than the objects of cults, but yet to a time which has not replaced the gods by anything new, and is still familiar with them and interested in them. Nor of course was *blót* [heathen sacrificial feast] given up. Heathenism was still very strong, though in Sweden rather than in Norway. It had not suffered that uprooting from ancient fanes [temples] and local habitations that is so fatal to it – as it proved in England.

The end of the period began with the violent apostolate of that great heathen figure and hero of the North – the christianizing king Ólaf Tryggvason. After his fall, and the fall of many of the greatest men through him or with him, there was a relapse into heathendom. But this was quickly ended by the no less vigorous but far wiser christianizing efforts of Ólaf the Holy, which at the time when Edward the Confessor was reigning in England left Norway completely christianized, and the heathen tradition destroyed.

The tenacity and conservatism of the North, however, can be measured not only by the efforts which had to be made by such great figures as the Ólafs, but in other smaller ways: such as the survival of the runes, so closely if accidentally associated with pagan traditions, even after the North had learned to write in Latin fashion. This happened chiefly in Sweden, but all over Scandinavia runes remained in use (through direct tradition, not revival) for such things as memorial inscriptions down to the sixteenth century.

Nonetheless, after 1050, certainly after 1100, poetry dependent on the heathen tradition was in old Scandinavia moribund or dead – and this means Skaldic verse whatever its subject, quite as much as lays actually dealing with myths, for the Skaldic verse and language depended upon a knowledge of these myths in writer and hearer, both of whom were normally what we should call aristocratic – nobles, kings and courtiers after the Northern fashion.

In Iceland it survived for some time. There the change over (about the year 1000) had been rather more peaceful and less embittered (a fact probably not unconnected with removal and colonization). In fact poetry became a profitable export industry of Iceland for a while; and in Iceland alone was anything ever collected or written down. But the old knowledge swiftly decayed. The fragments, much disjointed, were again collected – but in an antiquarian and philological revival of the twelfth and thirteenth centuries. Perhaps it would be more true to say, not antiquarian revival, but kindly burial. This was a new piety which pieced the fragments together without completely understanding them: indeed we often feel we understand them better. Certainly the old religion and its attendant mythology as a connected whole or anything like a 'system' (if it ever possessed one, as is, within limits, probable) has not been preserved at all, and was certainly not within the reach of the great prose artist, metrical expert, antiquarian and ruthless politician Snorri Sturluson in the thirteenth century. How much is lost can be appreciated by anyone who reflects how little we know now of even the major details of the extremely important temples and their 'cultus' and the priestly organization in Sweden or in Norway.

The 'Younger Edda' or 'Prose Edda' of Snorri Sturluson was a pious collection of fragments – to help in the understanding and making of verse which needed a knowledge of myths – when gentle, even tolerant and ironic, learning had supervened upon the struggle between religions.

After that the gods and heroes go down into their Ragnarök,* vanquished, not by the World-girdling serpent or Fenris-wolf, or the fiery men of Múspellsheim, but by Marie de France, and sermons, medieval Latin and useful information, and the small change of French courtesy.

Yet the sixteenth and seventeenth centuries, at the darkest hour, saw a resurrection after Ragnarök, almost as if there were fulfilled in it the words which the *Völva* [the sibyl who

---

* The Ragnarök is 'the fate of the Powers', 'the doom of the Gods' in the Norse mythology; assimilation to a distinct word *rökr*, meaning 'usk', 'twilight', led to the interpretaion *Götterdämmerung*, the 'ght of the Gods.

prophesies in the Eddaic poem *Völuspá*] speaks concerning the rearising of a new earth, and the return of men and gods to find and marvel at the golden pieces in the grass where once were the halls in which the gods had played at chess [see the tenth verse of the poem *The Prophecy of the Sibyl* given in Appendix B].

The discovery of the fallen pieces of the old splendour was often accidental, and the research which led to the recovery proceeded from various motives. In England theological zeal was powerfully blended with the historical and linguistic curiosity which it begot by accident. In the North this was not so. But whatever the motives the result was not only the rescue from the wreck of time of such fragments as we have, but swift recognition of their virtue, and regret for the loss of more. This was specially so with the 'Edda'.

The salvage from the ruins left by natural losses, accidents of time, the heedlessness and forgetfulness of men, and the ravages of war and fanaticism (whether theological or classical) was scanty. Nonetheless the eighteenth century seems to have marked its disapproval of these 'Gothic' bones dug from their graves by two fires which contrived to destroy some part of what had been saved, and narrowly missed destroying all the best. In 1728 in the fire at Copenhagen much of what had there been collected went up in smoke. Three years later the Cotton collection in London was partly burnt. *Beowulf* was scorched badly. But it escaped, just – for the embarrassment of later Schools of English. At Copenhagen the finder's own parchment transcript of the manuscript of the Elder Edda seems to have been among the losses. Lost it is at any rate. But the manuscript itself survived. Yet the gods and heroes nearly found a final and fatal Ragnarök, which would have left our knowledge and estimate of northern literature in a totally different state.

When the 'Elder Edda' is mentioned, we practically mean a single manuscript – no. 2365 4° in the Royal Collection in Copenhagen: now known as the *Codex Regius (of the Elder Edda)*. It contains 29 poems. There are 45 leaves of it left. After leaf 32 a gathering, probably of eight pages, has been lost.* There appear to have been no losses at beginning and end – where losses frequently occur.

This is all we know about this remarkable survivor of time, fire, and flood. In 1662 King Frederick III of Denmark sent the well-known Thormod Torfæus with an open letter to the celebrated Brynjólfr Sveinsson. Since 1639 Brynjólfr had been bishop of Skálaholt in Iceland, and had been a keen collector of manuscripts. Torfæus was commissioned to get his help in collecting for the king materials for ancient history, and any antiquities, curiosities, or rarities that could be found in Iceland. In 1663 the bishop sent the choicest of his collection to the king. Among these now priceless treasures was the Codex Regius. Where the bishop had found it, or what was its previous history is unknown, except that he had picked it up twenty years earlier: for on the front page he had written his monogram and a date (LL 1643, i.e. Lupus Loricatus = Brynjólfr), just as we

---

* My father thought it probable that the loss was due to robbery of the 'Long Lay of Sigurd' (see p.234), supposed to have been the chief constituent of the poetry in the lost gathering.

should scrawl our name and a date on a new and interesting acquisition from a second-hand bookshop.

Two hundred and fifty years have followed[*] – of examining, puzzling, construing, etymologizing, analysis, theorizing, arguing and sifting argument, of asserting and refuting, until, short as are its contents, Eddaic 'literature' has become a land and a desert in itself. From all this study, amidst a vast disagreement, certain things have reached, more or less, the stage of authoritative consensus of opinion.

We now know, at any rate, that this collection of poems should not be called *Edda* at all. This is a perpetuation of an act of baptism on the part of the bishop in which he acted *ultra vires*. The collection had no comprehensive title at all so far as we know or the manuscript shows. *Edda* is the title of one of the works of Snorri Sturluson (died 1241), a work founded on these very poems, and others now lost like them, and it is the title of that work only, by rights; a work which is concerned primarily, even in the earlier parts which are cast in narrative or dialogue form, with the technicalities of Northern poetry, which for us it rescued from oblivion. The name is therefore quite inapplicable to a collection of actual antique poems, collected largely for their merits as verse, not as exemplars of a craft.

Beyond this we can say little about the manuscript. It appears that the Codex Regius belongs palaeographically to say about 1270 (early in the latter half of the thirteenth century), and is itself apparently a copy of an original belonging to 1200 (some

---

[*]   A round figure! – rounded down, whether my father was counting from 1643 or 1663.

say earlier). It belongs in fact actually as we have it to a period thirty years after the death of Snorri; but even if it were not a fact that Snorri used these very poems substantially as we have them, it is clear enough internally that the matter, the manner, and the language of the poems entitles them to the name 'Elder'.

As for when they were written, we have no information other than an examination of the poems themselves will yield. Naturally the datings differ, especially in the case of individual poems. None of them, in point of original composition, are likely to be much older than 900 A.D. As a kind of central period which cannot possibly be extended in either direction we can say 850–1050 A.D. These limits cannot be stretched – least of all backwards. Nothing of them can have been cast into the form we know (or rather into the forms of which our manuscript offers us often a corrupt descendant), except for occasional lines, allusions, or phrases, before 800. Doubtless they were afterwards corrupted orally and scribally – and even altered: I mean that in addition to mere corruption producing either nonsense, or at least ill-scanning lines, there were actual variants current. But in the main these things were the products of individual authors, who, whatever they used of old tradition, even older poems, wrote new things which had not before existed.

The antiquity and origin of the mythology and legends met in the poems is another matter. In general it is not really so important to criticism (however attractive to curiosity) to know what answers can be made to this sort of question, as it is to remember that wherever they got their material the authors lived in the last centuries of heathenism in Norway and Iceland, and treated their material in the style and spirit of those lands and times. Even formal etymology has seldom much to say, attractive though I personally find it. Even when, as often happens, we can equate a name with its form in other Germanic languages it does not tell us much. Thus *Jörmunrekkr* is *Ermaníks*, and his name an echo of the history of the Goths, their power and ruin [see pp.322–23, note to stanza 86]; Gunnarr is Gundahari, and his story an echo of events in Germany in the fifth century [see Appendix A, pp.337–39]. But this does not tell us much of the state in which these tales first reached the North, or the paths (certainly various) they came by. And still less does it help us to unravel the literary problems concerning the various treatment of the Burgundian theme in Scandinavia.

But intriguing as all this questioning is, we may end on the note we struck before: it is not of the first importance. Far more important than the names of the figures, or the origins of the details of the story (except where this helps us to understand what is unintelligible or to rescue a text from corruption) is the atmosphere, colouring, style. These are products only in a very small degree of the origin of the themes: they chiefly reflect the age and country in which the poems were composed. And we shall not be far wrong in taking the mountains and fjords of Norway, and the life of small communities in that disconnected land, as the physical and social background of these poems – a life of a special sort of agriculture, combined with adventurous sea-faring and fishery. And the time: days of the fading of a special, individual, pagan culture, not elaborate materially, but in many ways highly civilized, a culture which had possessed not only (in some degree) an organized religion, but a store of partly organized and systematized legends and poetry. Days of a fading of belief, when in a sudden changing of the world the South went up in flames, and its plunder enriched the wooden halls of the Norse chieftains till they shone with gold. Then came Harald Fairhair, and a great kingship, and a court, and the colonization of Iceland (as an incident in a vast series of adventures), and the ruinous wars of Ólaf Tryggvason, and the dying down of the flame, into the gentle smoulder of the Middle Ages, taxes and trade-regulations, and the jog-trot of pigs and herrings.

It may be that it was with that characteristic flourish that my father ended this lecture; at any rate (though the manuscript text continues, and soon turns to a consideration of individual poems) it seems a good place to end it here.

I append here a number of notes and brief statements on various topics that are best treated separately, as follows.

§1 The 'Prose Edda' of Snorri Sturluson
§2 The Saga of the Völsungs (*Völsunga Saga*)
§3 The text of the poems
§4 The spelling of Norse names
§5 The verse-form of the poems
§6 Notes on the poems by the author

§1 THE 'PROSE EDDA' OF SNORRI STURLUSON

The name *Edda* properly belongs only to a celebrated work by the Icelander Snorri Sturluson (1179–1241). This is a treatise on the distinctive art of Icelandic poetry which in Snorri's day was dying out: the old metrical rules disregarded, the old mythological knowledge essential to it attacked by a clergy hostile to any survival of heathendom. This book, in its three parts, is a retelling in prose narrative of ancient myths and legends; an account of, and explanation of, the strange diction of the old 'court poetry'; and exemplification of its verse-forms.

In my father's lecture (p.29) he noted that the application of the name *Edda* by Bishop Brynjólf of Skálaholt to the poems of the great Codex that he acquired in 1643 was without historical justification. In Brynjólf's time it had come to be supposed among Icelanders interested in the ancient literature that there must have been 'an older *Edda*' from which Snorri's work was derived. Brynjólf himself wrote in a letter in 1641, before he knew of the existence of the Codex: 'Where now are those huge treasuries of all human knowledge written by Sæmund the Wise, and above all that most noble Edda, of which we possess now, beyond the name, scarcely a thousandth part; and that indeed which we do possess would have been utterly lost, had not the epitome of Snorri Sturluson left to us rather the shadow and footprints than the true body of that ancient Edda.'

Sæmund the Wise (1056–1133) was a priest whose prodigious learning became a legend, but for the title *Sæmundar Edda* that Brynjólf gave to the Codex there was no foundation.

Thus arose the conception of the two *Eddas*, the Poetic or Elder Edda and the Prose or Younger Edda. Why Snorri's work was named *Edda* is not known, but there have been several explanations: by some it is related to the word *óðr* in the sense 'poem, poetry', as if it meant 'Poetics', by others derived from the place Oddi in south-west Iceland, a centre of Icelandic learning where Snorri grew up.

From the 'Poetic Edda' emerged the adjective *Eddaic* (and *Eddic*), used in contrast to *Skaldic* (a modern derivative from the Old Norse word *skáld* meaning 'poet'). Of Skaldic verse my father wrote in his lecture on the Elder Edda (p.20): 'It was not until relatively late that "kings" in the North were rich enough or powerful enough to hold splendid court, and when this did come about . . . verse developed its local brief, pithy, strophic, often dramatic form not into *epic*, but into the astonishing and euphonious but formal elaborations of Skaldic verse.' This 'court poetry', as it may also be called, was an extraordinarily intricate and distinctive art, with extreme elaboration of verse-forms subject to rules of exacting strictness: 'elaborations', in my father's words, 'in which various kinds of internal and final full-rhyme and half-rhyme both vocalic and consonantal are interwoven with the principles of "weight" and stress and alliteration, with the deliberate object of utilizing to the full the vigour, force and rolling beat of the Norse tongue.' To which must be added the huge poetic vocabulary, and the extraordinary cultivation (described below) of the device of the 'kenning'.

'To us,' he wrote, 'thinking of the Elder Edda, "Eddaic" means the simpler, more straightforward language of the heroic and mythological verse, in contrast to the artificial language of the Skalds. And usually this contrast is thought of as one of age as well: old simplicity of good old Germanic days, unhappily given up in a new taste for poetry become an elaborate riddle.

'But the opposition between "Eddaic" and "Skaldic" verse is quite unreal as one of *time,* as between older and younger, as of a fine old popular manner being pushed out by a younger, newer fashion. They are related growths, branches on the same tree, essentially connected, even possibly sometimes by the same hands. Skalds can be found to write in *fornyrðislag,* the oldest of old metres; Skaldic kennings can be found in Eddaic lays.

'All that remains true of this contrast of age is the fact that the simpler metres, e.g. *fornyrðislag* and the style that goes with it, are far older, much closer, for instance, to other Germanic things, to Old English verse, than the specially Skaldic verse and manner. The Eddaic poems we have belong to the same period as Skaldic, but the metrical traditions and style they employ carries on still, without fundamental alteration, something of the common Germanic tradition. Old and new in metre rubbed shoulders – it was as we have seen already a transition period, a period of poise between old and new, not maintainable for long [see p.23].'

It is the highly artificial Skaldic poetry that is the subject of Snorri's instruction in his *Edda,* and indeed by far the greater part of what survives of it owes its survival to him. In the second part of the book, *Skáldskaparmál* ('Poetic Diction'), he treats above all of kennings, with a great number of exemplifying verses by named skalds: but very many of these kennings are wholly incomprehensible without a knowledge of the myths and legends to which they allude – and such themes are not characteristically the subject of the Skaldic poems themselves. In the first part of the *Edda* (the *Gylfaginning*) Snorri drew extensively on Eddaic poetry; and in the *Skáldskaparmál* also he told the stories on which certain kennings rest. The following is a single example.

> *Hvernig skal kenna gull?* How shall gold be named?
>
> Thus: by calling it the Fire of Ægir; the Pine-needles of Glasir; the Hair of Síf; the Head-band of Fulla; Freyja's Tears; the Drop, or Rain, or Shower of Draupnir [Óðin's gold ring, from which dropped other rings]; Otter's Ransom; Forced Payment of the Æsir; . . .

Following such a list as this, Snorri gave explanations of these locutions.

> *Hver er sök til þess, at gull er kallat otrgjöld?* What is the reason that gold is called Otter's ransom?
>
> It is told that when the Æsir, Óðin and Loki and Hœnir, went out to explore the world they came to a certain river, and they went along the river to a waterfall; and by the waterfall was an otter . . .

And thus it is that we have the story of Andvari's Gold told both by the author of the *Völsunga Saga* and by Snorri Sturluson (see the Commentary on the Lay of the Völsungs, pp.188–91); but indeed Snorri here continued his narrative into a résumé of the whole history of the Völsungs.

It remains to add that the celebrity of Snorri's book in the centuries that followed, and most especially of the *Skáldskaparmál*, led, before the emergence of the Codex Regius, to the term *Edda* being widely used to mean, expressly, the technical rules of the old 'court' poetry, or 'Skaldic' verse. In those days poets complained of the tyranny of *Edda*, or offered apologies for their lack of proficiency in the art of *Edda*. In the words of Gudbrand Vigfússon: 'An untaught poet who called a spade a spade, instead of describing it by a mythological circumlocution, would be scouted as "Eddaless"' (*Eddu-lauss*, 'having no Eddaic art'). Thus the term 'Eddaic', as now used, *in opposition to* 'Skaldic', is a perfect reversal of its former meaning.

§2 THE SAGA OF THE VÖLSUNGS
(*Völsunga Saga*)

The Codex Regius of the Poetic Edda is a collection of poems of great diversity, composed by poets who lived centuries apart; but it was compiled and ordered with intelligent care. Most of the heroic poems are concerned with the story of the Völsungs and the Niflungs; and these the compiler of the collection arranged, so far as the diverse structure and scope of the individual lays allowed him, in a narrative sequence, adding explanatory passages in prose at the beginning and end of many of the lays, and narrative links in the course of them.

But much of the material thus arranged is of the utmost difficulty. Poems are disordered or defective, or even patchworks of different origin altogether, and there are very many obscurities of detail; while worst of all, the fifth gathering of the Codex Regius disappeared long ago (see p.28), with the loss of all Eddaic poetry for the central part of the legend of Sigurd.

In this situation, there is an essential aid to the understanding of the Northern legend. This is the *Völsunga Saga*, written, probably in Iceland, in the thirteenth century, though the oldest manuscript is much later: a prose tale of the fate of the whole Völsung race from the far ancestry of Sigmund, father of Sigurd, and continuing on to the fall of the Niflungs and the death of Atli (Attila) and beyond. It is founded both on Eddaic lays that survive and other sources now lost; and 'it is solely from the lays that it has used,' my father said in a lecture, 'that it derives its power and the attraction that it has for all those who come to it,' for he did not hold the author's artistic capacity in high regard.

This author was faced with wholly divergent traditions (seen in the preserved Eddaic lays) concerning Sigurd and Brynhild: stories that cannot be combined, for they are essentially contradictory. Yet he combined them; and in doing so produced a narrative that is certainly mysterious, but (in its central point) unsatisfying: as it were a puzzle that is presented as completed but in which the looked for design is incomprehensible and at odds with itself.

In the commentary that follows each poem in this book I have noticed many features in which my father departed from the *Völsunga Saga* narrative, more especially in the case of his Lay of the Völsungs, where the Saga is of much greater importance as a source. He seems not to have set down any critical account of the Saga as a whole, or if he did it has not survived; but comments of his on the author's work in individual passages will be found in the commentary (see pp.208–11, 221, 244–45).

§3 THE TEXT OF THE POEMS

It is at once obvious that the manuscript of the two lays is a fair copy intended to be final, for my father's handwriting is clear and uniform throughout, with scarcely any corrections made at the time of writing (and of very few of his manuscripts, however 'final' in intention, can that be said). While it cannot be shown to be the case, there is at any rate no indication that the two poems were not written out consecutively.

It is a remarkable fact that no more than a few pages survive of work on the poems preceding the final text, and those pages relate exclusively to the opening (*Upphaf*, the Beginning) of *Völsungakviða en nýja*, to section I 'Andvari's Gold', and to a small part of section II, 'Signý'. Beyond this point there is no trace of any earlier drafting whatsoever; but the earlier manuscript material is interesting, and I have discussed it in a note on p.246–49.

The final manuscript of the poems did however itself undergo correction at some later time. By a rough count there are some eighty to ninety emendations scattered through the two texts, from changes of a single word to (but rarely) the substitution of several half-lines; some lines are marked for alteration but without any replacement provided.

The corrections are written rapidly and often indistinctly in pencil, and all are concerned with vocabulary and metre, not with the substance of the narrative. I have the impression that my father read through the text many years later (the fact that a couple of the corrections are in red ball-point pen points to a late date) and quickly emended points that struck him as he went – perhaps with a view to possible publication, though I know of no evidence that he ever actually proposed it.

I have taken up virtually all these late corrections into the text given in this book.

There are two notable differences in the presentation of *Völsungakviða en nýja* and *Guðrúnarkviða en nýja* in the manuscript. One concerns the actual organization of the poem. The Lay of the Völsungs following the opening section *Upphaf* ('Beginning') is divided into nine sections, to which my father gave titles in Norse without translation, as follows:

I	Andvara-gull [Andvari's gold]
II	Signý
III	Dauði Sinfjötla [The Death of Sinfjötli]
IV	Fœddr Sigurðr [Sigurd born]
V	Regin
VI	Brynhildr
VII	Guðrún
VIII	Svikin Brynhildr [Brynhild Betrayed]
IX	Deild [Strife]

I have retained these titles in the text, but added translations, as above, to those which are not simply proper names. In the Lay of Gudrún, on the other hand, there is no division into sections.

To sections I, II, V, and VI in the Lay of the Völsungs, but not to the other five, explanatory prose head-notes are added (perhaps in imitation of the prose notes inserted by the compiler of the Codex Regius of the Edda).

The marginal indications of the speakers in both poems are given exactly as they appear in the manuscript, as also are the indications of new 'moments' in the narrative.

The second difference in presentation between the two poems concerns the line-divisions. In *Upphaf,* alone of the sections of the Lay of the Völsungs, but throughout the Lay of Gudrún, the stanzas are written in eight short lines: that is to say, the unit of the verse, the half-line or *vísuorð*, is written separately:

> Of old was an age
> when was emptiness

(the opening of *Upphaf*). But apart from *Upphaf* the whole of the Lay of the Völsungs is written in long lines (without a metrical space between the halves):

> Of old was an age when Ódin walked

(the opening of *Andvara-gull*). At the top of this page, however, my father wrote in pencil: 'This should all be written in short line form, which looks better – as in *Upphaf*.' I have therefore set out the text of the Lay of the Völsungs in this way.

§4 THE SPELLING OF NORSE NAMES

I have thought it best to follow closely my father's usage in respect of the writing of Norse names in an English context. The most important features, which appear in his manuscript of the poems with great consistency, are these:

The sound *ð* of voiced 'th' as in English 'then' is replaced by *d*: thus *Guðrún* becomes *Gudrún*, *Hreiðmarr* becomes *Hreidmar*, *Buðli* becomes *Budli*, *Ásgarðr* becomes *Ásgard*.

As two of these examples show, the nominative ending *-r* is omitted: so also *Frey, Völsung, Brynhild, Gunnar* for *Freyr, Völsungr, Brynhildr, Gunnarr*.

The letter *j* is retained, as in *Sinfjötli, Gjúki*, where it is pronounced like English 'y' in 'you' (Norse *Jórk* is 'York').

The only case where I have imposed consistency is that of the name of the god who in Norse is *Óðinn*. In his lecture notes my father naturally used the Norse form (which I have retained in the text of his lecture on the 'Elder Edda', p.22). In the carefully written manuscript of the 'New Lays', on the other hand, he 'anglicized' it, changing *ð* to *d*, but (as generally in all such cases) retaining the acute accent indicating a long vowel. But he used two forms, favouring one or the other in different parts of the Lay of the Völsungs: *Ódin* and *Ódinn*. But in section VI, *Brynhildr*, where the name occurs frequently in the form *Ódinn*, he wrote (stanza 8) *Ódinn bound me, Ódin's chosen*. This is because in the Norse genitive *nn* changes to *ns*: *Óðins sonr*, 'son of Ódin'.

43

Seeing that in section VIII, stanza 5, where the name is repeated, *Ódin dooms it; Ódinn hearken!,* my father later struck out the second *n* of *Ódinn,* and since it seems to me that inconsistency in the form of the name serves no purpose, I have settled for *Ódin.* In the case of the name that is in Norse *Reginn* my father wrote *Regin* throughout, and I have followed this.

§5 THE VERSE-FORM OF THE POEMS

The metrical form of these Lays was very evidently a primary element in my father's purpose. As he said in his letters to W.H. Auden, he wrote in 'the old eight-line *fornyrðislag* stanza', and I give here an abbreviated account of its nature.

There are three metres found in the Eddaic poems, *fornyrðislag*, *malaháttr*, and *ljóðaháttr* (on this last see the note to the Lay of the Völsungs, section V, lines 42–44, pp.211–13); but here we need only consider the first, in which most of the narrative poems of the Edda are composed. The name *fornyrðislag* is believed to mean 'Old Story Metre' or 'Old Lore Metre' – a name which, my father observed, cannot have arisen until after later elaborations had been invented and made familiar; he favoured the view that the older name was *kviðuháttr*, meaning 'the "manner" for poems named *kviða*', since the old poems in *fornyrðislag*, when their names have any metrical import, are usually called *-kviða*: hence his names *Völsungakviða* and *Guðrúnarkviða*.

The ancient Germanic metre depended, in my father's words, on 'the utilization of the main factors of Germanic speech, *length* and *stress*'; and the same rhythmical structure as is found in Old English verse is found also in *fornyrðislag*. That structure was expounded by my father in a preface to the revised edition (1940) of the translation of *Beowulf* by J.R. Clark-Hall, and reprinted in J.R.R. Tolkien, *The Monsters and the Critics and Other Essays* (1983). In that account he defined the nature of the Old English verse-structure in these words.

The Old English line was composed of two opposed word-groups or 'halves'. Each half was an example, or variation, of one of six basic patterns.

The patterns were made of *strong* and *weak* elements, which may be called 'lifts' and 'dips'. The standard lift was a *long stressed* syllable, (usually with a relatively high tone). The standard dip was an *unstressed* syllable, long or short, with a low tone.

The following are examples in modern English of normal forms of the six patterns:

A	falling-falling	*knights in | ármour*	
		4 1 4 1	
B	rising-rising	*the róar | ing séa*	
		1 4 1 4	
C	clashing	*on hígh | móuntains*	
		1 4 4 or 3 1	
D	*a* falling by stages	*bríght | árchàngels*	
		4 3 2 1	
	b broken fall	*bóld | brázenfàced*	
		4 3 1 2	
E	fall and rise	*híghcrèsted | hélms*	
		4 2 1 4 or 3	

A, B, C have equal feet, each containing a lift and dip. D and E have unequal feet: one consists of a single lift, the other has a subordinate stress (marked `) inserted.

These are the normal patterns of four elements into which Old English words naturally fell, and into which modern English words still fall. They can be found in any passage of prose, ancient or modern. Verse of this kind differs from prose, *not* in re-arranging words to fit a special rhythm, repeated or varied in successive lines, but in choosing the simpler and more compact word-patterns and clearing away extraneous matter, so that these patterns stand opposed to one another.

The *selected* patterns were all of approximately equal metrical *weight*[*]: the effect of loudness (combined with length and voice-pitch), as judged by the ear in conjunction with emotional and logical *significance*[†]. The line was thus essentially a *balance* of two equivalent blocks. These blocks might be, and usually were, of different pattern and rhythm. There was in consequence no common tune or rhythm shared by lines in virtue of being 'in the same metre'. The ear should not listen for any such thing, but should attend to the shape and balance of the halves. Thus *the róaring séa rólling lándward* is not metrical because it contains an 'iambic' or a 'trochaic' rhythm, but because it is a balance of B + A.

---

[*] To a full *lift* a value 4 may be given. The *subordinate stresses* (reduced in force and lowered in tone) that appear in such compounds as *highcrèsted* may be given value 2. But reduction also occurs in other cases. For instance, the second of two clashing stresses in a sentence; or of two juxtaposed words (of equal significance when separate), such as nouns and adjectives, tends to be reduced to approximate value 3. Using these rough values we see that the normal total value of each pattern is 10; C tends to be slightly lighter, and E to be slightly heavier.

[†] And so not purely phonetic, nor exactly measurable in figures (such as those used above) or by a machine.

These patterns are found also in *fornyrðislag*, and can be readily identified in my father's Norse lays: as for example in stanza 45 of the Lay of Gudrún (p.268), lines 2–6:

A	rúnes of héaling
D (*a*)	wórds wéll-gràven
B	on wóod to réad
E	fást bìds us fáre
C	to féast gládly

In the variations on the 'basic patterns' ('overweighting', 'extension', etc.) described in my father's account there are indeed differences in Old Norse from Old English, tending to greater brevity; but I will enter only into the most radical and important difference between the verse-forms, namely, that all Norse poetry is 'strophic', or 'stanzaic', that is, composed in strophes or stanzas. This is in the most marked contrast to Old English, where any such arrangements were altogether avoided; and my father wrote of it (see p.7): 'In Old English breadth, fullness, reflection, elegiac effect, were aimed at. Old Norse aims at seizing a situation, striking a blow that will be remembered, illuminating a moment with a flash of lightning – and tends to concision, weighty packing of the language in sense and form, and gradually to greater regularity of form of verse.'

'The norm of the strophe (for *fornyrðislag*),' he said, 'is four lines (eight half-lines) with a complete pause at the end, and also a pause (not necessarily so marked) at the end of the fourth half-line. But, at least as preserved, the texts in the manuscripts do not work out regularly on this plan, and great shufflement and lacuna-making has gone on among editors (so that one can never tell to a strophe or two what references refer to in different editions).'

Noting that this variability in the length of the strophes occurs in some of the earlier and least corrupt texts, and that '*Völundarkviða*, undoubtedly an ancient poem, is particularly irregular and particularly plagued by editors (who are much more daring and wilful in Old Norse than in Old English)', he accepted the view that, in the main, this freedom should be seen as an archaic feature. 'The strict strophe had not fully developed, any more than the strict line limited syllabically'; in other words, the strophic form was a Norse innovation, and developed only gradually.

In my father's Lays the strophic form is entirely regular, and the half-line tends to brevity and limitation of syllables.

Alliteration

Old Norse poetry follows precisely the same principles in the matter of 'alliteration' as does Old English poetry. Those principles were formulated thus by my father in his account of Old English metre cited earlier.

One full lift in each half-line must alliterate. The 'key alliteration' was borne by the *first lift* in the *second* half. (This sound was called by Snorri Sturluson *höfuðstafr*, whence the term 'head-stave' used in English books.) With the head-stave the stronger lift in the first half-line *must* alliterate, and both lifts may do so. In the second half-line the second lift *must not* alliterate.

Thus, in the opening section of the Lay of the Völsungs, *Upphaf*, in the thirteenth stanza, lines 5–6, *the deep Dragon /*

shall be doom of Thór, the *d* of *doom* is the head-stave, while in Snorri's terminology the *d* of *deep* and *Dragon* are the *stuðlar*, the props or supports. The *Th* of *Thór*, the second lift of the second half-line, does not alliterate. It will be seen that in *Upphaf* both lifts of the first half do in fact alliterate with the head-stave in the majority of cases.

It is important to recognize that in Germanic verse 'alliteration' refers, not to *letters*, but to *sounds*; it is the agreement of the *stressed elements* beginning with *the same consonant*, or with *no consonant*: all vowels 'alliterate' with one another, as in the opening line of *Upphaf*, *Of old was an age / when was emptiness.* In English the phonetic agreement is often disguised to the eye by the spelling: thus in the same stanza, where lines 5–6 alliterate on '*r*', *unwrought was Earth, / unroofed was Heaven;* or in stanza 8 of section IV of the Lay of the Völsungs, where lines 1–2 alliterate on the sound '*w*': *A warrior strange, / one-eyed, awful.*

The consonant-combinations *sk, sp,* and *st* will usually only alliterate with themselves; thus in the Lay of the Völsungs section IV, stanza 9, lines 3–4, *the sword of Grímnir /singing splintered* does not show alliteration on both lifts of the second half-line, nor does section V, stanza 24, line 3–4, *was sired this horse, / swiftest, strongest.*

§6 NOTES ON THE POEMS, BY THE AUTHOR

Together with the manuscript of the New Lays were placed some small slips of paper on which my father made some interpretative remarks about them. They were written very rapidly in ink or in pencil, and in the case of (iv) in pencil overwritten and added to in ink, clearly at the same time. It seems impossible to put any even relative date on them; a sense of distance and detachment may be artificial.

(i)

After the mythical introduction and the account of the Hoard, the Lay turns to the Völsung-family, and traces the history of Völsung, Sigmund, and Sigurd. The chief part is the tragedy of Sigurd and Brynhild, which is of interest for itself; but the whole is given unity as a study of the way in which a wilful deed of Loki, the purposeless slaying of Otr, and his ruthless method of extricating Ódin and himself from the peril into which this deed has brought them sets in motion a curse that at the last brings Sigurd to his death.

The full working of this curse is only hastened by Ódin's own interventions – to provide Sigurd with horse and weapon fit for his task, and to provide him with a fit bride, the fairest of all Ódin's Valkyries, Brynhild. (It appears that Ódin purposes through Sigurd to punish the family of Hreidmar (Fáfnir and Regin) for the exaction of the ransom of Otr.) In the story of Sigurd

Here this text breaks off.

(ii)

Grímhild, wife of Gjúki King of the Burgundians (or Niflungs), is the chief agent of evil, not because of any far-sighted plans of wickedness: she is rather an example of that wickedness that looks only to each situation as it occurs, and sticks at nothing to gain from it what seems immediately profitable. She is 'grey with wisdom' being a witch in lore and still more skilled in the reading of minds and hearts to use their weaknesses and follies. Her will dominates her daughter Gudrún and her oldest son Gunnar.

Gudrún is a simple maiden, incapable of any great plans for profit or vengeance. She falls in love with Sigurd, and for herself has no further motive. A sensitive but weak character, she is capable of disastrous speech or action under provocation. The occasions of this that are described are her fatal retort to the taunting of Brynhild, which more than anything is the immediate cause of Sigurd's murder, and in the sequel, the Slaying of the Niflungs, her terrible deeds at the end when driven to madness and despair.

Gunnar is a hot impatient character, dominated by Grímhild. Though not too stupid to perceive prudence, in cases of doubt or difficulty he becomes fey and reckless, turning to violence.

(iii)

After Sigurd was slain, Brynhild took her own life, and they were both burned on one pyre. Gudrún did not take her own life, but for grief was for a time half-witless. She would not look upon her kinsmen nor upon her mother, and dwelt apart in a house in the woods. There after a while she began to weave in a tapestry the history of the Dragon-hoard and of Sigurd.

Atli son of Budli became king of the Huns, ancient enemies of the Burgundians, who had before slain his father.* His power growing great becomes a threat to Gunnar, who is now king in his father Gjúki's stead; and as Högni his brother had foretold they miss now the valour of King Sigurd their sworn-brother.

* In the Lay of the Völsungs Gunnar sang of the slaying of Budli's brother by the Burgundians (VII.15); and the same is said in the Lay of Gudrún, stanza 4.

(iv)

This lay [i.e. *Guðrúnarkviða en nýja*] is a sequel to the Lay of Sigurd and assumes knowledge of it, though by the device of Gudrún's tapestry the history of the accursed Hoard and of Sigurd is brought to mind and outlined at the beginning.

In the former Lay it was told how the dominion of the Gods was from the first threatened with destruction. Ódin, Lord of Gods and Men, begets in the world many mighty men, whom he gathers in Valhöll to be his companions in the Last Battle. One family in especial he singles out, the Völsungs,* all of whom are his chosen warriors, and one, Sigurd son of Sigmund, is to be the chief of all, their leader in the Last Day; for Ódin hopes that by his hand the Serpent shall in the end be slain, and a new world made possible.

None of the Gods can accomplish this, but only one who has lived on Earth first as a mortal, and died. (This motive of the special function of Sigurd is an invention of the present poet, or an interpretation of the Norse sources in which it is not explicit.)

Evil is not, however, to be found only in the ever-watchful host of the Enemies of Gods and Men. It is found also in Ásgard itself in the person of Loki, by whose deeds, wilful, merely mischievous, or wholly malicious, the counsels and hopes of Ódin seem ever turned awry or defeated.

Yet Loki is seen ever walking the world at the left hand of Ódin, who does not rebuke him, nor dismiss him, nor refuse the aid of his cunning. At Ódin's right hand there walks another figure, a nameless shadow. It would seem that this poet (seeing that the Northern Gods represent but written large the ways of Men in the hostile world) has taken this old legend to symbolize Man's prudence and wisdom and its ever present accompaniment of folly and malice that defeats it, only to bring forth greater heroism and deeper wisdom; while ever at the right hand walks the shadow that is neither Ódin nor Loki but in some aspect Fate, the real story that must be blended of both. Yet Ódin is master of the Three and the final outcome will resemble rather the hope of Ódin than the malice (shorter sighted) of Loki. Ódin at times gives expression to this, saying that his hope looks out beyond the seeming disasters of this world. Though Ódin's chosen come all to an evil end or untimely death, that will only make them of greater worth for their ultimate purpose in the Last Battle.

* After *the Völsungs* my father wrote *(the Chosen)*, but struck this out. An etymological speculation on the origin of the name which (at any rate at one time) he favoured associated it with Germanic words meaning 'choose'.

On this in many ways mysterious writing see the commentary on the *Upphaf* of the Lay of the Völsungs, and the commentary on the first section of the poem, *Andvari's Gold*, stanza 1.

In conclusion, this seems a suitable place to refer to remarks of my father's that bear upon, but have no (at any rate overt) relation to, *Guðrúnarkviða en nýja*. In his introduction to lectures at Oxford on the Eddaic poem *Guðrúnarkviða en forna*, the Old Lay of Gudrún, he said that 'curiously enough' he was more interested in Gudrún, 'who is usually slighted, and considered as of secondary interest', than in Brynhild. By implication, he contrasted the long agony of Gudrún with the irruption of Brynhild, who soon departs, 'and her passion and death remain only in the background of the tale, a brief and terrible storm beginning in fire and ending in it.'

VÖLSUNGAKVIÐA EN NÝJA
eða
SIGURÐARKVIÐA EN MESTA

VÖLSUNGAKVIÐA EN NÝJA

UPPHAF
(Beginning)

1   Of old was an age
when was emptiness,
there was sand nor sea
nor surging waves;
unwrought was Earth,
unroofed was Heaven –
an abyss yawning,
and no blade of grass.

2   The Great Gods then
began their toil,
the wondrous world
they well builded.
From the South the Sun
from seas rising
gleamed down on grass
green at morning.

Upphaf

3 They hall and hallow
high uptowering,
gleaming-gabled,
golden-posted,
rock-hewn ramparts
reared in splendour,
forge and fortress
framed immortal.

4 Unmarred their mirth
in many a court,
where men they made
of their minds' cunning;
under hills of Heaven
on high builded
they lived in laughter
long years ago.

5 Dread shapes arose
from the dim spaces
over sheer mountains
by the Shoreless Sea,
friends of darkness,
foes immortal,
old, unbegotten,
out of ancient void.

6   To the world came war:
    the walls of Gods
    giants beleaguered;
    joy was ended.
    The mountains were moved,
    mighty Ocean
    surged and thundered,
    the Sun trembled.

7   The Gods gathered
    on golden thrones,
    of doom and death
    deeply pondered,
    how fate should be fended,
    their foes vanquished,
    their labour healed,
    light rekindled.

8   In forge's fire
    of flaming wrath
    was heaviest hammer
    hewn and wielded.
    Thunder and lightning
    Thór the mighty
    flung among them,
    felled and sundered.

Upphaf

9   In fear then fled they,
       foes immortal,
       from the walls beaten
       watched unceasing;
       ringed Earth around
       with roaring sea
       and mountains of ice
       on the margin of the world.

*

10   A seer long silent
       her song upraised –
       the halls hearkened –
       on high she stood.
       Of doom and death
       dark words she spake,
       of the last battle
       of the leaguered Gods.

11   'The horn of Heimdal
       I hear ringing;
       the Blazing Bridge
       bends neath horsemen;
       the Ash is groaning,
       his arms trembling,
       the Wolf waking,
       warriors riding.

12   The sword of Surt
smoketh redly;
the slumbering Serpent
in the sea moveth;
a shadowy ship
from shores of Hell
legions bringeth
to the last battle.

13   The wolf Fenrir
waits for Ódin,
for Frey the fair
the flames of Surt;
the deep Dragon
shall be doom of Thór –
shall all be ended,
shall Earth perish?

14   If in day of Doom
one deathless stands,
who death hath tasted
and dies no more,
the serpent-slayer,
seed of Ódin,
then all shall not end,
nor Earth perish.

Upphaf

15   On his head shall be helm,
in his hand lightning,
afire his spirit,
in his face splendour.
The Serpent shall shiver
and Surt waver,
the Wolf be vanquished
and the world rescued.'

*

16   The Gods were gathered
on guarded heights,
of doom and death
deep they pondered.
Sun they rekindled,
and silver Moon
they set to sail
on seas of stars.

17   Frey and Freyia
fair things planted,
trees and flowers,
trembling grasses;
Thór in chariot
thundered o'er them
through Heaven's gateways
to the hills of stone.

18   Ever would Ódin
on earth wander
weighed with wisdom
woe foreknowing,
the Lord of lords
and leaguered Gods,
his seed sowing,
sire of heroes.

19   Valhöll he built
vast and shining;
shields the tiles were,
shafts the rafters.
Ravens flew thence
over realms of Earth;
at the doors an eagle
darkly waited.

20   The guests were many:
grim their singing,
boar's-flesh eating,
beakers draining;
mighty ones of Earth
mailclad sitting
for one they waited,
the World's chosen.

*

I

ANDVARA-GULL
(Andvari's Gold)

Here first is told how Ódin and his companions were trapped in the house of the demon Hreidmar, and his sons. These dwelt now in the world in the likeness of men or of beasts.

1   Of old was an age
when Ódin walked
by wide waters
in the world's beginning;
lightfooted Loki
at his left was running,
at his right Hœnir
roamed beside him.

2   The falls of Andvari
frothed and murmured
with fish teeming
in foaming pools.

As a pike there plunged
his prey hunting
Dwarf Andvari
from his dark cavern.

3   There hunted hungry
Hreidmar's offspring:
the silver salmon
sweet he thought them.
Otr in otter's form
there ate blinking,
on the bank brooding
of black waters.

4   With stone struck him,
stripped him naked,
Loki lighthanded,
loosing evil.
The fell they flayed,
fared then onward;
in Hreidmar's halls
housing sought they.

5   There wrought Regin
by the red embers
rune-written iron,
rare, enchanted;

I Andvari's Gold

of gold things gleaming,
of grey silver,
there Fáfnir lay
by the fire dreaming.

Hreidmar 6 'Do fetters fret you,
folk of Ásgard?
Regin hath wrought them
with runes binding.
Redgolden rings,
ransom costly,
this fell must fill,
this fur cover!'

7 Lightshod Loki
over land and waves
to Rán came running
in her realm of sea.
The queen of Ægir
his quest granted:
a net she knotted
noosed with evil.

Loki 8 'What fish have I found
in the flood leaping,
rashly roaming?
Ransom pay me!'

Andvari 'I am Andvari.
     Óin begot me
     to grievous fate.
     Gold I bid thee!'

Loki 9 'What hides thy hand
      thus hollow bending?'
Andvari 'The ring is little –
     let it rest with me!'
Loki 'All, Andvari,
     all shalt render,
     light rings and heavy,
     or life itself!'

   10 (The Dwarf spake darkly
     from his delvéd stone:)
Andvari 'My ring I will curse
     with ruth and woe!
     Bane it bringeth
     to brethren two;
     seven princes slays;
     swords it kindles –
     end untimely
     of Ódin's hope.'

   11 In Hreidmar's house
     they heaped the gold.

I Andvari's Gold

Hreidmar   'A hair unhidden
            I behold there yet!
            Out drew Ódin
            Andvari's ring,
            cursed he cast it
            on accurséd gold.

Ódin   12   Ye gold have gained:
            a god's ransom,
            for thyself and sons
            seed of evil.'
Hreidmar   'Gods seldom give
            gifts of healing;
            gold oft begrudgeth
            the greedy hand!'

       13   Words spake Loki
            worse thereafter:
Loki   'Here deadly dwells
            the doom of kings!
            Here is fall of queens,
            fire and weeping,
            end untimely
            of Ódin's hope!'

Ódin   14   'Whom Ódin chooseth
            ends not untimely,

though ways of men
he walk briefly.
In wide Valhöll
he may wait feasting –
it is to ages after
that Ódin looks.'

Hreidmar 15 'The hope of Ódin
we heed little!
Redgolden rings
I will rule alone.
Though Gods grudge it
gold is healing.
From Hreidmar's house
haste now swiftly!'

*

II

SIGNÝ

Rerir was the son of the son of Ódin. After him reigned
Völsung, to whom Ódin gave a Valkyrie as wife. Sigmund and
Signý were their eldest children and twins. They had nine
sons beside. Sigmund was of all men the most valiant, unless
his sons be named. Signý was fair and wise and foresighted.
She was given unwilling and against her foreboding to Siggeir
king of Gautland, for the strengthening of the power of King
Völsung. Here is told how hate grew between Gauts and
Völsungs, and of the slaying of Völsung. The ten brothers of
Signý were set in fetters in the forest and all perished save
Sigmund. Long time he dwelt in a cave in the guise of a
dwarvish smith. By Signý was a fierce vengeance devised and
fulfilled.

1   On the coasts of the North
was king renowned
Rerir sea-roving,
the raven's lord.

Shield-hung his ships,
unsheathed his sword;
his sire of old
was son of Ódin.

2   Him Völsung followed
valiant-hearted,
child of longing,
chosen of Ódin.
Valkyrie fair
did Völsung wed,
Ódin's maiden,
Ódin's chosen.

3   Sigmund and Signý,
a son and daughter,
she bare at a birth
in his builded halls.
High rose their roofs,
huge their timbers,
and wide the walls
of wood carven.

4   A tree there towered
tall and branching,
that house upholding,
the hall's wonder;

II Signý

its leaves their hangings,
its limbs rafters,
its mighty bole
in the midst standing.

*

Völsung	5	'What sails be these
in the seas shining?
What ships be those
with shields golden?'
Signý		'Gautland's banners
gilt and silver
Gautland's greeting
grievous bearing.'

Völsung	6	'Wherefore grievous?
Are guests hateful?
Gautland's master
glorious reigneth.'
Signý		'For Gautland's master
glory endeth;
grief is fated
for Gautland's queen.'

*

7   Birds sang blithely
     o'er board and hearth,
     bold men and brave
     on benches sitting.
     Mailclad, mighty,
     his message spake there
     a Gautish lord
     gleaming-harnessed.

Gaut   8   'Siggeir sent me
              swiftly steering:
              fame of Völsung
              far is rumoured.
              Signý's beauty,
              Signý's wisdom,
              to his bed he wooeth,
              bride most lovely.'

Völsung   9   'What saith Sigmund?
                 Shall his sister go
                 with lord so mighty
                 league to bind us?'
Sigmund   'With lord so mighty
                 league and kinship
                 let us bind, and grant him
                 bride most lovely!'

*

II Signý

10 Ere summer faded
   sails came shining,
   ships came shoreward
   with shields gleaming.
   Many and mighty
   mailclad warriors
   to the seats of Völsung
   with Siggeir strode.

11 Birds sang blissful
   over boards laden,
   over Signý pale,
   Siggeir eager.
   Dark wine they drank,
   doughty princes,
   Gautland's chieftains;
   glad their voices.

12 Wan night cometh;
   wind ariseth;
   doors are opened,
   the din is silenced.
   A man there enters,
   mantled darkly,
   hoary-bearded,
   huge and ancient.

13   A sword he sweeps
from swathing cloak,
into standing stem
stabs it swiftly:

Grímnir   'Who dares to draw,
doom unfearing,
the gift of Grímnir
gleaming deadly?'

14   Doors clanged backward;
din was wakened;
men leapt forward
mighty-handed.
Gaut and Völsung
glory seeking
strove they starkly,
straining vainly.

15   Sigmund latest
seized it lightly,
the blade from bole
brandished flaming.
Siggeir yearning
on that sword gazing
red gold offered,
ransom kingly.

II Signý

Sigmund 16 'Though seas of silver
and sands of gold
thou bade in barter,
thy boon were vain!
To my hand made,
for me destined,
I sell no sword
to Siggeir ever.'

*

Signý 17 'My heart is heavy
my home leaving!
Signý's wisdom
Signý burdens.
From this wedding waketh
woe and evil –
break, sire, the bonds
thou hast bound me in!'

Völsung 18 'Woe and evil
are woman's boding!
Fate none can flee.
Faith man can hold.
Ships await thee!
Shame to sunder
the bridal bed,
the bounden word.

Signý 19   'Sigmund, farewell!
Siggeir calls me.
Weak might hath woman
for wisdom's load.
Last night I lay
where loath me was;
with less liking
I may lay me yet.'

20   'Hail! toft and Tree,
timbers carven!
Maid here was once
who is mournful queen.'
Wild blew the wind
waves white-crested.
On land of Völsung
she looked no more.

*

21   A ship came shining
to shores foaming,
gloomy Gautland's
guarded havens.
Sigmund lordly,
sire and kindred,
to fair feasting
fearless journeyed.

II Signý

Signý 22 'Father Völsung,
fairest kinsman!
Back my brethren!
This beach tread not!
A bitter drinking,
baleful meeting,
swords hath Siggeir
set to greet you.'

23 With thousand thanes,
thronging spearmen,
his guests welcomed
Gautland's master.
Ten times Völsung
towering wrathful
casque and corslet
clove asunder.

24 Through and through them
thrice went Sigmund;
as grass in Gautland
grimly mowed them.
His shield he shed:
with shining sword
smoking redly
slew two-handed.

*

25   Black the raven
by the body croaketh,
bare are Völsung's
bones once mighty.
In bonds the brethren
are bound living;
Siggeir smileth,
Signý weeps not.

Signý 26   'Sweet still is sight
while see one may!
A boon, my husband –
bid men linger!
Slay not swiftly
seed of Völsung!
For death is lasting,
though the doom tarry.'

Siggeir 27   'Wild and witless
words of Signý,
that pain and torment
plead for kindred!
Glad will I grant it,
grimly bind them
in the forest fettered,
faint and hungry.'

II Signý

28   In the forest fettered,
      faint and naked,
      her ten brethren
      torment suffered.
      There one by one
      a wolf rent them;
      by night after night
      another sought she.

Signý   29   'What found ye in the forest,
                  my fair servants?'
Servants   'Nine brothers' bones
                  under night gleaming;
                  yet were shackles broken,
                  she-wolf lying
                  torn and tongueless
                  by the tree riven.'

                     *

Signý   30   'Who hath deeply delved
                  this dark cavern?
                  Dwarvish master,
                  thy doors open!'
Sigmund   'Who knocks at night
                  at nameless doors?
                  In may enter
                  elvish maiden!'

31 Brother and sister
in a bed lying,
brief love, bitter,
blent with loathing!
Answer, earth-dweller –
in thy arms who lies,
chill, enchanted,
changed, elfshapen?

32 Back went Signý
to Siggeir's hall,
nine months brooding
no word speaking.
Wolves were wailing,
her women shuddering,
Signý silent,
when a son she bore.

*

Sigmund 33 'Who calls so clear
at cavern's doorway,
fords so fearless
the foaming stream?
Fair one, thy father
thy face gave not!
What bringest bound
in bast folded?'

II Signý

Sinfjötli 34 'My face is Völsung's,
father of Signý.
Signý sent me
a sword bearing.
Long years it lay
on the lap of Siggeir;
Sigmund drew it,
since hath no man.'

35 Thus son of Signý
came Sinfjötli,
to vengeance bred
of Völsung slain.
In the forest faring
far in warfare
long they laboured,
long they waited.

36 Wide they wandered
wolvish-coated,
men they murdered,
men they plundered.
Daylong slept they
in dark cavern
after dreadful deeds
of death in Gautland.

37   Moon was shining,
men were singing,
Siggeir sitting
in his sounding hall.
Völsung vanquished
voices chanted;
wolves came howling
wild and dreadful.

38   Doors were opened,
din fell silent.

Gautar   'Eyes we see there
like eager fire!
wolves have entered,
watchmen slaying!
Flames are round us
fire-encircled.'

39   Sigmund stood there
his sword wielding,
and Signý's son
at his side laughing.

*Sigmund
& Sinfjötli*   'Pass may no man,
prince nor servant!
In pain shall perish
pride of Siggeir.'

II Signý

Sigmund 40   'Come forth, Signý,
                   sister fairest!
                   Gautland's glory
                   grimly endeth.
                   Glad the greeting,
                   grief is over;
                   avenged is Völsung
                   valiant-hearted!'

Signý 41   (Sigmund's sister
                   Signý answered:)
                   'Son Sinfjötli,
                   Sigmund father!
                   Signý comes not,
                   Siggeir calls her.
                   Where I lay unwilling
                   I now lay me glad;
                   I lived in loathing,
                   now lief I die.'

*

DAUÐI SINFJÖTLA
(The Death of Sinfjötli)

1   Ships they laded
    with shining gear,
    gems and jewels,
    joys of Gautland.
    Wild blew the winds,
    waves were foaming;
    they viewed afar
    the Völsung shore.

2   Long ruled Sigmund,
    sire and uncle;
    Sinfjötli sat
    at his side proudly.
    There towered the tree,
    tall and ancient,
    birds in the branches
    were blithe again.

III The Death of Sinfjötli

3   Ever Grímnir's gift
gleamed in warfare;
at Sigmund's side
Sinfjötli strode.
Hard, handlinkéd,
helm and corslet
glasswhite glittered
with grey silver.

4   Seven kings they slew,
their cities plundered;
wide waxed their realm
the world over.
Of women fairest
in war taken
a wife took Sigmund;
woe she brought him.

5   Sinfjötli came
sailing proudly
ships goldladen
to the shore steering.

Sigmund   'Hail! Ódin's son,
eager-hearted!
War no longer!
Wine is pouring.'

6 In came the queen
  evil pondering –
  her sire was slain
  by Sinfjötli – :

Queen 'Hail! Völsung fell,
  valiant-hearted!
  Weary art thou.
  Wine I bring thee.

7 Steep stands the horn,
  Stepson thirsty!'

Sinfjötli 'Dark seems the drink,
  deadly blended!'
  Sigmund seized it,
  swiftly drained it;
  no venom vanquished
  Völsung's eldest.

Queen 8 'Beer I bring thee
  brown and potent!'

Sinfjötli 'Guile there gleameth
  grimly blended!'
  Sigmund seized it,
  swiftly drank it;
  that prince of men
  poison harmed not.

III The Death of Sinfjötli

Queen 9 'Ale I offer thee,
eager Völsung!
Völsungs valiant
at venom blench not;
heroes ask not
help in drinking –
if drink thou darest,
drink Sinfjötli!'

10 Dead Sinfjötli
drinking stumbled.
Sigmund 'Woe! thou witchwife
weary-hearted!
Of the seed of Völsung
in Signý's child
the fairest flower
fades untimely!'

11 There sorrowladen
Sigmund raised him,
in arms caught him;
out he wandered.
Over wood and wild
to the waves foaming
witless strayed he
to the waves roaring.

Boatman 12 'Whither bringest thou
thy burden heavy?
My boat is ready
to bear it hence.'
A man there steered,
mantled darkly,
hooded and hoary,
huge and awful.

13 Alone was Sigmund
by the land's margin;
in Valhöllu
Völsung feasted:
Völsung 'Son's son welcome,
and son of daughter!
But one yet await we,
the World's chosen.'

*

IV

FŒDDR SIGURÐR
(Sigurd Born)

1   Alone dwelt Sigmund
     his land ruling;
     cold was his bower,
     queenless, childless.
     In songs he heard
     of sweetest maiden,
     of Sigrlinn's beauty,
     Sváfnir's daughter.

2   Old was Sigmund,
     as an oak gnarléd;
     his beard was grey
     as bark of ash.
     Young was Sigrlinn
     and yellow-gleaming
     her locks hung long
     on lissom shoulder.

3 Seven sons of kings
 sued the maiden:
 Sigmund took her;
 sails were hoisted.
 The Völsung land
 they viewed afar,
 the windy cliffs,
 the waves foaming.

Sigmund 4 'Say me, Sigrlinn,
 sweeter were it
 young king to wed
 and yellow-bearded,
 or wife of a Völsung,
 the World's chosen
 in my bed to bear,
 bride of Ódin?'

*

Sigrlinn 5 'What sails be these
 in the seas shining? –
 the shields are scarlet,
 ships uncounted.'
Sigmund 'Seven sons of kings
 seeking welcome!
 Grímnir's gift shall
 gladly meet them!'

IV Sigurd Born

6 High sang the horns,
  helms were gleaming,
  shafts were shaken,
  shields them answered.
  Vikings' standards,
  Völsung's banner
  on strand were streaming;
  stern the onslaught.

7 Old was Sigmund
  as the oak gnarléd;
  his sword swung he
  smoking redly.
  Fate him fended
  fearless striding
  with dew of battle
  dyed to shoulder.

8 A warrior strange,
  one-eyed, awful,
  strode and stayed him
  standing silent,
  huge and hoary
  and hooded darkly.
  The sword of Sigmund
  sang before him.

9   His spear he raised:
sprang asunder
the sword of Grímnir,
singing splintered.
The king is fallen
cloven-breasted;
lords lie round him;
the land darkens.

10   Men were moaning,
the moon sinking.
Sigrlinn sought him,
sadly raised him:

Sigrlinn   'Hope of healing
for thy hurts I bring,
my lord beloved,
last of Völsungs.'

Sigmund 11   'From wanhope many
have been won to life,
yet healing I ask not.
Hope is needless.
Ódin calls me
at the end of days.
Here lies not lost
the last Völsung!'

IV Sigurd Born

12   Thy womb shall wax
with the World's chosen,
serpent-slayer,
seed of Ódin.
Till ages end
all shall name him
chief of chieftains,
changeless glory.

13   Of Grímnir's gift
guard the fragments;
of the shards shall be shaped
a shining blade.
Too soon shall I see
Sigurd bear it
to glad Valhöll
greeting Ódin.'

14   Cold came morning
o'er the king lifeless
and woeful Sigrlinn
her watch keeping.
Ships came sailing
to the shore crowding,
rovers northern
to the red beaches.

15   The bride of Sigmund
as a bondwoman
over sounding seas
sadly journeyed.
Wild blew the winds,
waves them lifted;
she viewed afar
the Völsung land.

16   Wind was wailing,
waves were crying,
Sigrlinn sorrowful,
when a son she bore.
Sigurd golden
as a sun shining,
forth came he fair
in a far country.

Woman 17   'O woman woeful
in war taken,
who was thy husband
while his house lasted?
What father begot
such fair offspring? –
grey steel glitters
in his gleaming eyes.'

IV Sigurd Born

Sigrlinn 18 'The sire of Sigurd
Sigmund Völsung;
Seed of Ódin
songs shall call him.'

Woman 'Fair shall be fostered
that father's child;
his mother be mated
to a mighty king.'

*

V

REGIN

The king of that land took Sigrlinn to wife. Sigurd was sent
to be fostered by Regin, of whom it has been told above.
Regin dwelt now in the forest and was deemed wise in many
other matters than smithwork. Regin egged Sigurd to slay
Fáfnir. With the sword Gram and the horse Grani, of which
it is here spoken, he accomplished this, though Regin had
concealed from him both the great power of Fáfnir and the
nature of the hoard that the serpent guarded. Here also are
given the dark words of Regin in which the undermeaning
is that the real cause of the serpent's death is Regin, who
should therefore have the gold (though this he has promised, at least in large share, to Sigurd); but that Regin should
slay the slayer of his brother. Sigurd deeming him only
weighed with the thought of his guilt in brother-murder,
dismisses his words with scorn. Nor does Sigurd heed the
dragon's words concerning the curse, thinking them merely
the device of greed to protect the gold even though its
guardian be slain. This indeed was the dragon's chief
purpose in revealing the curse at the hour of his death. Yet
that curse began to work swiftly.

V *Regin*

1 The forge was smoking
in the forest-darkness;
there wrought Regin
by the red embers.
There was Sigurd sent,
seed of Völsung,
lore deep to learn;
long his fostering.

2 Runes of wisdom
then Regin taught him,
and weapons' wielding,
works of mastery;
the language of lands,
lore of kingship,
wise words he spake
in the wood's fastness.

Regin   3 'Full well couldst thou wield
wealth and kingship,
O son of Sigmund,
a sire's treasure.'
Sigurd   'My father is fallen,
his folk scattered,
his wealth wasted,
in war taken!'

Regin 4   'A hoard have I heard
on a heath lying,
gold more glorious
than greatest king's.
Wealth and worship
would wait on thee,
if thou durst to deal
with its dragon master.'

Sigurd 5   'Men sing of serpents
ceaseless guarding
gold and silver
greedy-hearted;
but fell Fáfnir
folk all name him
of dragons direst,
dreaming evil.'

Regin 6   'Dragons all are dire
to the dull-hearted;
yet venom feared not
Völsung's children.'

Sigurd   'Eager thou urgest me,
though of age untried –
tell me now truly
why thou tauntest me!'

*

V Regin

Regin 7 'The falls of Andvari
frothed and spouted
with fish teeming
in foaming pools.
There Otr sported,
mine own brother;
to snare salmon
sweet he thought it.

8 With stone smote him,
stripped him naked,
a robber roving
ruthless-handed;
at Hreidmar's house
hailed my father,
that fairest fell
for food offered.

9 There wrought Regin
by the red embers
rough iron hewing
and runes marking;
there Fáfnir lay
by the fire sleeping,
fell-hearted son,
fiercely dreaming.

(Hreidmar) 10   "Redgolden rings,
　　　　　　　　　ransom costly,
　　　　　　　　　this fell must fill,
　　　　　　　　　this fur cover."
　　　　　　　　　From the foaming force
　　　　　　　　　as a fish netted
　　　　　　　　　was Dwarf Andvari
　　　　　　　　　dragged and plundered.

　　　　　11   All must Andvari,
　　　　　　　　　all surrender,
　　　　　　　　　light rings and heavy,
　　　　　　　　　or life itself.
　　　　　　　　　In Hreidmar's house
　　　　　　　　　heaped he laid them,
　　　　　　　　　gold ring on gold,
　　　　　　　　　a great weregild.

(Regin & 12   "Shall not brethren share
Fáfnir)　　　　　in brother's ransom
　　　　　　　　　their grief to gladden? –
　　　　　　　　　gold is healing."
(Hreidmar)　　　"The wreathéd rings
　　　　　　　　　I will rule alone,
　　　　　　　　　as long as life is
　　　　　　　　　they leave me never!"

V Regin

13   Then Fáfnir's heart
fiercely stung him;
Hreidmar he hewed
in his house asleep.
Fáfnir's heart
as a fire burneth:
part nor portion
he pays to Regin.

14   In dragon's likeness
darkling lies he;
deep his dungeons,
and dread he knows not.
A helm of horror
his head weareth
on Gnitaheiði
grimly creeping.'

Sigurd 15   'With kin unkindly
wert thou cursed Regin!
His fire and venom
affright me not!
Yet why thou eggest me,
I ask thee still –
for father's vengeance ,
or for Fáfnir's gold?'

Regin 16 'A sire avenged
were sweet to Regin;
the gold thy guerdon,
the glory thine.
A sword for Sigurd
will the smith fashion,
the blade most bitter
ever borne to war.'

*

17 The forge was smoking,
the fire smouldered.
Two swords there fashioned
twice he broke them:
hard the anvil
hewed he mightily –
sword was splintered,
smith was angered.

Sigurd 18 'Sigrlinn, say me,
was sooth told me
of gleaming shards
of Grímnir's sword?
Sigmund's son
now seeks them from thee –
now Gram shall Regin
guileless weld me!'

V Regin

19   The forge was flaring,
the fire blazing:
a blade they brought him
with blue edges;
they flickered with flame,
as it flashed singing –
the cloven anvil
clashed asunder.

20   The Rhine river
ran by swiftly;
there tufts of wool
on the tide he cast.
Sharp it shore them
in the sheer water:
glad grew Sigurd,
Gram there brandished.

Sigurd 21   'Where lies the heath
and hoard golden?
Now rede me Regin
of roads thither!'
Regin   'Far lies Fáfnir
in the fells hiding –
a horse must thou have,
high and sturdy.'

22   In Busiltarn ran
blue the waters,
green grew the grass
for grazing horse.
A man them minded
mantled darkly,
hoary-bearded,
huge and ancient.

23   They drove the horses
into deep currents;
to the bank they backed
from the bitter water.
But grey Grani
gladly swam there:
Sigurd chose him,
swift and flawless.

Man 24   'In the stud of Sleipnir,
steed of Ódin,
was sired this horse,
swiftest, strongest.
Ride now! ride now!
rocks and mountains,
horse and hero,
hope of Ódin!'

*

V Regin

25   Gand rode Regin
and Grani Sigurd;
the waste lay withered,
wide and empty.
Fathoms thirty fell
the fearful cliff
whence the dragon bowed him
drinking thirsty.

26   In deep hollow
on the dark hillside
long there lurked he;
the land trembled.
Forth came Fáfnir,
fire his breathing;
down the mountain rushed
mists of poison.

27   The fire and fume
over fearless head
rushed by roaring;
rocks were groaning.
The black belly,
bent and coiling,
over hidden hollow
hung and glided.

28   Gram was brandished;
grimly ringing
to the hoary stone
heart it sundered.
In Fáfnir's throe
were threshed as flails
his writhing limbs
and reeking head.

29   Black flowed the blood,
belching drenched him;
in the hollow hiding
hard grew Sigurd.
Swift now sprang he
sword withdrawing:
there each saw other
with eyes of hate.

Fáfnir 30   'O man of mankind!
What man begot thee?
Who forged the flame
for Fáfnir's heart?'

Sigurd   'As the wolf I walk
wild and lonely,
no father owning,
a flame bearing.'

V Regin

Fáfnir 31   'A wolf was thy sire –
full well I know it!
Who egged thee eager
to mine undoing?'

Sigurd   'My sire was Sigmund,
seed of Völsung;
my heart egged me,
my hand answered.'

Fáfnir 32   'Nay! Regin wrought this,
rogue and master!
O son of Sigmund!
sooth I tell thee:
my guarded gold
gleams with evil,
bale it bringeth
to both my foes.'

Sigurd 33   'Life each must leave
on his latest day,
yet gold gladly
will grasp living!'

Fáfnir   'Fools! saith Fáfnir –
with fate of woe
this gold is glamoured.
Grasp not! Flee thou!'

Sigurd 34   'A fool, saith Sigurd,
              could not fend himself
              with helm of horror –
              hell now seize him!'
              In the heather had hidden
              as a hare cowering
              the fear-daunted smith;
              forth now crept he.

Regin 35   'Hail! O Völsung
              victory-crownéd,
              of mortal men
              mightiest hero!'
Sigurd   'In the halls of Ódin
              more hard to choose!
              many brave are born
              who blades stain not.'

Regin 36   'Yet glad is Sigurd,
              of gold thinking,
              as Gram on the grey
              grass he wipeth!
              'Twas blood of my brother
              that blade did spill,
              though somewhat the slaying
              I myself must share.'

V Regin

Sigurd   37   'Far enow thou fleddest,
               when Fáfnir came.
               This sword slew him,
               and Sigurd's prowess.'
Regin   'This sword I smithied.
               Yet would serpent live,
               had not Regin's counsel
               wrought his ending!'

Sigurd   38   'Nay, blame not thyself,
               backward helper!
               Stout heart is better
               than strongest sword.'
Regin   'Yet the sword I smithied,
               the serpent's bane!
               The bold oft are beaten
               who have blunt weapons.'

         39   Thus heavy spake Regin
               Ridil unsheathing,
               fell Fáfnir's heart
               from the flesh cleaving.
               Dark blood drank he
               from the dragon welling;
               deep drowsing fell
               on dwarvish smith.

Regin 40   'Sit now, Sigurd!
          Sleep o'ercomes me.
          Thou Fáfnir's heart
          at the fire roast me.
          His dark thought's dwelling
          after drink potent
          I fain would eat,
          feast of wisdom.'

     41   Sharp spit shaped he;
          at shining fire
          the fat of Fáfnir
          there frothed and hissed.
          To tongue he touched
          testing finger –
          beasts' cry he knew,
          and birds' voices.

*

first bird 42   'A head shorter
          should hoary liar
          go hence to nether hell!
          The heart of Fáfnir
          I whole would eat
          if I myself were Sigurd.'

V Regin

second bird 43   'Who a foe lets free
          is fool indeed,
          when he was bane of brother!
          I alone would be lord
          of linkéd gold,
          if my wielded sword had won it.'

first bird 44   'A head shorter
          should hiding dwarf
          deprived of gold perish!
          There Regin rouses
          in rustling heather;
          Vengeance he vows for brother.'

*

45   Round turned Sigurd,
          and Regin saw he
          in the heath crawling
          with hate gleaming.
          Black spilled the blood
          as blade clove him,
          the head hewing
          of Hreidmar's son.

46   Dark red the drink
          and dire the meat

whereon Sigurd feasted
seeking wisdom.
Dark hung the doors
and dread the timbers
in the earth under
of iron builded.

47   Gold piled on gold
there glittered palely:
that gold was glamoured
with grim curses.
The Helm of Horror
on his head laid he:
swart fell the shadow
round Sigurd standing.

48   Great and grievous
was Grani's burden,
yet lightly leaped he
down the long mountain.
Ride now! ride now
road and woodland,
horse and hero,
hope of Ódin!

*

V Regin

49 Ever wild and wide
the wandering paths;
long lay the shadow
of lone rider.
Birds in the branches
blithe were singing:
their words he heard,
their wit he knew not.

Raven 50 'High stands a hall
on Hindarfell,
fire it fenceth
flaming-tonguéd;
steep stands the path,
stern the venture,
where mountains beckon
to mighty heart.'

Finch 51 'A maid have I seen
as morning fair,
golden-girdled,
garland-crownéd.
Green run the roads
to Gjúki's land;
fate leads them on,
who fare that way.'

Raven 52 'Slumber bindeth
the sun-maiden
on mountain high,
mail about her.
Thorn of Ódin
is thrust in bosom –
to what shall she wake,
woe or laughter?'

Finch 53 'The Gjúkings proudly,
Gunnar and Högni,
there rule a realm
by Rhine-water.
Gudrún groweth
golden-lovely,
as flower unfolded
fair at morning.'

Raven 54 'Too peerless proud
her power wielding,
victory swaying
as Valkyrie,
she heard nor heeded
hests of Ódin,
and Ódin smote
whom Ódin loved.'

*

VI

BRYNHILDR

Here is told of the awakening of Brynhild by Sigurd.
Doomed by Ódin to go no longer to warfare but to wed, she
has vowed to wed only the greatest of all warriors, the
World's chosen. Sigurd and Brynhild plight their troth, amid
great joy, although of her wisdom she foresees that great
perils beset Sigurd's path. They depart together, but the pride
of Brynhild causes her to bid Sigurd depart and come back to
her only when he has won all men's honour, and a kingdom.

1   Ever wide and wild
the wandering path;
long lay the shadow
of lone rider.
Ever high and high
stood Hindarfell,
mountain mighty
from mist rising.

2   A fire at crown,
      fence of lightning,
      high to heavenward
      hissed and wavered.
      Greyfell Grani,
      glory seeking,
      leaped the lightning
      lightning-sinewed.

3   A wall saw Sigurd
      of woven shields,
      a standard streaming
      striped with silver;
      a man there war-clad,
      mailclad, lying,
      with sword beside him,
      sleeping deadly.

4   The helm he lifted:
      hair fell shining,
      a woman lay there
      wound in slumber;
      fast her corslet
      as on flesh growing –
      the gleaming links,
      Gram there clave them.

*

VI Brynhild

Brynhild 5   'Hail! O Daylight
awakening   and Day's children!
           Hail, Night and Noon
           and Northern Star!
           Hail, Kingly Gods,
           Queens of Ásgard!
           Hail, Earth's bosom
           all-abounding!

      6   Hands of healing,
           hear and grant us,
           light in darkness,
           life and wisdom;
           to both give triumph,
           truth unfailing,
           to both in gladness
           glorious meeting!'

*

Brynhild 7   'Brynhild greets thee,
           O brave and fair!
           What prince hath pierced
           my pale fetters?'
   Sigurd   'A man fatherless,
           yet man-begotten,
           here red from battle
           raven-haunted.'

Brynhild 8 'Ódin bound me,
Ódin's chosen;
no more to battle,
to mate doomed me.
An oath I uttered
for ever lasting,
to wed but one,
the World's chosen.'

Sigurd 9 'In the halls of Ódin
it were hard to choose
man there mightiest,
most renownéd.'
Brynhild 'Yet one they wait for,
in wide Valhöll,
the serpent-slayer,
seed of Ódin.'

Sigurd 10 'Seed of Ódin
is Sigmund's child,
and Sigurd's sword
is serpent's bane.'
Brynhild 'Hail, son of Sigmund,
seed of Völsung!
Warriors wait for thee
in wide Valhöll.'

VI Brynhild

Sigurd 11 'Hail, bright and splendid!
Hail, battle-maiden,
bride of Völsung
Brynhild chosen!'
Troth in triumph
twain there plighted
alone on mountain;
light was round them.

Brynhild 12 'A beaker I bring thee,
O battle-wielder,
mighty-blended
mead of glory,
brimmed with bounty,
blessed with healing,
and rimmed with runes
of running laughter.'

Sigurd 13 'I drink, all daring:
doom or glory;
drink of splendour
dear the bearer!'
Brynhild 'Dear the drinker!
Doom and glory
both me bodeth,
thou bright and fair!'

Sigurd 14 'I flee nor flinch,
though fey standing,
words of wisdom,
woe, or gladness.'

Brynhild 'Words of wisdom
warning darkly
hear thou and hold,
hope of Ódin!

15 Be slow to vengeance,
seed of Völsung!
In swearing soothfast,
the sworn holding.
Grim grow the boughs
in guile rooted;
fair flowers the tree
in faith planted!

16 Where the witch-hearted
walks or houses
linger not, lodge not,
though lone the road!
Though beauty blindeth
bright as morning,
let no daughter of kings
thy dreams master!

VI Brynhild

17 Hail, Sigmund's son!
Swift thy glory,
yet a cloud meseems
creepeth nigh thee.
Long life, I fear,
lies not before thee,
but strife and storm
stand there darkly.'

Sigurd 18 'Hail, Brynhild wise!
Bright thy splendour
though fate be strong
to find its end.
Faith ever will I hold
firm, unyielding,
though strife and storm
stand about me.'

19 Faith then they vowed
fast, unyielding,
there each to each
in oaths binding.
Bliss there was born
when Brynhild woke;
yet fate is strong
to find its end.

*

20 Ever wild and wide
the wandering paths;
on roads shining
went riders two.
High towered the helm;
hair flowed in wind;
mail glinted bright
on mountain dark.

Brynhild 21 'Here, Sigmund's son,
swift and fearless,
is our way's parting,
to woe or joy.
Here, lord, I leave thee,
to my land turning;
hence Grani bears thee
glory seeking.'

Sigurd 22 'Why, Brynhild wise,
bride of Völsung,
when at one are the riders
do our ways sunder?'

Brynhild 'I was queen of yore,
and a king shall wed.
Lands lie before thee –
thy lordship win!'

VI Brynhild

23   To her land she turned
lonely shining;
green ran the roads
that Grani strode.
To her land she came,
long the waiting;
in Gjúki's house
glad the singing.

*

VII

GUÐRÚN

Guðrún   1   'O mother, hear me!
Mirth is darkened,
dreams have troubled me,
dreams of boding.'

Grímhild   'Dreams come most oft
in dwindling moon,
or weather changing.
Of woe think not!'

Guðrún   2   'No wind, nor wraith
of waking thought –
a hart we hunted
over hill and valley;
all would take him,
'twas I caught him:
his hide was golden,
his horns towering.

VII Gudrún

3   A woman wildly
on the wind riding
with a shaft stung him,
shooting pierced him;
at my knees he fell
in night of woe,
my heart too heavy
might I hardly bear.

4   A wolf they gave me
for woe's comfort;
in my brethren's blood
he bathed me red.
Dreams have vexed me,
direst boding,
not wind or weather
or waning moon.'

Grímhild   5   'Dreams oft token
the dark by light,
good by evil,
Gudrún daughter!
Lift up thine eyes
eager shining!
Green lie the lands
round Gjúki's house.'

Gudrún 6 'The roads run green
to the Rhine-water!
Who rides here lone,
arrayed for war?
His helm is high,
his horse fleeting,
his shield is shining
with sheen of gold!'

7 Thus Gudrún gazed,
Gjúki's daughter,
from wall and window
in wonder looking.
Thus Sigurd rode,
seed of Völsung,
into Gjúki's courts
gleaming-harnessed.

8 There Gjúki dwelt
his gold dealing
in Niflung land,
the Niflung lord.
Gunnar and Högni
were Gjúki's sons,
mighty princes;
men them hearkened.

VII Gudrún

9   There Grímhild dwelt,
       guileful in counsel,
       grimhearted queen
       grey with wisdom,
       with lore of leechcraft,
       lore of poison,
       with chill enchantment
       and with changing spells.

10   As ravens dark
       were those raven-friends;
       fair their faces,
       fierce their glances.
       With Huns they waged
       hate and warfare,
       gold ever gathering
       in great dungeons.

11   Silent they sat
       when Sigurd entered
       Gunnar greeting,
       Gjúki hailing.
Gjúki   'Who comes unbidden
       in battle's harness,
       helm and hauberk,
       to halls of mine?'

Sigurd 12 'The son of Sigmund,
Sigurd Völsung,
a king's son cometh
to kingly house.
Fame of Niflungs
far is rumoured,
not yet hath faded
fame of Völsung.'

13 There swift for Sigurd
seat was ordered;
the feast grew fair,
folk were mirthful.
There Gunnar grasped
his golden harp;
while songs he sang
silence fell there.

Of these 14 By mighty Mirkwood
things sang on the marches of the East
Gunnar the great Goth-kings
in glory ruled.
By Danpar-banks
was dread warfare
with the hosts of Hunland,
horsemen countless.

VII Gudrún

15 Horsemen countless
hastened westward;
the Borgund lords
met Budli's host.
In Budli's brother
their blades reddened
the glad Gjúkings,
gold despoiling.

Of these 16 Then Sigurd seized
things sang the sounding harp;
Sigurd hushed they hearkened
in the hall listening.
The waste lay withered
wide and empty;
forth came Fáfnir,
fire around him.

17 Dark hung the doors
on deep timbers;
gold piled on gold
there glittered wanly.
The hoard was plundered,
helm was lifted,
and Grani greyfell
grievous burdened.

18   High Hindarfell,
      hedged with lightning,
      mountain mighty
      from mists uprose.
      Brynhild wakened,
      bright her splendour –
      song fell silent,
      and Sigurd ended.

19   By Gjúki's chair
      Grímhild hearkened,
      of Gudrún thinking
      and the golden hoard.
      Gunnar and Högni
      gladly bade him
      in league and love
      long to dwell there.

*

20   The Borgund lords
      their battle furnished;
      banners were broidered,
      blades were sharpened.
      White shone hauberks,
      helms were burnished;
      under horses' hooves
      Hunland trembled.

VII Gudrún

21   Grim was Gunnar
      on Goti riding;
      under haughty Högni
      Hölkvir strode;
      but fleeter was Grani,
      foal of Sleipnir;
      flamed all before
      the fire of Sigurd.

22   Foes were vanquished,
      fields were wasted,
      grimly garnered
      Gram the harvest.
      Where Gjúkings rode
      glory won they,
      ever glory Sigurd
      greater conquered.

23   Wide waxed their realm
      in world of old;
      Dane-king they slew,
      doughty princes.
      Dread fell on folk;
      doom they wielded;
      victory rode ever
      with the Völsung lord.

24   High they honoured him,
in heart loved him,
Hun-gold gave him
in the hall sitting.
But his heart remembered
house of Völsung,
and Sigmund slain
on sands afar.

25   A host he gathered,
help of Gjúkings;
to the sea he rode
and sails hoisted.
His ship was shining
with shields and mail;
it was dragon-headed,
dire and golden.

26   As fire and tempest
to his father's land
came Sigurd sailing;
the sand was reddened.
Clashed the cloven
casque and hauberk;
shields were splintered,
shorn was corslet.

VII Gudrún

27 Men learned there lived yet
    line of Völsung!
    Now of Völsung land
    was a Völsung lord.
    But the house once high
    was hollow, roofless;
    the limbs were rotten
    of their leafy tree.

28 A man there walked
    mantled darkly,
    his beard was flowing,
    and blind his eye:
Grímnir   'Grímnir hails thee,
    glorious Völsung!
    Far hence hath flown
    the fate of Sigurd.

29 Where Sigmund drew
    sword of Grímnir,
    Gram shall shine not.
    Go thou, Völsung!
    Now king thou art
    of kings begotten,
    a bride calls thee
    over billowing seas.'

*

30 His fleet went forth
    with flaming sails;
    goldladen ships
    came glad to shore.
    Steeds went striding,
    stonefire glinted,
    horns were sounded;
    home rode Sigurd.

31 A feast they fashioned,
    far proclaimed it,
    their highroofed halls
    hung with splendour;
    boards and beakers,
    benches, gilded;
    mead poured and ale
    from morn to eve.

32 A king sat Sigurd:
    carven silver,
    raiment gleaming,
    rings and goblets,
    dear things dealt he,
    doughty-handed,
    his friends enriching,
    fame upraising.

VII Gudrún

33 (There spake Grímhild
to Gjúki's ear:)

Grímhild   'How long shall last
league unbounden?
Here is worthiest lord
of world's renown!
Were a daughter offered,
he would dwell for ever,
our strength in strife,
standing bulwark.'

Gjúki   34   'The gifts of kings
are gold and silver;
their daughters fair
are dearly wooed!'

Grímhild   'Gifts oft are given
to greedy hand;
wives oft are wooed
by worthless men!'

35 Sigurd sat silent;
the singing heard not
but in heart Brynhild
bright with splendour:
'A queen was I once,
and a king shall wed.'

Soon, thought he, soon
I will seek my own.

*

36   Grímhild went forth
to guarded bower;
deep horn she filled
that was darkly written.
She drink of power
dreadly blended;
it had strength of stone,
it was stained with blood.

Grímhild   37   'Hail, guest and king!
Good go with thee!
Drink now deeply
dear love's token!
A father hast thou found,
and fond mother,
brothers sit nigh thee.
O bravest, hail!'

38   Deep drank Sigurd,
drained it laughing,
then sat unsmiling,
the singing heard not.

VII Gudrún

> In came Gudrún
> golden-lovely,
> as moon uprising
> marvellous shining.

39   In came Gudrún
> gleaming-robéd,
> as flower unfolded
> fair at morning.
> Sigurd wondered,
> silent gazing;
> his mind was glamoured,
> mood confounded.

*

VIII

SVIKIN BRYNHILDR
(Brynhild Betrayed)

1   Brynhild abode
a blossomed summer,
homing harvest,
hoary winter.
A year followed year;
yearning seized her:
the king came not;
cold weighed her heart.

2   Of her wealth and splendour
wide spread the word;
kings came riding,
her courts thronging.
Her mood was troubled,
her mind darkened;
fell greeting found they,
and few returned.

VIII *Brynhild Betrayed*

3   One armed and mantled
    as ancient king
    wild steed there rode
    than wind fleeter.
    Spear upholding
    spiked with lightning
    her hall he entered,
    hailed her darkly:

King 4   'Bond unbroken
    shall be bounden oath,
    dreed and endured
    be doom appointed.
    Brynhild full soon
    shall bridal drink;
    choosing not the slain,
    shall choose the living.

5   Brynhild must drink
    the bridal feast,
    ere winters two
    o'er the world be passed.
    A queen thou wert,
    a king shalt wed:
    Ódin dooms it;
    Ódin hearken!'

6   Fire forth blossomed,
    flames were kindled,
    high up-leaping
    hissed and wavered.
    In hall standing
    hedged with lightning,
    'one only', thought she
    'can enter now!'

                *

7   In Gjúki's house
    glad the singing.
    A feast they fashioned,
    far men sought it.
    To blissful Gudrún
    the bridal drank
    there golden Sigurd
    glorious shining.

8   Morning woke with mirth,
    merry came evening;
    harp-strings were plucked
    by hands of cunning;
    mead poured and ale,
    men were joyful,
    of peerless kings
    praise uplifting.

VIII Brynhild Betrayed

9   Oaths swore Sigurd
for ever lasting,
a bond of brotherhood
in blood mingled,
help in venture,
in hate and battle,
in need and desire,
nowhere failing.

10   Gunnar and Högni
gladly swore it,
as Grímhild counselled
grey with wisdom.
Gunnar and Högni
good they deemed it;
glad was Gudrún
gleaming-lovely.

11   Gudrún walked in joy,
gladness round her;
mornings came with mirth,
mirth at sleeping.
Sigurd dwelt as king
sweet days and nights;
high hope he had,
yet in heart a shadow.

*

12   Wide went the word
of woman mighty,
of Brynhild queen
bright in splendour.
Grímhild hearkened,
grimly pondered,
of Gunnar thinking
and of Gjúki's power.

Grímhild 13   'Hail, Gjúki's son!
Good go with thee!
Fair flowers thy state,
thy fame riseth.
Who could woo as he wills,
a wife yet lacketh,
though his might few match,
or might of friends.'

Gunnar 14   'Lo! Gjúkings' mother
grey in counsel,
what wife shall Gunnar
woo or look for?
Fairest must be woman,
of fame mightiest,
that Gunnar seeketh
his gold dealing.'

VIII Brynhild Betrayed

Grímhild   15   'Of the one fairest
fame is rumoured:
Brynhild the queen
bright in splendour.
Wide walks the word
of her wealth and might;
though high nor humble
her halls enter.'

Gunnar   16   'Proud and peerless
in peril woven,
a queen would she be,
our courts' glory!
Gunnar Gjúki's son
glory seeking
at thy rede shall ride
to her realm afar.'

Grímhild   17   'The son of Sigmund
thy sister holds,
Sigurd the mighty
is thy sworn brother.
At right hand in aid
he shall ride with thee;
counsels potent
shall my cunning find you.'

*

146

18   Gunnar rode Goti,
on Grani Sigurd,
Högni Hölkvir,
horse night-swarthy.
Steeds were striding,
stonefire glinting,
high wind rushing
over helm and mane.

19   Over fell and lowland
and forest gloomy,
over rocks and rivers
their roads led them.
Golden gables
gleaming saw they;
a light was lifted
o'er the land afar.

20   Fire forth blossomed,
flames up-leaping,
trees of lightning
twisted branching.
Gunnar smote Goti:
the ground spurning
he reared him backward,
nor rowel heeded.

VIII Brynhild Betrayed

21   Sigurd unsmiling
silent waited,
in his shrouded heart
a shadow deepened:

Sigurd   'For what waits Gunnar,
Gjúking fearless?
Here the queen dwelleth
that our quest seeketh!'

Gunnar 22   'A boon grant me,
O blood-brother!
Goti will not bear me,
now Grani lend me!'
Gunnar smote Grani:
on the ground moveless
grey-hewn he stood
as of graven stone.

23   Gunnar rode not
the glittering flame.
Oaths swore Sigurd,
all fulfilled them.
In hope or hate
help unfailing,
he Grímhild's counsel
grim refused not.

24 Counsels potent
    had her cunning furnished
    of chill enchantment
    and changing spell.
    In Gunnar's likeness
    on Grani leaped he;
    gold spurs glinted,
    Gram was brandished.

25 The earth shivered;
    angry roaring
    fire flaming-tongued
    flashed heavenward.
    With sword smitten
    snorting leaped he,
    Grani greyfell;
    the ground trembled.

26 The fire flickered;
    flame wavered,
    sank to silence
    slaked and fading.
    Swart lay the shadow
    of Sigurd riding
    in helm of terror
    high and looming.

VIII Brynhild Betrayed

27   Sigurd stood there
        on sword leaning;
        Brynhild waited
        a blade holding.
        There helméd maiden
        of helméd king
        name demanded:
        night fell round them.

Sigurd 28   'Gunnar Gjúki's son
        greets and hails thee.
        As my queen shalt thou ride
        my quest fulfilling.'
        As on swaying seas
        a swan glimmering
        sat she sore troubled
        seeking counsel:

Brynhild 29   'What shall I answer
        in hour o'ershadowed,
        Gunnar, Gunnar,
        with gleaming eyes?'
Sigurd   'Redgolden rings,
        Rhineland treasure,
        mighty brideprice
        shall be meted thee!'

Brynhild 30　'Gunnar, speak not
of golden rings!
Swords were me dearer
to slay my loves.
Art thou all men's master,
all surpassing? –
to only such
will I answer give.'

Sigurd 31　'Yea, swords hast thou reddened,
swords yet shalt wield;
and oaths hast thou sworn,
and oaths shalt keep.
Thy wall is ridden,
thy wavering fire:
thou art doomed him to wed
who dared to pass.'

32　In a bed them laid
Brynhild, Sigurd;
a sword them sundered
set there naked.
Gram lay between
gleaming sheathless,
fate lay between
forged unyielding.

VIII Brynhild Betrayed

33 Dawn came on earth,
day grew round them.
From sleeping finger
he slipped her ring,
and Andvari's gold,
old, enchanted,
on Brynhild's hand
bound in token.

Sigurd   34 'Wake thou! wake thou!
Wide is daylight.
I ride to my realm
to array the feast.'
Brynhild   'Gunnar, Gunnar,
with gleaming eyes,
on day appointed
I shall drink with thee.'

*

IX

DEILD
(Strife)

1 On day appointed
dawn rose redly,
sun sprang fiery
southward hasting.
Bridal to Brynhild
blissful drank he,
Gunnar Gjúki's son,
gold unsparing.

2 All surpassing,
proud and ardent,
Brynhild sat there,
a bride and queen.
All men's master,
all surpassing,
in came Sigurd
as sun rising.

IX Strife

3 By Gudrún's side,
 Gjúki's daughter,
 she saw him seated –
 a silence fell.
 As stone graven
 stared she palely,
 as cold and still
 as carven stone.

4 From shrouded heart
 the shadows parted;
 oaths were remembered
 all unfulfilled.
 As stone carven,
 stern, unbending,
 he sat unsmiling
 no sign making.

5 Clamour rose again,
 clear the singing.
 Men were joyful –
 mirth they deemed it.
 In that hall beheld they
 heroes mightiest,
 and kings and queens
 crowned in splendour.

*

6   Forth rode Sigurd,
the forest seeking,
to hunt the hart;
horns were sounded.
To the Rhine-river,
to running water,
queens went comely
with combs of gold.

7   Their locks they loosened.
Long one waded
to deeper pools
darkly swirling:

Brynhild   'The water that hath washed
thy wan tresses
shall not flow unfitting
over fairer brow!'

Gudrún 8 'More queenly I,
more kingly wed! –
fame all surpasses
he that Fáfnir slew!'

Brynhild   'Worth all surpasses
who my wavering fire,
flaming lightning
fearless vanquished!'

IX Strife

9 (Grim laughed Gudrún
Grímhild's daughter:)

Gudrún   'True spake the tongue
of truth unwitting!
Thy wavering fire
wildly flaming
he rode unrecking
who that ring gave thee –
did Gunnar get it
on Gnitaheiði?

10 Andvari's ring,
old, enchanted,
is on Brynhild's hand
bound in token.
Did Gunnar give me
the gleaming ring
from thy hand he drew,
now here on mine!'

11 Coldhued as death
the queen was stricken,
strode swift from stream
as stone silent;
from Rhine-river,
from running water,
her bower sought she
brooding darkly.

12 Dim fell evening,
    dusk was starless;
    her mind was as night
    as she mourned alone;
    alone, lightless,
    made lamentation:
Brynhild 'Fell! fell the fates
    that forged our days!

13 Mine own must I have
    or anguish suffer,
    or suffer anguish
    Sigurd losing.
    Yet he is Gudrún's
    and Gunnar's I:
    foul wrought the fates
    that framed my life!'

14 Daylong lay she
    drinking nor eating,
    as in dead slumber
    or dreadful thought.
    Her maidens marvelled –
    she minded not,
    Gunnar sought her;
    grim she heard him.

IX Strife

15 Then spake Brynhild
from bitter pondering:
Brynhild 'Whence came the gold
here gleaming pale?
Who holds the ring
from my hand taken?'
Nought spake Gunnar,
no word answered.

Brynhild 16 'King men call thee!
A coward rather,
from fire flinching,
fearful, quaking!
From witch-woman's
womb thou camest.
Woe to Grímhild,
woe's contriver!'

Gunnar 17 'Vile words to use,
thou Valkyrie,
thou slayer of men,
and sword-hearted!'
Brynhild 'If sword I had,
I would slay thee now,
for thy secret treason,
for thy sundered oaths!

18   Him only loved I
who all surpassed;
an oath uttered,
him only to wed,
him only to wed
who mine ardent fire
vanquished valorous;
I am vow-breaker.

19   I am oath-breaker,
dishonoured, humbled;
I am love-bereaved
and life-curséd.
In thy halls shalt thou hear
never happy voices,
no queen in thy courts
shall comely walk.'

20   Long there lay she
in lamentation;
afar heard folk
her fell mourning.
Gudrún she spurned,
Gunnar scorning,
and Högni mocking;
hate was kindled.

*

159

IX Strife

21 From the hunt rode Sigurd
    home returning,
    found halls unlit
    and hearts darkened.
    They brought him to seek her
    for sorrow's healing;
    his mood was loath,
    on the morrow went he.

Sigurd 22 'Hail, O sunlight
    and sun's rising!
    Sleep no longer
    and sorrow cast thou!'

(He draws back the coverlet from Brynhild and wakes her, as before he had done.)

Brynhild 'I slept on mountain,
    I sleep no more!
    Accursed be thy words,
    cruel forswearer!'

Sigurd 23 'What grief ails thee
    amid good liking,
    who to glorious Gunnar
    wert gladly wed?'

Brynhild 'Gladly! gladly!
    Grim thou mockest me.
    Him only I loved,
    who all surpassed.'

Sigurd   24   'Yet glory no less
                hath Gjúki's son,
                my blood-brother,
                best renownéd.
                Well he loves thee,
                lord unfearing –
                look now and learn
                light yet shineth!'

Brynhild 25   'Nay, Fáfnir Sigurd
                fearless conquered;
                my wavering fire
                he waded twice;
                twice he waded
                tongues of lightning:
                so great glory
                never Gunnar earned.'

Sigurd   26   'That twice he waded,
                who told thee so?
                Sigurd hath not said it –
                why saist thou this?'
Brynhild   'Gloom was round us.
                Thy gleaming eyes,
                thine eyes gleaming
                anguish gave me.

161

IX Strife

27   Veils of darkness
they vanquished me.
I am life-curséd
and love-bereaved.
Yet I curse thee too,
cruel forswearer,
who rendered to another
the ring taken.

28   Gudrún I curse
for cruel reproach
of bed broken
and body yielded.
Thy glory alone
seems good to thee;
of all women the worst
thou weenest me.'

Sigurd 29   'Woe worth the words
by women spoken!
Woe worth the while
this work began!
Webs enwound me
woven dreadly,
my mind shadowing,
my mood darkening.

30   Long I loved thee,
      long desiring.
      Thee only would I hold,
      now all I know.
      My mood mastering,
      my mind wielding,
      I sat unsmiling,
      no sign making.

31   This solace sought I,
      that I saw thee still,
      the one hall walking
      though wife of other.'

Brynhild   'Too late! too late,
      love thou speakest!
      To allay this evil
      there leech is none.'

Sigurd 32   'Is hope all fallen,
      is healing vain?
      Must fate fierce-hearted
      thus find its end?'

Brynhild   'This hope only,
      this heart's comfort –
      that Sigurd forsworn
      a sword should bite!'

IX Strife

Sigurd 33   'Swords lightly sleep,
              soon may I feel them!
              Then would Brynhild die –
              bitter would she deem it.'
Brynhild   'Well fall the words
              from woe's maker!
              Little light in life
              hath he left to me.'

Sigurd 34   'Yet Gunnar would I slay,
              Gudrún forsake,
              from death thee to keep,
              our doom o'ercoming!'
Brynhild   'I am wife of one,
              I wed no other.
              No lord will I love,
              and least Sigurd!'

                     *

        35   Forth went Sigurd
              filled with anguish,
              his heart was swollen
              in heaving breast.
              Mail-rings clutched him,
              marred his breathing,
              to his flesh cutting
              fiercely straining.

36   There stood Gudrún
           gleaming-lovely:

Gudrún   'Sleeps yet Brynhild,
           sickness bearing?'

Sigurd   'Brynhild sleeps not,
           brooding darkly.
           She broodeth darkly
           our bale and doom.'

37   Gudrún wanly
           grasped him weeping:

Gudrún   'What doth Brynhild brood,
           what bale purpose?'

Sigurd   'Thou shouldst know it,
           needless asking.
           Woe worth the words
           by women spoken!'

38   (Then spake Gunnar
           gloomy-hearted:)

Gunnar   'What hope of healing
           harm's amending?
           Shall we gold offer,
           gold and silver?'

Sigurd   'Gold and silver
           let Gunnar offer!
           Her lord alone
           her leech must be.'

IX Strife

39   Then Gunnar offered
gold and silver,
gold and silver
gleaming-hoarded.

Brynhild   'Gunnar, speak not
of gold and silver;
swords were me dearer
to slay my life.

40   All men's master,
all surpassing,
such only ever
shall earn my love.
Than thy liege lower
thou art less become,
a Völsung's squire,
a vassal's servant!

41   From thy bed parting,
at thy board humbled
I will leave thee alone
to laughter of men,
if life thou allowest
to liege forsworn,
if thou slay not Sigurd,
thy sister's lord.'

Gunnar 42 'Fell-hearted thou,
and foe of peace!
I oaths have sworn
for ever lasting,
bonds of brotherhood
in blood mingled;
though Brynhild bid it,
I may break them not.'

Brynhild 43 'Oaths too I swore
for ever lasting –
light thou heldest them!
I am love-betrayed.
Sigurd thou sent me,
thy sworn brother.
My bed he entered,
by my body laid him,
betrayed thy trust,
betraying me.

44 To Gudrún he told it,
Gudrún knoweth.
In shame am I shrouded,
and shamed art thou!'
Gunnar came forth
grievous-hearted,
daylong he sat,
deeply brooding.

IX Strife

45 From mood to mood
his mind wandered,
from shame to shame
shorn of friendship.
Högni called he
to hidden counsel,
his true brother,
whom he trusted well.

Gunnar 46 'Evil wrought Sigurd:
oaths he swore me,
oaths he swore me,
all belied them;
betrayed my trust,
whom I trusted most,
truth forswearing,
whom most true I deemed.'

Högni 47 'Brynhild beguiles thee
baleful-hearted,
woe devising
to woe stings thee;
loathing Gudrún,
her love grudging,
thy love loathing,
she lies to thee.'

Gunnar 48   'Brynhild, Brynhild,
I better hold her
than all women,
than all treasure.
I will life sooner leave
than lose her now,
than live lonely
for laughter of men.

49   Let us slay Sigurd –
forsworn is he!
Let us lords be alone
of our lands again!
Let us slay Sigurd,
this sorrow ending,
and masters make us
of his mighty hoard!'

Högni 50   'Woe worth the words
by women spoken!
Lords unassailed
our league made us.
The might of Sigurd
we shall mourn later,
and the sister-sons
this sire had got us.'

IX Strife

51   To Gotthorm turning,
Grímhild's offspring,
greyhearted lord,
Gunnar hailed him:

Gunnar   'No oaths thou sworest,
no oaths heedest.
With his blood unblended
his blood now spill!'

52   Gold he promised him
and great lordship;
his bastard blood
burned with hunger.
Snake's flesh they took,
seethed it darkly,
wolf-meat gave him,
wine enchanted.

53   Drunk with madness,
dire and wolvish,
he grinned and gnashed
his grinding teeth.
Of guile unworthy,
no guile dreaming,
yet doom foreboding,
drear went Sigurd.

54   To the forest fared he,
falcon loosing,
with hounds hunting,
for harm's solace.
Gotthorm rode there,
and Grani marked he,
assailing Sigurd,
with searing words.

Gotthorm 55 'O werewolf's son
and war-captive,
what huntest here
where hart roameth –
thou wooer of women
and wife-marrer,
who wouldst lord all alone
our lands and queens!'

56   Sword touched Sigurd
swart-red flushing;
white blanched the knuckles
on hilt clenching:
Sigurd 'Thou drunken dog,
doom hangs nigh thee!
Now slink to kennel!
Sleep may mend thee.'

IX Strife

57   Gotthorm he left
to grind his teeth;
back rode Sigurd
foreboding ill.
Night fell starless,
none were waking;
asleep was Gudrún
by Sigurd dreaming.

58   Dawn came wanly:
drunk with hatred
there Gotthorm stalked
as glowering wolf.
Sword leaped naked,
sleeping stabbed him,
pierced through to pillow,
pinned in anguish.

59   Forth sprang the wolf
by fear blinded
of awful eyes
that opened wide.
Gram was brandished,
gleaming handled,
hissing hurled aloft
at hasting beast.

60   At the door he tumbled
dreadly crying;
there hell took him
hewn asunder.
Forth crashed the head,
feet fell backward;
blood ran darkly
on bower threshold.

61   In sweet embrace
to sleep she went,
to grief unending
Gudrún wakened,
to her bliss drowning
in blood flowing.
in flowing blood
of fairest lord.

62   Breast white and bare
she beat so sore
that Sigurd raised him
from soaking pillow:

Sigurd   'My wife, weep not
for woe foredoomed!
Brothers remain to thee –
blame them lightly!

IX Strife

63   Brynhild wrought this:
best she loved me,
worst she dealt me,
worst belied me.
I Gunnar never
grieved nor injured;
oaths I swore him,
all fulfilled them!'

64   Dead fell Sigurd;
dreadly Gudrún
cried in anguish,
called him vainly.
Swords rang on wall,
and sleepers shivered;
geese screamed shrill
in green meadow.

65   Then laughed Brynhild
in her bed listening
with whole heart once –
the house shuddered –
Gudrún hearing
in grief's torment.
Gunnar answered
grimly speaking:

Gunnar   66   'Little thou laughest
for delight of soul,
O fell-hearted!
Fey I deem thee.
Thy colour blancheth,
cold thy cheeks are;
cold thy counsels
and accursed thy redes.'

Brynhild   67   'Cursed are the Niflungs,
cruel forswearers.
Oaths swore Sigurd,
all fulfilled them.
Ye all shall find
evil fortune,
while all men's honour
he for ever holdeth.

68   Bonds of brotherhood
in blood mingled
with murder kept ye;
he remembered them.
A sword lay naked
set between us,
Gram lay grimly
gleaming sheathless.

IX Strife

69   Now life no longer
will I live with you;
of love ye robbed me
with lying counsels.
Shorn I leave you,
shame enduring,
of faith and friendship,
of fame on earth.'

70   In arms he took her,
anguished begged her
her hand to stay,
hope to look for.
She thrust them from her
who thronged round her,
longing only
for her last journey.

71   (Högni only
withheld her not:)

Högni   'Little would I hinder
her last journey,
so she bide in that land
never born again.
Crooked came she forth
from curséd womb

to man's evil
and our mighty woe.'

*

72   Gold corslet she took,
gleaming hauberk,
helm set on head,
in hand a sword.
On the sword she cast her,
sank down wounded:
thus Brynhild ended
her bright splendour.

Brynhild 73   'A boon I beg thee,
this boon at last!
Pile high a pyre
on the plain builded;
shields hang round it
and shining cloths,
blood pour over it
for us brightly shed!

74   A hawk at each hand,
a hound at feet,
there harnessed set ye
our horses slain.

IX Strife

At his side lay me,
sword between us,
naked gleaming
as on night of yore.

75 Burn there Brynhild
in the blazing fire
who in flames awoke
to fell sorrow.
In flames send forth
that fairest lord
now as sun setting
who as sun did rise!'

76 Flames were kindled,
fume was swirling,
a roaring fire
ringed with weeping.
Thus Sigurd passed,
seed of Völsung,
there Brynhild burned:
bliss was ended.

*

77 On the hell-way hastened
the helméd queen,

never born again
from bleak regions.
In Valhöllu
Völsungs feasted:
'Son's son welcome,
seed of Ódin!'

78   Thus soon came Sigurd
the sword bearing
to glad Valhöll
greeting Ódin.
There feasts he long
at his father's side,
for War waiting,
the World's chosen.

79   When Heimdall's horn
is heard ringing
and the Blazing Bridge
bends neath horsemen,
Brynhild shall arm him
with belt and sword,
a beaker bear him
brimmed with glory.

80   In the day of Doom
he shall deathless stand

IX Strife

> who death tasted
> and dies no more,
> the serpent-slayer,
> seed of Ódin:
> not all shall end,
> nor Earth perish.

81 On his head the Helm,
    in his hand lightning,
    afire his spirit,
    in his face splendour.
    When war passeth
    in world rebuilt,
    bliss shall they drink
    who the bitter tasted.

82 Thus passed Sigurd,
    seed of Völsung,
    hero mightiest,
    hope of Ódin.
    But woe of Gudrún
    through this world lasteth,
    to the end of days
    all shall hear her.

*

COMMENTARY
on
VÖLSUNGAKVIÐA EN NÝJA

COMMENTARY

on

VÖLSUNGAKVIÐA EN NÝJA

The subtitle *Sigurðarkviða en mesta* means 'The Longest Lay of Sigurd': see p.234.

Throughout the commentary the poem *Völsungakviða en Nýja* is referred to as 'the Lay' or occasionally 'the Lay of the Völsungs', and the *Völsunga Saga* as 'the Saga'. The name 'Edda' always refers to the 'Elder Edda' or 'Poetic Edda'; the work of Snorri Sturluson is named the 'Prose Edda'.

The nine sections of the poem following the Upphaf are referred to by Roman numerals and the stanzas by Arabic numerals: thus 'VII.6' refers to stanza 6 in the section 'Gudrún'. Notes are related to stanzas, not lines; and a general note on the section precedes notes to individual stanzas.

UPPHAF

This prelude to the Lay of the Völsungs echoes and reflects the most famous poem of the Edda, the *Völuspá*, in which the *Völva*, the wise woman or sibyl, recounts the origin of the world, the age of the youthful Gods, and the primeval war;

Upphaf

prophesies the Ragnarök, the Doom of the Gods; and after it the renewal of the Earth, rising again out of deep waters (see the third part of my father's poem *The Prophecy of the Sibyl*, given in Appendix B at the end of this book).

But the images of the *Völuspá* are here ordered to an entirely original theme: for the sibyl declares (stanzas 13–15) that the fate of the world and the outcome of the Last Battle will depend on the presence of 'one deathless who death hath tasted and dies no more'; and this is Sigurd, 'the serpent-slayer, seed of Ódin', who is 'the World's chosen' for whom the mailclad warriors wait in Valhöll (stanza 20). As is made explicit in my father's interpretative note (iv) given on p.53–54, it is Ódin's hope that Sigurd will on the Last Day become the slayer of the greatest serpent of all, *Miðgarðsormr* (see note to stanza 12 below), and that through Sigurd 'a new world will be made possible'.

'This motive of the special function of Sigurd is an invention of the present poet', my father observed in the same brief text. An association with his own mythology seems to me at least extremely probable: in that Túrin Turambar, slayer of the great dragon Glaurung, was also reserved for a special destiny, for at the Last Battle he would himself strike down Morgoth, the Dark Lord, with his black sword. This mysterious conception appeared in the old Tale of Turambar (1919 or earlier), and reappeared as a prophecy in the *Silmarillion* texts of the 1930s: so in the *Quenta Noldorinwa*, 'it shall be the black sword of Túrin that deals unto Melko [Morgoth] his death and final end; and so shall the children of Húrin and all Men be avenged.' Very remarkably a form of this conception is found in a brief essay of my father's from near the end of his life, in which he wrote that Andreth the Wise-woman of the House of Bëor had prophesied that 'Túrin in the Last Battle should return from the Dead, and before he left the Circles of the World for ever should challenge the Great Dragon of Morgoth, Ancalagon the Black, and deal him the death-stroke.' The extraordinary transformation of Túrin is seen also in an entry in *The Annals of Aman,* where it is said that the great constellation of Menelmakar, the Swordsman of the Sky (Orion), 'was a sign of Túrin Turambar, who should come into the world, and a foreshadowing of the Last Battle that shall be at the end of Days.'*

Beyond this, in the absence (so far as I know) of any other writing of my father's bearing on his enigmatic conception of Sigurd, I think that speculation on its larger significance would fall outside the editorial limits that I have set for myself in this book.

My father's Ódin does indeed retain his ancient character of gathering his 'chosen' to Valhöll to be his champions at the Ragnarök, and in the Lay of the Völsungs he appears against Sigmund, Sigurd's father, and disarms him in his last fight, so that he is slain (IV.8–11). In Norse legend a belief is expressed that Ódin, faithless, ambiguous, and sinister, desiring strife

---

* For references and citations from volumes of *The History of Middle-earth* on this matter see *The Peoples of Middle-earth* (1996), pp.374–75; and for the entry in the *Annals of Aman* see *Morgoth's Ring* (1993), pp.71, 76.

Upphaf

among kinsmen, turning against his favourites at the last and felling those whom he has favoured, has reason for his conduct: he needs his own, needs his favourites against the day of the Ragnarök (see the note to IX.77–78).

But from the extraordinary complex of ideas that surround Ódin in Northern antiquity – suggesting layer upon layer of shifting belief and symbolism – a God is glimpsed in my father's work who has retained little of the subtle, sinister, and enigmatic deity of ancient writings: the god of war, lord of the Valkyries; exciter of madness; the initiate, the lord of the gallows, the self-sacrificed, the master of obscene magic, the inspiration of poetry; the shape-changer, the old one-eyed man, the faithless friend, and on the Last Day the victim of the Wolf. 'Weighed with wisdom woe foreknowing' (*Upphaf* 18), and seen by my father, referring to his own poem and to his treatment of the old legend, as symbolizing prudence and wisdom beside the malice and folly of Loki, Ódin seems more like Manwë of his own mythology; and he calls them both 'Lord of Gods and Men'.

1   On this stanza see p.246. It echoes the third stanza of the *Völuspá*; and citing the Norse verse in a lecture my father followed it with this first stanza of the *Upphaf*, with some differences: 'shivering waves', 'unraised heaven'.

11 It is told by Snorri in the Prose Edda that Heimdal *(Heimdallr)* was the warden or sentinel of the Gods

(Æsir), dwelling beside Bifröst ('the quaking path'), the rainbow bridge between Ásgard, the realm of the Æsir, and Midgard, the world of Men (see note to 12), which he guards against the rock-giants; but at the Ragnarök (the Doom of the Gods) Bifröst will be crossed by the hosts coming from the fiery land of Múspell, and will break beneath them. The red part of the bow is blazing fire. Heimdal's horn is the Gjallarhorn, whose blast is heard over all the worlds; and he will blow it at the Ragnarök.

The Ash is Yggdrasill, the World Tree, whose branches stretched out over earth and heaven. The Wolf is Fenrir (named in stanza 13), whom the Gods chained; but at the Ragnarök Fenrir will break his chains and devour Óðin.

12 Surt (*Surtr*): the great demon of fire, at the Ragnarök coming out of Múspell, the land of fire, against the Gods.

The 'slumbering Serpent' is *Miðsgarðsormr*, the Serpent of Midgard, who lay coiled through all the seas encompassing Midgard, the world of Men. The Norse name *Miðgarðr* corresponds to Old English *Middan-geard, Middan-eard*, which lie behind the later form *Middle-earth*.

The 'shadowy ship' is Naglfar, made of dead men's nails.

13 Frey *(Freyr):* the chief god of fertility, of peace and plenty, in Norway and Sweden; Freyja (stanza 17) was his sister.

The 'deep Dragon' is the Serpent of Midgard: see note on stanza 12.

I

ANDVARA-GULL
(Andvari's Gold)

For the story in §I of the Lay of the Völsungs the sources are
the Eddaic poem known as *Reginsmál*, the Lay of Regin,
which is indeed less a poem than fragments of old verse
pieced together with prose; a passage in Snorri Sturluson's
version of the Völsung legend in the Prose Edda; and the
Völsunga Saga. The few verses in *Reginsmál* that bear on this
part of the narrative (dialogue between Loki and Andvari,
and between Loki and Hreidmar after the gold had been paid
over) are here and there a model for the Lay, but only lines
5–6 in stanza 8 are a translation (*Andvari ek heiti, Óinn hét
minn faðir*).

Apart from this, *Andvara-gull* in the Lay is a new poem. It
is very allusive, and deliberately so, and I give here in abbreviated form the course of the story as it is known from the prose
narratives: for the most part the two versions differ little.

It is told that three of the Æsir, Óðin, Hœnir, and Loki,
went out into the world, and they came to a waterfall known
as the Falls of Andvari, Andvari being the name of a dwarf
who fished there in the form of a pike (Snorri says nothing of
Andvari at this point). At that place there was an otter that
had caught a salmon, and was eating it on the river bank; but
Loki hurled a stone at the otter and killed it. Then the Æsir
took up the salmon and the otter and went on their way until

they came to the house of a certain Hreidmar. Snorri describes him as a farmer, a man of substance, greatly skilled in magic; in the Saga he is simply an important and wealthy man; whereas in the headnote to this section of the Lay he is 'a demon'.

The Æsir asked Hreidmar for lodging for the night, saying that they had enough food with them, and they showed Hreidmar their catch; but the otter was Hreidmar's son Otr, who took the form of an otter when he was fishing (the name *Otr* and the Norse word *otr* 'otter' being of course the same). Then Hreidmar called out to his other sons, Fáfnir and Regin, and they laid hands on the Æsir and bound them, demanding that they should ransom themselves by filling the otter-skin with gold, and also covering it on the outside with gold so that no part of it could be seen.

Here the prose versions separate. According to Snorri (who had not previously mentioned Andvari) Ódin now sent Loki to Svartálfaheim, the Land of the Dark Elves; it was there that he found the dwarf Andvari who was 'as a fish in the water', and Loki caught him in his hands. In the Saga, on the other hand, Loki's errand was to seek out Rán, the wife of the sea-god Ægir, and get from her the net with which she drew down men drowning in the sea; and with that net he captured the dwarf Andvari, who was fishing in his falls in the form of a pike. This is the story that my father followed (stanza 7).

Andvari ransomed himself with his hoard of gold, attempting to keep back a single little gold ring; but Loki saw it and took it from him (stanza 9). In Snorri's account only,

I Andvari's Gold

Andvari begged to keep the ring because with it he could multiply wealth for himself, but Loki said that he should not have one penny left.

Andvari declared that the ring would be the death of any who possessed it, or any of the gold. According to Snorri, 'Loki said that this seemed very well to him, and he said that this condition should hold good, provided that he himself declared it in the ears of those who should receive the ring.' Then Loki returned to Hreidmar's house, and when Ódin saw the ring he desired it, and took it away from the treasure. The otter-skin was filled and covered with the gold of Andvari, but Hreidmar looking at it very closely saw a whisker, and demanded that they should cover that also. Then Ódin drew out Andvari's ring (*Andvaranaut*, the possession of Andvari) and covered the hair. But when Ódin had taken up his spear, and Loki his shoes, and they no longer had any need to fear, Loki declared that the curse of Andvari should be fulfilled. And now it has been told (Snorri concludes) why gold is called 'Otter's ransom' (*otrgjöld*) or 'forced payment of the Æsir' (*nauðgjald ásanna*): see p.36.

An important difference between the two prose versions is that Snorri began his account of the Völsung legend with 'Andvari's Gold', whereas in the Saga this story is introduced much later, and becomes a story told by Regin (son of Hreidmar) to Sigurd before his attack on the dragon. But although my father followed Snorri in this, he nonetheless followed the Saga in giving a brief retelling of 'Andvari's Gold' by Regin to Sigurd in the fifth section of the poem, with a number of verse-lines repeated from their first occurrence (see V.7–11).

1 Of all the Northern divinities *Loki* is the most enigmatic; ancient Norse literature is full of references to him and stories about him, and it is not possible to characterize him in a short space. But since Loki only appears here in these poems, and in my father's words concerning him given on p.54, it seems both suitable and sufficient to quote Snorri Sturluson's description in the Prose Edda:

> 'Also counted among the Æsir is Loki, whom some call the mischief-maker of the Æsir, the first father of lies, and the blemish of all gods and men. Loki is handsome and fair of face but evil in his disposition and fickle in his conduct. He excels all others in that cleverness which is called cunning, and he has wiles for every circumstance. Over and over again he has brought the gods into great trouble, but often got them out of it by his guile.'

In this stanza he is called 'lightfooted Loki', and in Snorri's version of the story of Andvari's Gold it is said, as already noted, that after the payment of the ransom to Hreidmar Ódin took up his spear 'and Loki his shoes'. Elsewhere Snorri wrote of 'those shoes with which Loki ran through air and over water'.

Of the god *Hoenir* no more is said in the Lay than that while Loki went on the left side of Ódin, Hœnir

I Andvari's Gold

> went on his right. In my father's somewhat mysterious interpretation given on p.54 (iv) he calls the companion of Ódin who walks on his right hand 'a nameless shadow', but this must surely be Hœnir, or at least derived from him. However, if there is no end to what is told of Loki in the Norse mythological narratives, very little can now be said of Hœnir; and to my understanding, there is nothing in the vestiges that remain that casts light on the 'nameless shadow' that walks beside Ódin.

6   Ásgard is the realm of the Gods (Æsir).

7   Rán: the wife of the sea-god Ægir; see p.189.

8   'I bid thee': I offer thee.

13–15   In these concluding stanzas the references to the hope of Ódin, and Ódin's choice, have of course no counterparts in the Norse texts.

II
SIGNÝ

This is a rendering in verse of elements of the narrative of the earlier chapters of the *Völsunga Saga*. No old poetry recounting or referring to this story exists apart from a single half-stanza (see the note to stanzas 37–39), but this section of the Lay of the Völsungs can be seen as an imagination of it. It is a selection of moments of dramatic force, and many elements of the prose Saga are omitted; in particular the most savage features of the story are eliminated (see notes to stanzas 30–32, 37–39).

The *Gauts* of the headnote to this section are the *Gautar* of Old Norse, dwelling in *Gautland,* a region of what is now southern Sweden, south of the great lakes. The name *Gautar* is historically identical with the Old English *Geatas,* who were Beowulf's people.

1–2　These two stanzas are an extreme reduction of the opening chapters of the Saga which tell of Völsung's immediate ancestry in a prosaic fashion: my father clearly found this unsuited to his purpose.

2　'child of longing': Rerir's wife was for long barren.

4　In the Saga the tree in the midst of King Völsung's hall is named the Barnstock, and is said to have been an apple-tree.

7　'Birds sang blithely': the birds were sitting in the boughs of the great tree that upheld the hall; so again in stanza 11, and see III.2.

10　King Siggeir and many other guests came to the wedding feast held in King Völsung's hall.

12–13　In the Saga the old man is described in terms that make it plain that he was Ódin, but he is not named. Here in the Lay he is *Grímnir* 'the Masked', a name of Ódin that does not appear at all in the Saga but is derived from the Eddaic poem *Grímnismál.*

II Signý

The 'standing stem' in 13 line 3 is the trunk of the Barnstock, into which Ódin thrust the sword.

14 'Gaut and Völsung': Völsung's children and race are often called *Völsungar*, Völsungs, as in the name of the Saga, and in the head-note to this section.

16 This was the beginning of hatred and the motive for Siggeir's attack on Völsung and his sons when they came to Gautland as his guests (21–23); Siggeir was enraged at Sigmund's answer, but (in the words of the Saga) 'he was a very wily man, and he behaved as if he were indifferent'.

'bade': offered (so also 'I bid thee' in I.8); 'boon': request.

17–22 It is told in the Saga that on the day following the night of the wedding feast ('last night I lay / where loath me was', 19) Siggeir left very abruptly and returned with Signý to Gautland, having invited Völsung and his sons to come as his guests to Gautland three months later (21). Signý met them when they landed to warn them of what Siggeir had prepared for them (22), but (according to the Saga) Völsung would not listen to Signý's entreaty that he return at once to his own land, nor to her request that she should be allowed to stay with her own people and not return to Siggeir.

20 'toft': homestead.

29　In the Saga the sons of Völsung were set in stocks in the forest to await the old she-wolf who came each night. Signý, on the tenth day, sent her trusted servant to Sigmund, who alone survived, to smear honey over his face and to put some in his mouth. When the wolf came she licked his face and thrust her tongue into his mouth; at which he bit into it. Then the wolf started back violently, pressing her feet against the stocks in which Sigmund was set, so that they were split open; but he held on to the wolf's tongue so that it was torn out by the roots, and she died. 'Some men say,' according to the Saga, 'that the wolf was King Siggeir's mother, who had changed herself into this shape by witchcraft.'

While in the Saga the stocks are an important element in the story at this point, in the Lay there is no suggestion of stocks, but only of fetters and shackles; the wolf is 'torn and tongueless', but 'by the tree riven'. See the note on stanzas 30-32.

30–32　This passage is very greatly condensed, and elements in the Saga essential to the narrative are passed over. Thus in the Saga, Signý found Sigmund in the woods, and it is explicit that they decided that he should make a house for himself under the ground, where Signý would provide for his needs. There is nothing in the Saga to explain Signý's words in the Lay 'Dwarvish master, thy doors open!' In the opening prose passage of this section (p.72) it is said that 'Sigmund dwelt in a cave in the guise of a dwarvish smith.'

II Signý

In this connection it is curious, if nothing more, to observe that in William Morris' poem *The Story of Sigurd the Volsung* Sigmund's dwelling is explicitly 'a stony cave' that was once 'a house of the Dwarfs'. It is also said in that poem (see the note to stanza 29) that by Siggeir's orders the men who led the sons of Völsung into the forest cut down the greatest oak-tree that they could find and bound them to it 'with bonds of iron'; and when the wolf came for Sigmund he 'burst his bonds' and slew it with his hands.

Signý had two sons by Siggeir, and when the elder was ten years old she sent him out to Sigmund in the forest to be a help to him should he attempt to avenge Völsung; but the boy, told by Sigmund to make the bread while he himself went out for firewood, was frightened to touch the bag of flour because there was something alive in it. When Sigmund told Signý about this she told him to kill the boy, since he had no heart; and Sigmund did so. The next year Signý sent her second son by Siggeir out into the woods, and things went in the same way.

After that Signý changed shapes with a sorceress, and the sorceress slept with Siggeir for three nights in Signý's form, while Signý slept with her brother. The son born to them was named Sinfjötli.

33 On lines 5–6 of this stanza see the note to 35–36.

'bast': flexible bark, used for making baskets, and for tying.

33–34 In the Saga Sigmund subjected Sinfjötli to the same test as Siggeir's sons, and when he came back to the underground house Sinfjötli had baked the bread, but he said that he thought that there had been something alive in the flour when he started kneading it. Sigmund laughed, and said that Sinfjötli should not eat the bread he had baked, 'for you have kneaded in a great venomous snake.' There is no mention in the Saga of Sinfjötli's bringing Sigmund's sword (see note to 37–39).

35–36 A long passage is devoted in the Saga to the ferocious exploits of Sigmund and Sinfjötli in the forest, where they became werewolves; and it is an important point that Sigmund thought that Sinfjötli was the son of Signý and Siggeir (cf. 33 'Fair one, thy father / thy face gave not'), possessing the energy and daring of the Völsungs but the evil heart of his father.

37–39 In the Saga Sigmund and Sinfjötli entered Siggeir's hall and hid themselves behind ale barrels in the outer room; but the two young children of Siggeir and Signý were playing with golden toys, bowling them across the floor of the hall and running along with them, and a gold ring rolled into the room where Sigmund and Sinfjötli sat. One of the children, chasing the ring, 'saw where two tall, grim men were sitting, with overhanging helms and shining mailcoats'; and he ran back and told his father.

Signý, hearing this, took the children into the outer room and urged Sigmund and Sinfjötli to kill them, since

II Signý

they had betrayed their hiding-place. Sigmund said that he would not kill her children even if they had given him away, but the terrible Sinfjötli made light of it, slew both children, and hurled their bodies into the hall. When Sigmund and Sinfjötli had at last been captured Siggeir had a great burial-mound made of stones and turf; and in the midst of the mound there was set a huge stone slab so that when they were put into it they were separated and could not pass the slab, but could hear each other. But before the mound was covered over Signý threw down a bundle of straw to Sinfjötli, in which was meat. In the darkness of the mound Sinfjötli discovered that Sigmund's sword was thrust into the meat, and with the sword they were able to saw through the stone slab.

I have said that there is no old poetry treating this story save for one half-stanza, and those verses are cited by the author of the Saga at this point:

> ristu af magni
> mikla hellu,
> Sigmundr, hjörvi,
> ok Sinfjötli.

'They cut with strength the great slab, Sigmund and Sinfjötli, with the sword'.

When they got out of the mound it was night, and everyone was asleep; and bringing up wood they set fire to the hall.

40–41   It was now, when Sigmund told Signý to come
forth, that in the Saga she revealed the truth about
Sinfjötli – this is no doubt implied in stanza 41 of the
Lay, 'Son Sinfjötli, Sigmund father!' In her last words,
according to the Saga, before she went back into the fire,
she declared that she had worked so mightily to achieve
vengeance for Völsung that it was impossible for her
now to live longer.

III

DAUÐI SINFJÖTLA
(The Death of Sinfjötli)

There intervenes now in the Saga, after the deaths of Signý
and Siggeir, the history of Helgi Hundingsbani, an originally
independent figure who had been connected to the Völsung
legend by making him the son of Sigmund and Borghild
(only referred to as 'the Queen' in this section of the Lay). In
this the Saga follows the 'Helgi lays' of the Edda; but in his
poem my father entirely eliminated this accretion, and Helgi
is not mentioned.

The sources for this section of the Lay are the Saga and a
short prose passage in the Edda entitled *Frá dauða Sinfjötla*
(Of Sinfjötli's death): the compiler of the Codex Regius of
the Edda evidently wrote this, in the absence of any verses, in
order to conclude the histories of Sigmund and Sinfjötli.
There are no important differences between the Lay and the
old narratives.

III The Death of Sinfjötli

1–2 In the Saga Sigmund, returning to his own land, drove out a usurper who had established himself there.

3 'Grímnir's gift': see II.12–13 and note.

4 In *Frá dauða Sinfjötla* and in the Saga Sigmund's queen is named Borghild; in the Lay she is given no name (perhaps because my father regarded the name Borghild as not original in the legend, but entering with the 'Helgi' connection). It is not said in the sources that she was taken in war.

6 In both sources Sinfjötli slew Borghild's brother, not her father; they were suitors for the same woman. In the Saga it is told that Borghild wished to have Sinfjötli driven out of the land, and though Sigmund would not allow this he offered her great riches in atonement; it was at the funeral-feast for her brother that Sinfjötli was murdered.

7 It is told in the Saga, at the time of the bread-making incident, when Sinfjötli kneaded in a poisonous snake (see note to II.33–34), that Sigmund could not be harmed by poison within or without, whereas Sinfjötli could only withstand poison externally; the same is said in *Frá dauða Sinfjötla* and in the Prose Edda.

9–10 In both sources Sigmund said to Sinfjötli, when Borghild offered him drink for the third time: *Láttu grön sía, sonr* ('Strain it through your beard, my son'). Sigmund was very drunk by then, says the Saga, 'and that is why he said it'.

12 The boatman was Ódin (the verses describing him here are repeated in varied form in IV.8). This is not said in the old sources. In those texts the boatman offered to ferry Sigmund across the fjord, but the boat was too small to take both Sigmund and the body of Sinfjötli, so the body was taken first. Sigmund walked along the fjord, but the boat vanished. The Saga tells that Borghild was banished, and died not long after.

13 *in Valhöllu*: the Norse dative inflexion is retained for metrical reasons.

IV

FŒDDR SIGURÐR
(Sigurd born)

After the expulsion of Borghild Sigmund took another wife very much younger than himself (IV.2), and she was the mother of Sigurd. In the Saga and in *Fra dauða Sinfjötla* her name was Hjördis, the daughter of King Eylimi; whereas in the Lay she is Sigrlinn. This difference depends on the view that a transference of names took place: that originally in the Norse legends Hjördis was the mother of Helgi (see the note to III), while Sigrlinn was Sigmund's wife and Sigurd's mother. After this transference Sigrlinn became the mother of Helgi (and so appears in the Eddaic poem *Helgakviða Hjörvarðssonar*, the Lay of Helgi son of Hjörvarð) and Hjördis became the mother of Sigurd. In the German poem *Nibelungenlied*, written about the beginning of the thirteenth

IV Sigurd born

century, Sieglind (Sigrlinn) was King Siegmund's queen, the mother of Siegfried (Sigurd).

The narrative in this section of the Lay has been changed and reduced from that in the Saga (to which there is no poetry corresponding in the Edda). In the Saga, King Lyngvi was a rival to Sigmund for the hand of Hjördis, but Hjördis rejected him; and it was Lyngvi, not the seven suitors, 'sons of kings', of the Lay (stanzas 3 and 5), who came with great force against Sigmund in his own land.

Hjördis accompanied only by a bondwoman was sent into the forest and remained there during the fierce battle. In the Saga as in the Lay (stanzas 8–9) Ódin appeared, and Sigmund's sword ('Grímnir's gift', 5) broke against the upraised spear of the god, and he was slain (on the significance of Ódin's intervention see the note on the section *Upphaf*, pp.185–86).

As in the Lay, in the Saga Hjördis (Sigrlinn) found Sigmund where he lay mortally wounded on the battlefield, and he spoke to her, saying that there was no hope of healing and he did not wish for it, since Ódin had claimed him (stanza 11); he spoke also of Sigurd, her son unborn, and told her to keep the shards of the sword, which should be made anew.

Immediately upon Sigmund's death, a further fleet came in to the shore, commanded, it is said in the Saga, by Alf son of King Hjálprek of Denmark (stanza 14 of the Lay, where the newcomers are not named). Seeing this Hjördis ordered her bondwoman to exchange clothes with her, and to declare that she was the king's daughter. When Alf returned with the women, still disguised, to his own country the truth of the subterfuge emerged. Alf promised to marry Hjördis after her child was born, and so it came about that Sigurd was brought up in King Hjálprek's household. In the Lay the curious story of the disguising of Sigrlinn (Hjördis) is reduced to the words 'The bride of Sigmund / as a bondwoman / over sounding seas / sadly journeyed'.

11 'wanhope': despair.

13 In the Saga Sigmund named the sword that should be made from the shards *Gramr*; this appears in the next section of the Lay, V.18.

V

REGIN

The sources of the story in this section of the Lay are not only the *Völsunga Saga* but also poems of the Edda on which the Saga drew: the conclusion of *Reginsmál* (see the note to section I, p.188), and *Fáfnismál*; the story is also briefly told by Snorri Sturluson in the Prose Edda, whereby he explains why 'gold' is called in poetry 'the abode of Fáfnir' and 'Grani's burden'.

There is little, in strictly narrative terms, in this part of the Lay that is not found in these sources, and in places (notably in the dialogue between Sigurd and Regin after Fáfnir's death) the tenor of the verses of *Fáfnismál* is followed; but only here and there do they correspond at all closely.

V Regin

The legend of 'Andvari's gold' as told in section I of the
Lay does not extend beyond the departure of the Æsir from
Hreidmar's house after the payment of the ransom for his son
Otr. In the note to that section (p.190) I have noticed that
Snorri Sturluson in his version of the Völsung legend began
with 'Andvari's gold', whereas in the Saga it is not introduced
until much later, and enters as a story told by Regin himself,
son of Hreidmar, to Sigurd before his attack on the dragon.
In this section of the Lay we reach that point.

After telling that Sigurd grew up in the house of King
Hjálprek the Saga says no more than that Regin became his
fosterfather, and that he taught Sigurd many accomplish-
ments, including a knowledge of runes and many languages
(see stanza 2). Snorri, on the other hand, continues the story
of Hreidmar and the gold of Andvari beyond the point
where my father left it at the end of section I of the Lay.

'What more is to be said of the gold?' Snorri wrote, and
then told this story. Hreidmar took the gold, but his other
sons Fáfnir and Regin claimed for themselves some part of
the blood-money paid for their brother. Hreidmar would
give them nothing ('Redgolden rings I will rule alone', I.15);
and Fáfnir and Regin slew their father. Then Regin
demanded that Fáfnir should share the treasure with him
equally, but Fáfnir replied that there was small chance of
that, since he had killed his father for the sake of it; and he
told Regin to be gone, or else he would suffer the same fate
as their father.

Then Fáfnir took the helm which Hreidmar had owned, and set it upon his head – the helm which is called *œgishjálmr*, Helm of Terror: all living things fear it. Then Fáfnir going up onto Gnitaheiði made himself a lair; and he turned himself into a dragon, and laid himself down upon the gold (as Glaurung did in Nargothrond). But Regin fled away, and came to King Hjálprek, and became his smith; Sigurd was his fosterson.

Having already told the story of the origin of the hoard, Snorri continued now with the story of Regin's dealings with Sigurd and the slaying of Fáfnir. With that story this section of the Lay is concerned; but before reaching it, as noted earlier (see pp.190–91), my father followed the Saga in introducing here the story of Andvari's gold (or, in the case of the Lay, re-introducing it) as a story told by Regin in answer to Sigurd's demanding why he egged him on to slay Fáfnir. In this second appearance of the story in the Lay verse-lines are repeated or nearly repeated in a characteristic way (compare I.2–6, 9 with V.7–11), but the Æsir are excluded, and Loki is replaced by a nameless 'robber roving ruthless-handed' (8). In V.12–14, however, Regin's tale now brings in the slaying of Hreidmar (by Fáfnir – that Regin had a part in it is not mentioned, either in the Saga or in the Lay), the strife between the sons, and the transformation of Fáfnir into a dragon 'on Gnitaheiði'.

An important element in the story as told in the Saga is entirely absent from this section of the Lay. After the making of the sword Gram and the acquisition of the horse Grani, Sigurd declared to Regin that he would not attack Fáfnir until he had avenged his father; and setting out with a great

V Regin

host and fleet provided by King Hjálprek he achieved this in a bloody battle in which he slew King Lyngvi. But a form of the story of Sigurd's revenge appears in the Lay at a later point in the narrative (VII.24–29).

14　Gnitaheiði: this name in Old Norse is *Gnitaheiðr*, of which the second element is Old Norse *heiðr* 'heath', and it is variously anglicized as 'Gnitaheid', 'Gnitaheith', or 'Gnitaheath'. In my father's poems it appears several times but always in the combination 'on Gnitaheiði'. This may be a retention of the dative case, or it may be a use of the modern Icelandic form of the word, which is *heiði*.

17–18　It was Sigurd who broke the two swords by striking them on an anvil; whereupon, according to the Saga, he went to his mother and asked whether it were true that Sigmund had entrusted to her the fragments of his sword, and she gave them to him. On the name Gram (*Gramr*) see the note to IV.13.

20　Both Snorri Sturluson and the Saga know of Sigurd's testing of the sharpness of Gram by its cutting of the tuft of wool when it drifted in the water onto the sword's edge; but only in the Lay is the river called the Rhine (*Rín* in Norse).

'sheer': clear.

21 'Now rede me': Now give me counsel.

22–24   Only in the Saga is this story found of how Sigurd came to possess his grey horse Grani (very frequently named in poems of the Edda). The old man is once again Ódin (with the description here compare II.12, III.12, IV.8).

The name *Busiltarn* is derived from the Saga; the Norse form is *Busiltjörn*, which was the form first written by my father in the manuscript of the Lay, later corrected in pencil. The English word *tarn*, a small lake, is derived from the Norse word; but in the Saga the Busiltarn is said to be a river, as it clearly is also in the Lay.

Sleipnir was the name of Ódin's eight-legged horse.

25   Gand: Regin's horse is not named elsewhere, but this must be the Old Norse word *gandr* (contained in 'Gandalf'). Its original or primary meaning is uncertain, but it has reference to sorcery and magic, both beings and things, and especially to the staff used in witchcraft; it is also use of wolves. The word *gandreið* is used of the witches' nocturnal ride.

In a lecture on the text of *Fáfnismál* my father remarked on the huge height of the cliff from which Fáfnir drank as a good detail in the Saga absent from the poem, since Sigurd thus 'first got a notion of what he was in for.'

26   'long there lurked he': i.e. Sigurd. In the prose preamble to *Fáfnismál* in the Codex Regius, as also in the Saga and in Snorri Sturluson's brief account, Sigurd dug a pit in the

V Regin

path which the dragon took when he crawled to the water (the 'hollow' of stanzas 26–27, 29, which is not said to have been made by Sigurd); in the Saga an old man (Óðin) came to Sigurd while he was digging it and advised him to dig other trenches to carry off the dragon's blood. On this matter my father noted in a lecture:

> Óðin and his advice, however, do not appear very intelligible, and the intrusion of Óðin has perhaps been imitated from other places (e.g. the choosing of Grani). The several pits do not seem of much use, for in any case Sigurd has got to be in *one*, and it is only in the one in which he is (immediately under the wound) that the blood is likely to pour down. The Saga version is due to harping on Óðin, and to an appreciation that the inherited plot did not paint Sigurd's dragon-slaying (which is later referred to as his great title to fame) in the best light. It could not be altered in manner, and therefore the dragon and his poisonousness must be magnified; but it is not successfully done.

His view was that the original significance of the pit was to enable Sigurd to escape the blast of flame which passed over his head (cf. 27, lines 1–3).

30 In *Fáfnismál*, repeated in the Saga, Sigurd, in answer to Fáfnir's question, replies that he is called *göfugt dýr*, that is 'noble beast'; and a prose note at this point in the Codex Regius explains that 'Sigurd concealed his name,

because it was believed in ancient times that the word of a dying man might have great power if he cursed his foe by his name.' My father observed that this note was 'doubtless perfectly correct for the original writer of the poem, whose audience were probably sufficiently of the "ancient times" not to need the explanation!' He said also that 'the mysterious words *göfugt dýr* are probably meant to be obscure, even nonsensical', though they might be 'a riddling way of saying "man".'

33 'glamoured': enchanted.

34 Sigurd's words in this stanza refer to the *œgishjálmr* 'Helm of Terror' which Heidmar possessed and which Fáfnir took to wear himself: see p.205, and stanza 14. At the words 'hell now seize him!' Fáfnir died.

36–41 My father declared the 'undermeaning' of Regin's 'dark words' in his preamble to this section of the Lay; and in notes for a lecture (written in pencil at great speed and now not entirely legible) he discussed in detail the relationship in this episode between the Saga and *Fáfnismál*, seeking to determine not only how the writer of the Saga compressed and modified the verses but why he did so. I give here, with some slight editing, a part of this discussion, since it well illustrates his critical treatment of such problems in the Edda.

He begins with a summary of the dialogue of Regin and Sigurd after the death of Fáfnir in the Saga (I give references to the stanzas and lines of the Lay in brackets).

V Regin

After the death of Fáfnir Regin came to Sigurd and said: 'You have won a great victory: your glory from it will be eternal' [35, 1–4]. Then Regin is suddenly or affects to be suddenly stricken with disquiet – 'he looks upon the ground for a long while' and says with great emotion 'it is my brother you have killed and I cannot be accounted innocent of this' [36, 5–8]. Sigurd dries his sword on the grass, and simply replies 'you were a long way off at the time when I tested the sword' (implying therefore 'innocent enough!') [37, 1–4].

Regin counters with the fact that he made the sword [37, 5]; Sigurd counters with 'brave heart is better than sharp sword in battle' [38, 3–4].

Regin does not rebut this, but repeats again 'with great emotion' almost his exact words 'You slew my brother, &c.' Then Regin cut out the dragon's heart, drank the dragon's blood, and asked Sigurd as a sole boon (no sort of reason for which is given) to roast the heart for him.

The repetition by Regin of the words 'You killed my brother and I can hardly be accounted innocent' is *not* a feature of *Fáfnismál*. Does it serve an artistic purpose – or is it just accidental, due to some confusion in the saga-writer's source, or in the handing down of the saga? It is probably intentional, and perhaps not bad. The saga-writer has constructed a picture of Regin, already plotting Sigurd's removal, and trying as it were to justify himself to himself. Scornfully relieved of any share of responsibility by Sigurd, he contents himself with mere repetition – he adheres to his remorse, and to his 'You slew my brother' (i.e. his vengeance).

After such words Sigurd should have needed no *igður* [the birds whose voices he could understand, see 41, 8 and 43, 1–3]. That the brother of one you had slain was unsafe was learnt almost at the mother's knee, certainly on the father's lap, in Scandinavia – especially when he went out of his way to point it out to you.

There is a curious absence of explanation of the reason why Sigurd must roast the heart. The real reason is of course that Sigurd must cook the heart so as to hear the birds. *Fáfnismál* supplies a not overwhelming but sufficient reason – *ek mun sofa ganga* [I shall go to sleep] (we may presume, after the potent draught of dragon's blood) [39, 5–8, and 40]. Whether there ever was a better reason – connected with this remnant of very ancient belief, the eating of flesh and drinking of blood (of foes especially) to obtain their wisdom and power [40, 5–8; 46, 1–4] we perhaps can no longer say.

It may be noted that Snorri Sturluson says that Regin expressly proposed to Sigurd as terms of reconciliation for the slaying of Fáfnir, that he roast the heart for him.

39   Ridil: Old Norse *Riðill*, Regin's sword; Snorri names it *Refill*.

42–44   In *Fáfnismál* there are seven stanzas ascribed (in a prose linking-passage) to the words of the birds (of a kind

V Regin

called *igður*, of uncertain meaning) chattering in the thicket, whose voices Sigurd could at once understand after the blood from the dragon's heart touched his tongue; but these stanzas are in two different metres. The poem *Fáfnismál* is not in the verse-form *fornyrðislag* in which the greater number of the poems of the Edda are written, but in *ljóðaháttr*. In this metre the stanza falls into two halves of three lines each, of which the third line in each half usually has three stressed elements and double (or treble) alliteration within itself. Only three of the 'bird-verses' are in *ljóðaháttr*, the others being in *fornyrðislag*; and my father argued forcefully and in detail that the *fornyrðislag* verses come from another poem (see further the note to 49–54).

The three *ljóðaháttr* verses, he held, are spoken by two birds, with two main motives selected : gold, fear of treachery, and gold repeated. This is the basis for these three stanzas in the Lay (though the suggestion in 42, 5–6 that Sigurd should eat Fáfnir's heart himself is introduced from one of the other verses); but – rather oddly – they are cast in *ljóðaháttr*, thus apparently marking them out as intrusive, since the Lay is in *fornyrðislag*.

To illustrate the form as it appears in Old Norse I give here the first of the three *ljóðaháttr* verses with a close translation:

Höfði skemra   láti hann inn hára þul
Fara til heljar heðan!
Öllu gulli   þá kná hann einn ráða,
fjölð, því er und Fáfni lá.

(Shorter by a head, / let him send the grey-haired wizard / hence to hell! All the gold / then can he possess alone, / the wealth, that under Fáfnir lay.)

46–48   In the Saga Sigurd ate some only of the dragon's heart, and some he set aside. The purpose of this is seen later in the saga, where it is told that at some time after the wedding of Sigurd and Gudrún 'Sigurd gave Gudrún some of Fáfnir's heart to eat, and thereafter she was far more grim than before, and wiser also.' This element is excluded from the Lay; my father considered it 'a late piece of machinery to explain Gudrún's tangled psychology.'

These verses derive from a prose passage in *Fáfnismál*, closely similar to that in the Saga, which tells that after the death of Regin Sigurd rode on Grani following the tracks of Fáfnir to his lair, which was standing open. The doors and door-posts were of iron, as were all the beams of the house, which was dug down into the earth (46). Sigurd found there a vast store of gold and filled two great chests with it; he took the Helm of Terror and a golden mailcoat and many other precious things, and he loaded them onto Grani; but the horse would not move until Sigurd leaped upon his back.

V Regin

49 'their wit he knew not': this very unusual use of the word 'wit' seems in the context to be equivalent to 'meaning', 'signification'.

49–54 In *Fáfnismàl*, after Sigurd has slain Regin and eaten the dragon's heart he hears the *igður* again; and these five verses are again in *fornyrðislag* (see the note to 42–44). There is no indication of how many birds spoke, but the first two verses concern Gudrún, and the last three concern a Valkyrie on the mount of Hindarfell, surrounded by fire, sleeping: Ódin stabbed her with the thorn, for she had felled a warrior against his command. See the note on 54 below.

My father held that these verses, like the previous 'bird-verses' in *fornyrðislag*, came from a poem 'which enlarged on the situation, and probably attempted through the bird-tradition to tell more of the tale'- a trace of a poem that attempted 'to compress a great deal of the story into one situation.' While accepting that 'it is useless to discuss which bird says what', he thought the guess that one bird speaks the verses concerning Gudrún and a second those about the Valkyrie 'as good as any'.

In the Lay he did however retain this second group of 'bird-verses' (or more accurately, composed verses that echo their meaning), and gave them to a raven (those about the Valkyrie) and a finch (those about Gudrún), and interlaced them. But he displaced them to *follow* Sigurd's entry into Fáfnir's lair and his loading Grani with the treasure that he found there, so that these birds are speaking of things that may lie ahead for Sigurd as he rides away from Gnitaheiði; whereas in *Fáfnismál* the prose passage cited in the note to 46–48 follows the second group of 'bird-verses'.

54 'her power wielding, / victory swaying as Valkyrie'. In northern legend and poetry the course and outcome of battles was governed by Valkyries, demonic warrior-women sent out as emissaries of Óðin.

The word *Valkyrja* means 'chooser of the slain': it is given to them to determine who is to die, and to award victory. Perhaps the most striking example of this conception is found in the *Hákonarmál*, a poem composed in the tenth century on the death of King Hákon the Good of Norway, son of King Harald Fairhair. The poem opens thus:

> Göndul and Skögul Gautatýr sent
> to choose who of kings of Yngvi's race
> should go to Óðin and dwell in Valhöll.

Göndul and Skögul are Valkyries; Gautatýr is a name of Óðin. In the poem King Hákon is pictured sitting on the ground with his shield rent and his mailshirt gashed, listening to the words of the Valkyries.

V Regin

> Then said Göndul, as she leant on the shaft of her spear,
> 'Now will the might of the Gods grow greater,
> since they have summoned Hákon with a great host
>   to their dwellings.'

> The king heard what the Valkyries were saying
> as they sat on their horses, thoughtful their
>   countenance,
> with helms on their heads and their shields held
>   before them.

Then Hákon speaks to the Valkyrie named Skögul:

> 'Why have you decided the battle thus, Geirskögul?
> We have deserved victory of the Gods.'
> 'We have brought it about,' said Skögul, 'that you
>   have held the field, and your foes have fled
>   away.

> Now we must ride to the green homes of the Gods,
> to tell to Ódin that a mighty king is coming to him.'

VI

BRYNHILDR

In the note to V. 46–48 I have given the content of the prose passage provided in the Codex Regius describing how Sigurd entered Fáfnir's lair and took from it the great treasure of gold, which he loaded in chests on his horse Grani. This passage is treated in editions of the Edda as the conclusion of the poem *Fáfnismál*; but in fact it continues without break or new title into the story of Sigurd's encounter with the Valkyrie asleep on Hindarfell, and this part is treated as the prose introduction to a strange work to which the name *Sigrdrífumál* is given.

This latter part of the prose passage, which is found in closely similar form in the Saga, tells that Sigurd rode up onto Hindarfell (*Hindarfjall*) and turned south. On the mountain he saw a great light, as of a fire burning, and it lit up the sky; and when he came to it there stood a shield-wall (*skjaldborg*), and above it a banner. Sigurd went in to the *skjaldborg*, and saw a man there lying asleep, with all his armour and weapons. First he took the helmet from his head; and then he saw that it was a woman. The hauberk was so tight that it seemed to have grown into the flesh. Then with his sword Gram he cut the hauberk from the neck and along both sleeves, and he took the hauberk off her; and she woke, and sat up, and saw Sigurd.

It will be seen that stanzas 2–4 of the Lay follow the content of this prose passage quite closely, with the 'wall of woven shields', the standard, and 'her corslet fast as on flesh growing'; but the leaping of the flames by Grani is an addition in the Lay, taken from Sigurd's second visit to Brynhild, when he came to her in Gunnar's shape. On the occasion of his first coming to her the sources say no more than that he 'went in' to the *skjaldborg*. This word, which is found both in the Saga and in the prose passage in the Edda, is often interpreted to mean here a tower, or a fortress, but my father

VI Brynhild

referred in other writing to Brynhild having 'surrounded herself with a wall of flame'.

With the Valkyrie's first words to Sigurd the verses of the so-called *Sigrdrífumál* begin:

> Hvat beit brynju?
> Hvi brá ek svefni?
> Hverr feldi af mér
> fölvar nauðir?

> What bit the mail?
> How am I roused from sleep?
> Who has cast down from me
> the pale bonds?

Then in this opening verse Sigurd replied that the son of Sigmund with the sword of Sigurd had cut her free. This verse is in *fornyrðislag*, but the poem that follows is in *ljóðaháttr* (see note to V.42–44), with a few stanzas in *fornyrðislag*. The Valkyrie celebrates her awakening in verse that is echoed in the Lay in stanzas 5–6, and then says:

> Long did I sleep,   long was I cast in sleep,
>   long are the ills of men!
> Óðin ordained it   that I could not break
>   the runes of slumber.

There follows then in the Codex Regius manuscript another prose passage beginning 'She named herself Sigrdrífa, and she was a Valkyrie'; she told Sigurd that two kings had fought, that Ódin had promised victory to one of them, but the Valkyrie had felled him in the battle. In retribution for this 'Ódin stabbed her with the sleep-thorn' (as in the words of the Raven in V.52), and said that never again should she win victory in battle, but that she should wed. 'And I said to Ódin that in return I made a vow that I would marry no man who knew fear' (the same words are used in the Saga). In the version of Snorri Sturluson she vowed to wed none but the man who should dare to ride through the fire that surrounded her dwelling. In her oath in the Lay (VI.8) the original text had 'world's renown': I have adopted the late change to 'chosen' and capitalized the 'w'.

The name Sigrdríf or Sigrdrífa of the sleeping Valkyrie has given rise to a great deal of speculative discussion. In the last of the five 'bird-verses' that constitute the end of *Fáfnismál* (and which are represented in the Lay by stanzas V.50–54) there is a reference to 'the sleep of Sigrdríf', and in the prose passage just cited she is twice named Sigrdrífa. It has been supposed that this name is unreal, a misunderstanding on the part of the compiler of the Codex Regius, who took the word in the *Fáfnismál* verse to be a proper name, whereas it is in fact a descriptive term of a Valkyrie, perhaps meaning 'giver of victory', used of Brynhild. In the Saga the Valkyrie on Hindarfell is called Brynhild; while Snorri Sturluson says that she named herself Hildr (which means 'battle'), but adds that 'she is called Brynhild, and she was a Valkyrie'.

VI Brynhild

On the other hand, it has been held that 'Sigrdrífa' and 'Brynhild' were originally two distinct beings who came later to be identified; and thus 'Sigrdrífa' becomes an element in the most intractable problem of the Norse Völsung legend, the treatment in the sources of Brynhild in two altogether distinct and incompatible ways. The Lay itself provides no evidence of my father's view of the name 'Sigrdrífa', which does not occur in it. See further the Note on Brynhild, p.243.

The prose passage in the Codex Regius ends, after the Valkyrie's words to Sigurd concerning her vow, by his asking her 'to teach him wisdom', and there follows a stanza in which Brynhild brings him ale brewed with good spells and *gamanrúna*, which may be translated as 'joyful runes' or 'gladness runes'. On this is founded stanza 12 in the Lay: the last lines of this, 'rimmed with runes of running laughter', suggest that my father was thinking of runes graven on the cup.

Of the *Sigrdrífumál* he remarked: 'This poem, more than almost any other in the Edda, is a composite thing of more or less accidental growth, and not as one poet left it'; and following the verse about the bringing of ale there is a long series of verses concerned with rune-lore (the magical use of runes, for example victory-runes, speech-runes, wave-runes, birth-runes, and the places on which they should be carved). 'It does not need much persuasion', he said, to 'convince one that all this stuff is *accretion*. It has no connection with Sigurd's later life. Its cause is *gamanrúna*. It is very interesting and important, but it does not concern the Völsungs.'

It is remarkable that the author of the *Völsunga Saga* included all these verses of runic lore, as verses, in his text. My father saw in this a good example of the saga-writer's method: 'Nearly all of this has no point or significance for the tale, is probably a late addition, is not fit for prose; here was a chance if anywhere for omission, if the compiler had been inspired with a truly artistic purpose.'

There is naturally no vestige of these verses in the Lay. In the Eddaic poem the Valkyrie now gave to Sigurd a series of eleven counsels. This element appears, though in greatly reduced form, in the Lay (stanzas 15–16); my father believed them to be, unlike the rune-lore verses, part of the original poem, since they can for the most part be related to Sigurd's story.

No more is to be learned from the *Sigrdrífumál* about the first meeting of Sigurd and the Valkyrie beyond her counsels to him, for no more of the poem is preserved: it is here that the 'great lacuna' of the Poetic Edda begins. This is the calamitous loss from the Codex Regius of a whole gathering, probably of eight leaves (see p.28): my father guessed that those leaves contained perhaps 200–300 stanzas. For this vitally important part of the Völsung legend there is no Eddaic poetry, except for four *fornyrðislag* stanzas quoted in the *Völsunga Saga*; and thus from this point the sources are the Saga and the very brief version in Snorri Sturluson's Prose Edda. The lacuna ends, in terms of the Lay, at stanza 46 in its last section.

VI Brynhild

My father believed that the troth-plighting of Sigurd and Brynhild (stanza 19), which is found in the Saga immediately after a prose paraphrase of the counsels, derived from the lost conclusion of the *Sigrdrífumál*.

20–23   The Saga, after the words 'and this they swore to each other with oaths', continues at once 'Now Sigurd rides away'. The conclusion of this section of the Lay, referred to in the prose preamble that precedes it ('They depart together, but the pride of Brynhild causes her to bid Sigurd depart and come back to her only when he has won all men's honour, and a kingdom'), is a development altogether peculiar to the Lay.

VII
GUÐRÚN

When in the Lay Sigurd parted from Brynhild his journey took him by intention to the land of the Gjúkings, as is seen from the words (VI.23) 'green ran the roads / that Grani strode' together with those of the Finch (V.51) 'Green run the roads / to Gjúki's land'. So it is also in Snorri's greatly condensed account.

In the Saga, on the other hand, he rode from Hindarfell until he came to the house of a great lord named Heimir. He was married to Brynhild's sister Bekkhild, who stayed at home and did fine needlework, whereas Brynhild wore helmet and hauberk and went to battle (hence their names, Norse *bekkr* 'bench', of the long seats in an old Scandinavian hall, and *brynja* 'hauberk, coat of mail'). Sigurd stayed in that house for a long time in high honour.

We are then told that Brynhild was Heimir's foster-daughter, and that she had come back to his house and was living apart and working on a tapestry that showed the deeds of Sigurd, the slaying of the dragon, and the taking of the treasure. One day Sigurd's hawk flew up to a high tower and settled by a window. Sigurd climbed up after it, and saw within a woman of great beauty working on a tapestry of his deeds, and he knew that it was Brynhild.

On the next day he went to her, and at the end of a strange conversation she said to him: 'It is not fated that we should dwell together; I am a shield-maiden and I wear a helmet among the warrior-kings. To them I give aid in battle; and battle is not hateful to me.' But when Sigurd said that if this were so 'the pain that lies therein is harder to bear than a sharp sword' Brynhild replied that she would muster men for battle, 'but you will wed Gudrún, Gjúki's daughter.' 'No king's daughter shall beguile me,' said Sigurd; 'I am not double-hearted; and I swear by the gods that I shall have you or no woman else.' Then Brynhild spoke in the same way; and Sigurd gave her a gold ring, *ok svörðu nú eiða af nýju*, 'and they renewed their oaths'. Then Sigurd left her, and the chapter in the Saga ends.

Brynhild is here the daughter of King Budli (*Buðli*) and the sister of Atli (Attila), and Snorri says the same.

Of this extraordinary development in the story of Sigurd and Brynhild there is no trace in the Lay; but I postpone

VII Gudrún

discussion of the treatment of this part of the legend by the author of the Saga to the end of my commentary on the Lay (Note on Brynhild, p.241).

The Saga now turns to the kingdom of Gjúki, which lay 'south of the Rhine', to his wife Grímhild (described as a sorceress, and of a grim disposition), his three sons Gunnar, Högni, and Gotthorm, and his daughter Gudrún (*Guðrún*). It is told that one day Gudrún spoke to one of her waiting-women and told her that she was downcast because of a dream.

With Gudrún's dream the Lay takes up at the beginning of section VII, but my father treated this episode very differently from the form it has in the Saga. In the latter, Gudrún dreamt that she had in her hand a marvellous hawk with golden feathers: she cared for nothing more than that hawk, and she would rather lose all her wealth than lose it. The woman interpreted the dream to mean that some king's son would come to ask for Gudrún; he would be a fine man and she would greatly love him. Then Gudrún said: 'It grieves me that I do not know who he is; but let us go to seek Brynhild, for she will know.'

And so they did. Gudrún and her attendants came to Brynhild's hall, which was all adorned with gold and stood on a hill. There Gudrún related to Brynhild her dream: but not the dream that she had spoken about before, for now she told of the great stag with golden hair which appears in the Lay. But in his poem (VII.1–5) my father combined and interwove the two episodes, rejecting the dream of the hawk;

and the interpreter of Gudrún's dream(s) is neither the waiting-woman nor Brynhild, but Grímhild, her mother. The dream of the stag in the Lay (VII.2–4) derives in content from the Saga, but there is an important difference. In the Saga Gudrún says to Brynhild that it was 'you' who shot down the stag at her feet, and it was 'you' who gave her a wolf-cub which spattered her with her brothers' blood; whereas in the Lay it is 'a woman wildly / on the wind riding' who brought down the golden hart, and it was an unidentified 'they' who gave her the wolf.

In the Saga, when Gudrún has recounted her dream, Brynhild says to her: 'I will explain it as it will come to pass. Sigurd, whom I chose to be my husband, will come to you. Grímhild will give him mead that is drugged, which will bring great affliction to us all. You will have him, but you will soon lose him; then you will be wedded to King Atli. You will lose your brothers, and then you will slay Atli.' Then Gudrún expressed her sense of 'overwhelming sorrow' to know such things, and returned to her father's house.

It may be that this episode was derived by the writer of the Saga from a poem in which the substance of the story was told prophetically, as is seen elsewhere in the Edda; but as a simple element in the narrative, recording Brynhild's power of foretelling, it is grotesque. As my father observed, 'Foreknowledge is a dangerous element in a tale.' In the Lay he of course got rid in its entirety of Gudrún's visit to Brynhild, and Grímhild offers no interpretation of the dream, but tries to calm her with soothing words about the weather (as does the waiting-woman in the Saga) and the idea

VII Gudrún

that 'dreams oft token / the dark by light, / good by evil'. Gone too are Brynhild's sister Bekkhild; Atli son of Budli likewise disappears as Brynhild's brother. Where Brynhild dwelt after she parted from Sigurd we are not told: 'to her land she turned / lonely shining', 'to her land she came, / long the waiting' (VI.23). At the beginning of VIII she is seen in her courts of 'wealth and splendour', awaiting Sigurd (1–2).

In the Saga, as in the Lay, Sigurd now arrives at King Gjúki's halls, riding on Grani with his treasure. He was received with honour; and he rode abroad with Gunnar and Högni and was foremost among them. Grímhild observed how deeply he loved Brynhild, and how much he spoke of her, but she thought how fine a thing it would be if he, with his great qualities and his vast riches, should marry Gudrún and remain among them. She prepared therefore a potion and gave it to Sigurd to drink; and with that drink he lost all memory of Brynhild.

In the Lay, at the feast held on his arrival, a new element enters in the songs sung to the harp by Gunnar (of war between the Goths and the Huns, 14–15), and by Sigurd (of Fáfnir and the golden hoard, and of Brynhild on Hindarfell, 16–18); and there is an account of a campaign led by Sigurd to the old land of the Völsungs in vengeance for the death of Sigmund (24–29). In the Saga this took place far earlier, and was carried out with the aid of King Hjálprek (see pp.205–6), whereas in the Lay he was aided by the Gjúkings. Ódin appears here in the Lay as he does in the Saga, but his rôle is altogether different. In the Saga (deriving from verses of *Reginsmál*) the ships were caught in a great storm, but Ódin stood on a headland and called to them, and when they took him on board the storm abated. In the Lay (28–29) he appears at the end of the fighting, accosting Sigurd at the old house of Völsung, now roofless and the great tree that upheld it dead, to warn him that his fate does not lie in the land of his ancestors; but Ódin says 'Now king thou art / of kings begotten, / a bride calls thee / over billowing seas', and after his return Sigurd recalls the words of Brynhild, 'a queen was I once, / and a king shall wed' (VI.22, VII.35).

8   'Niflung land, Niflung lord', and 12 'Niflungs': on the name *Niflungar* Snorri Sturluson was specific: *Gjúkingar, þeir eru ok kallaðir Niflungar*, 'the Gjúkings, who are also called Niflungs'. In this commentary, conceived fairly strictly as an elucidation of the treatment of the Norse Völsung legend in my father's Lay, it is unnecessary to enter even cursorily into the deep matter of origins that lies behind the name Niflungs (German *Nibelungen*, Nibelungs); but something is said of this in Appendix A, pp.356–63.

14 Mirkwood: Not occurring in the Saga, the Norse name *Myrkviðr*, Anglicized as 'Mirkwood', was used of a dark boundary-forest, separating peoples, and is found in poems of the Edda in different applications; but it seems probable that in its origin it represented a memory in heroic legend of the great forest that divided the land of

VII Gudrún

the Goths from the land of the Huns far off in the south and east. This is what the name means in the Eddaic poem *Atlakviða*, the Lay of Atli (Attila), whence its appearance here in the Lay.

Danpar: Like Mirkwood, this name is not found in the Saga, but occurs in *Atlakviða* and elsewhere in Old Norse poetry (see further the note to stanza 86 in the Lay of Gudrún). It is a survival of the Gothic name of the Russian river Dnieper.

15 'Borgund lords': This expression occurs again in stanza 20. My father derived it from the notable words in a verse of the *Atlakviða*, where Gunnar is called *vin Borgunda*, lord of the Burgundians. Nowhere else in Norse is Gunnar recognised as a Burgundian, nor is the word found as the name of a people; but very remarkably the same expression is found in one of the fragments of the Old English poem *Waldere*, where Guðhere is called *wine Burgenda*. Both the Old Norse *Gunnarr* and the Old English *Guðhere* are descended from the name of the historical Burgundian king Gundahari, who was killed by the Huns in the year 437. For an account of the historical origins of the Gjúkings see Appendix A.

Budli's brother: in the Saga the killing of the brother of King Budli, father of Atli and Brynhild, by the Gjúkings is mentioned at a later point in the narrative.

28 'and blind his eye': Ódin had only one eye: according to
the myth that he gave up one of his eyes as a pledge in
order to gain a drink from the spring of Mímir, the water
of wisdom at the root of the Tree of the World.

38 It is not said in the Lay as it is in the Saga that after drinking Grímhild's potion Sigurd lost all memory of
Brynhild: 'he drained it laughing, / then sat unsmiling';
but the meaning is clear from IX.4.

39 'glamoured': a word used in V.33 and 47: 'enchanted', in
the sense of being brought under a spell.

VIII
SVIKIN BRYNHILDR
(Brynhild Betrayed)

In the Saga the wedding of Sigurd to Gudrún follows, and the
swearing of brotherhood between Sigurd and the sons of
Gjúki (stanzas 7–10 in the Lay); it is said that by this time he
had dwelt among the Gjúkings for two and a half years. After
they were wedded Sigurd gave Gudrún some of Fáfnir's heart
to eat: see the note to V.46–48. They had a son named
Sigmund.

The coming of Ódin to Brynhild among the suitor kings
(2–5) is peculiar to the Lay. It seems (stanza 6) that it was
only after his coming that the fire rose about her hall, and
that Brynhild conceived it as a barrier against all comers save
Sigurd. The description of the fire in the Lay resembles that

VIII Brynhild Betrayed

in VI.2, when on Hindarfell Sigurd saw Brynhild's fire as a 'fence of lightning' that 'high to heavenward / hissed and wavered'.

In the Saga there follows Grímhild's counselling of Gunnar to woo Brynhild (stanzas 12–17 in the Lay); and Sigurd is said to have been as eager for the match as were Gjúki and his sons. But they rode first to King Budli, Brynhild's father, to gain his assent before they went to the hall of Heimir, Brynhild's fosterfather (see p.223). Heimir said that her hall was not far off, and that he thought that she would only marry the man who would ride through the fire that blazed about it. In the Lay Budli and Heimir are of course eliminated.

The story in the Saga of the refusal of Gunnar's horse to enter the fire, the loan of Grani, the refusal of Grani to bear Gunnar, and the shape-changing taught them by Grímhild, is followed in the Lay; the Saga here quotes two stanzas from an unknown poem concerning the sudden roaring of the fire and the trembling of the earth as Sigurd entered it, and its sinking down again (followed in stanzas 25–26 in the Lay).

The substance of the dialogue between Sigurd and Brynhild (28–31) is mostly derived from the Saga: her doubt as to how to answer, his promise of a great bride-price, her demand that he slay all who had been her suitors (stanza 30, lines 3–4), and his reminder of her oath. It is strongly implied in stanza 31 that Brynhild had vowed to wed none but the man who dared to pass through the fire, and at this point in the Saga Sigurd explicitly reminds her that she has sworn to go with the man who should do so. With this is to be compared Brynhild's words to Sigurd on Hindarfell (VI.8):

> An oath I uttered
> for ever lasting,
> to wed but one,
> the World's chosen.

We must understand that in Brynhild's thought the one who rides the fire must be 'the World's chosen', and that is Sigurd; but it is Gunnar, and she is 'sore troubled', and in her doubt likened to a swan 'on swaying seas'.

In the Saga Sigurd in Gunnar's form remained three nights with Brynhild, and they slept in the same bed; but he laid the sword Gram between them, and when she asked him why he did so, he replied that it was fated that he should hold his bridal thus, or else get his death.

An important distinction between the Saga and the Lay lies in what is said of the exchange of rings. In the Saga it was told (see p.223) that at their meeting in Heimir's halls 'Sigurd gave her a gold ring', though nothing more is said of it, and now it is said that at his departure 'he took from her the ring Andvaranaut that he had given her, and gave her another ring from Fáfnir's hoard'. In the Lay (33), on the other hand, he took from her while she slept the ring that she wore on her finger and put Andvaranaut in its place. In this the Lay follows Snorri's account: 'in the morning he gave Brynhild as

VIII Brynhild Betrayed

bridal gift the same gold ring which Loki had taken from Andvari, and took another ring from her hand for remembrance'. See further IX.9–10 and note.

After this, in the Saga, Sigurd rode back through the fire, and he and Gunnar changed into their own semblances; but Brynhild went back to her fosterfather Heimir and told him what had happened, and of her doubt: 'He rode through my flickering fire . . . and he said that he was named Gunnar; but I said that only Sigurd would do that, to whom I swore faith on the mountain.' Heimir said that things must rest as they were; and she said 'Áslaug, Sigurd's daughter and mine, shall be brought up here with you'. My father regarded the introduction of Áslaug as a 'grievous damage' to the story (and see p.242, (6)). It was unquestionably an invention made in order to link together Sigurd and Brynhild and the most celebrated viking of legend, Ragnar Loðbrók: in the largely fabulous *Ragnars Saga* Áslaug is said to be one of his wives and the mother of several of his numerous viking sons.

4   'dreed' : submitted to, endured.

    'choosing not the slain': a reference to Brynhild as Valkyrie.

17 In line 6 'thee' refers to Gunnar; in line 8 'you' is plural and refers to Gunnar and Sigurd.

20 'rowel': a spiked revolving disc at the end of a spur.

29 'meted': allotted, apportioned.

IX

DEILD

(Strife)

As I have said (p.221), the great lacuna in the Codex Regius caused the loss of all ancient Norse poetry for the central part of the legend of Sigurd. The manuscript does not take up again until near the end of a lay of Sigurd which is known as the *Brot (af Sigurðarkviðu)*, the 'Fragment' (of a lay of Sigurd). Only some 20 stanzas of this poem are preserved, and these come late in the development of the tragedy, after 'the quarrel of the queens', as they washed their hair in the waters of the Rhine. My father noted that it can be seen from what is left of the *Brot* that there has been lost the greater part of 'an old and very vigorous poem – for example the supreme vigour and economical force of

> *Mér hefir Sigurðr*
> *selda eiða,*
> *eiða selda,*
> *alla logna . . .'*

These words of Gunnar's come almost at the beginning of the preserved part of the *Brot*, and are closely echoed in the Lay, IX.46.

What was contained in the pages removed from the Codex Regius has been much discussed. An important factor is the existence in the manuscript of a poem named *Sigurðarkviða*

233

IX Strife

en skamma, 'the Short Lay of Sigurd'; but this is 71 stanzas long – almost the longest of all the heroic lays of the Edda. This title must have been used in contrast to something else, very probably in the same collection. My father's view of the matter was closely argued but tentatively expressed; as he said, 'one must remember that all this sort of thing (like the dating of individual poems, on which each scholar with equal certitude seems to give a different opinion) is very "guessy" and dubious.' He thought it possible that there were three Sigurd lays: *Sigurðarkviða en skamma,* preserved in the Codex Regius; *Sigurðarkviða en meiri,* 'the Greater (Longer) Lay of Sigurd', which is totally lost; and 'an ancient, terse, poem, concentrated chiefly on the Brynhild tragedy', of which the conclusion is preserved in the *Brot.* (To his own poem he gave an alternative title, written under the primary title on the first page of the manuscript of the Lay, *Sigurðarkviða en mesta,* 'the Longest Lay of Sigurd', for in it the whole history is told.)

However this may be, for almost all the narrative from Sigurd's coming to the court of the Burgundians (Niflungs, Gjúkings) to the beginning of the *Brot* (Gunnar's declaration to Högni that Sigurd had broken his oaths) we are largely dependent on the *Völsunga Saga,* for Snorri tells the story with great brevity, and the preserved Sigurd lay, *Sigurðarkviða en skamma,* is chiefly concerned with the deaths of Sigurd and Brynhild. In my father's view, it can be assumed that in so far as the relevant chapters of the Saga had an Eddaic basis they depended on poetry very closely similar to that carried away in the lacuna of the Codex Regius.

Thus, to recapitulate, Eddaic poetry concerning the deaths of Sigurd and Brynhild is preserved, most importantly, in *Sigurðarkviða en skamma,* and in the conclusion (the *Brot* or Fragment) of another Sigurd lay. They were used, of course, by the writer of the Saga, and my father wove his version from these sources independently.

3–4   At the end of the feast of the bridal of Gunnar and Brynhild, according to the Saga, Sigurd remembered all his oaths to Brynhild, but he made no sign. There is no suggestion in the Saga of what is implied in stanza 3.

6–11   The quarrel between Brynhild and Gudrún when they washed their hair in the river follows the story as told by Snorri Sturluson and in the Saga, except in the matter of the rings that revealed the truth to Brynhild: see the note to 9–10. A long dialogue between Brynhild and Gudrún which follows in the Saga is eliminated in the Lay.

9–10   As I have noted earlier (p.231), in the Saga Sigurd in Gunnar's form took the ring Andvaranaut from Brynhild and gave her another from Fáfnir's hoard, whereas in the Lay, following Snorri Sturluson, this is reversed. So here, in Snorri's words: 'Gudrún laughed, and said: "You think that it was Gunnar who rode through the flickering fire? But I think that he who slept with you was the one who gave me this gold ring; but the gold ring which you wear on your hand and which

IX Strife

you received as a wedding gift is called Andvaranaut; and I do not think that Gunnar got it on Gnitaheiði.'" On Gnitaheiði see V.14.

12–20 Brynhild's withdrawal to her bedchamber in black silence, lying like one dead, and her words with Gunnar when he came to her, derive in a general way from the Saga; but the long reproach that in the Saga she casts at him differs greatly from the equivalent passage in the Lay (stanzas 15–19). In the Saga she began, when at last prevailed upon by Gunnar to speak, by asking him: 'What have you done with the ring I gave you, which king Budli gave me at our last parting, when you Gjúkings came to him and vowed to harry and burn unless you gained me?' Then she said that Budli had given her two choices, to wed as he wished, or to lose all her wealth and his favour; and seeing that she could not strive with him she promised to wed the one who would ride through her fire on the horse Grani with Fáfnir's hoard. This further confusion arising from the 'doubled' view of Brynhild is once again eliminated in the Lay, as are other details of the story in the Saga: the fettering of Brynhild by Högni after her threat to kill Gunnar, and her tearing of her tapestry apart.

20 Lines 3–4: In the Saga Brynhild ordered the door of her chamber to be set open so that her lamentations could be heard far off.

21–34 The dialogue between Sigurd and Brynhild derives most of its elements from that in the Saga, but in the Lay it is much more compressed and coherent. In the Saga Brynhild does not curse Gudrún, and Sigurd does not say that he would even be willing to kill Gunnar.

26 In the Saga Brynhild said that she wondered at the man who came into her hall, and she thought that she recognised Sigurd's eyes, but she could not see clearly because 'her fortune was veiled'.

27 Lines 7–8: see VIII.33 lines 3–4 and IX.10 lines 5–8.

29 Lines 1, 3: 'Woe worth': A curse upon; 'Woe worth the while': A curse upon the time. Again in stanzas 37, 50.

30 Lines 7–8: 'I sat unsmiling, no sign making': see IX.3–4.

35 Here in the Saga the writer quoted a verse from a poem that he called *Sigurðarkviða*, in which it is said that Sigurd's grief was so great that the links of his mailshirt snapped. Of this verse my father remarked that he did not believe it to come from the same hand as the *Brot*, and so attributed it to the otherwise wholly lost '*Sigurðarkviða en meiri*' (see p.234). In the Lay the extravagant idea is characteristically reduced.

39–40 Stanzas 39 lines 5–8 and 40 lines 1–4 echo VIII.30.

39–50 Elements in the arrangement of dialogue are altered in the Lay, and the development set in a clearer light and sharper focus. Brynhild's lie to Gunnar, that Sigurd had

IX Strife

possessed her (43), leads to his words to Högni (46): 'oaths he swore me, all belied them', which are almost the first words of the *Brot* (see p.233).

51–64   There were two distinct versions of the story of the murder of Sigurd, each represented in poems of the Edda. In the *Brot* he was slain out of doors, and Högni had a part in it (despite his perception that Brynhild had lied to Gunnar, which is seen in a verse of the *Brot* that is echoed in stanza 47 of the Lay); but in *Sigurðarkviða en skamma* and other poems he was slain by Gotthorm in his bed (see further pp.243–44). The compiler of the Codex Regius put in a prose note about this at the end of the *Brot*:

> In this poem is told of the death of Sigurd, and here the story is that they slew him out of doors; but some say that they slew him within doors, in his bed, sleeping. But German men say that they slew him out in the forest; and so also it is told in *Guðrúnarkviða en forna* (the Old Lay of Gudrún) that Sigurd and the sons of Gjúki had ridden to the council place when he was slain. But all are agreed in this, that they broke their troth to him, and fell upon him when he was lying down and unprepared.

The Saga follows the story of his death as he slept in the house, and the Lay likewise adopts this version, but introduces (54–57) a brief episode in which Gotthorm encountered Sigurd as he hunted in the forest, and hailed him abusively – perhaps to give colour to what is said in the Saga, and repeated in stanzas 52–3 – that the diet of wolf and snake on which he was fed made him exceedingly bold and fierce.

51 Grímhild's offspring: the author of the Saga regarded Gotthorm (*Gottormr*) as a full brother of Gunnar and Högni, and had Gunnar say that they should persuade Gotthorm to do the deed, because he was young and had sworn no oath. My father here followed a tradition, found in the poem *Hyndluljóð*, that Gotthorm was the half-brother of Gunnar and Högni, being 'Grímhild's offspring'; Snorri Sturluson, also, says that Gotthorm was Gjúki's stepson.

58–59 In the Saga, Gotthorm went twice to Sigurd's chamber in the morning, but Sigurd looked at him, and Gotthorm dared not attack him on account of his piercing gaze; when he came the third time Sigurd was asleep.

67–69 These stanzas echo the concluding verses of the *Brot*, which does not extend to the death of Brynhild.

73 In the Saga, following *Sigurðarkviða en skamma*, Brynhild dying foretold all the later history of Gudrún; this has no place in the Lay.

77 Lines 5–7 are an exact repetition of lines 3–5 in III.13, where the 'son's son' is Sinfjötli, except that the reading there is *Völsung*, not *Völsungs*. The plural form here is clear, but may nonetheless be erroneous. On the form *Valhöllu* see the note to III.13.

IX Strife

77–82   The concluding passage is of course peculiar to the Lay. With stanzas 79–81 cf. *Upphaf*, the opening section of the Lay, stanzas 11, 14–15.

77–78   In a fragmentary poem of the tenth century on the death of the ferocious Eirik Blood-axe, son of King Harold Fairhair and brother of Hákon the Good (see the note on V.54) there is a remarkable image of the coming of an 'Ódin hero' to Valhöll. The poem opens with Ódin declaring that he has had a dream in which he was preparing Valhöll to receive a company of the slain. There is a great noise of many men approaching the hall, and Ódin calls on the dead heroes Sigmund and Sinfjötli to rise up quickly and go to meet the dead king who is coming, saying that he believes it to be Eirik.

Sigmund says to Ódin: 'Why do you hope for Eirik, rather than for other kings?' And the god replies: 'Because he has reddened his sword in many lands.'

Then Sigmund asks: 'Why have you robbed him of victory, when you knew him to be brave?' And Ódin answers: 'Because it cannot be clearly known. . .' – and then (at any rate as the text stands) he breaks off, and concludes: 'The grey wolf is gazing at the dwellings of the Gods' (see the commentary on the *Upphaf* ('Beginning'), pp.185–86.

Note on Brynhild

In what follows I set out, with minor editing, the content of some notes of my father's, written very rapidly in soft pencil and difficult to read, on his interpretation of the tangled and contradictory narratives that constitute the tragedy of Sigurd and Brynhild, Gunnar and Gudrún. I will repeat here what I have said in my Foreword, that there is nothing in these or any other notes for his lectures on Old Norse literature that bears on the question of whether he had written, or intended to write, poems on the subject of the Völsung legend; but that views expressed in the lectures may illuminate, naturally enough, his treatment of the sources in his Lays.

In my commentary on the last part of the Lay I referred (p.234) to my father's belief that the fragment of a Sigurd lay known as the *Brot,* with which the Codex Regius takes up again after the lacuna, is the conclusion of 'an ancient, terse, poem, concentrated chiefly on the Brynhild tragedy'. For this poem he used in his notes the title *Sigurðarkviða en forna,* 'the Old Lay of Sigurd'. In notes for a lecture on the content of the lacuna he suggested (following the great scholar Andreas Heusler) that the poem probably began with Sigurd's coming to the halls of Gjúki, and his reception; his oath of brotherhood with the king's sons; and his wedding with Gudrún: all this probably brief and *without reference to Sigurd's previous knowledge of Brynhild.* He proposed that the chief elements of the conception of Brynhild in that poem were these.

(1) A semi-magical personage, ultimately derived from a Valkyrie legend.

(2) She surrounded herself with a wall of flame, and vowed only to wed the hero who rode it – intending it to be Sigurd.

(3) The wall of flame *is* ridden by Sigurd, but under the appearance of Gunnar. The oath holds her. She comforts herself with the thought of Gunnar's deed.

(4) Her comfort fails and her pride is mortally wounded when she discovers that it was Sigurd after all who rode the flame: in addition she has been tricked into breaking her oath to wed the actual rider.

(5) Her vengeance takes this form: she cannot have Sigurd now, and therefore she will destroy him (and so mortally wound Gudrún, the natural object of her hate); but she will by this very act avenge herself on Gunnar by involving him in a dreadful oath-breaking – so that after all is over, Sigurd dead, and she about to follow, she can turn and say, 'Sigurd is pure of all such vileness, you Gunnar alone are shamed' [this is the end of the *Brot,* echoed in stanzas IX.67–69 in the Lay].

(6) To do this she *lies* terribly against Sigurd and herself. She accuses him of broken faith when he lay in her bed after the riding of the flame. This was her only means of getting Gunnar to slay him [see stanzas IX. 43, 46, and 49 of the Lay]. Later she reveals the truth [stanza 68, lines 5–8].

That is why Áslaug is such a fatal addition in the Saga, even if she was begotten upon the mountain-top, not at the second riding of the flame (see p.232).

I think that we should accept (he wrote) such a conception for the poem, of which the twenty stanzas of the *Brot* are all that are left, and for one of the oldest lines of tradition. The resolution of the Brynhild-Valkyrie difficulty does not lie in the assumption that one was mortal (Brynhild) and the other a Valkyrie from an older 'myth', which later became confused. The solution, I think, is that the Valkyrie is the one essential part of the whole story, which is always present. [In a separate note my father wrote: 'Brynhild cannot be a "human" character mythicized (or confused with a Valkyrie Sigrdrífa). She is a Valkyrie humanized.']

But she was treated in at least two different ways. There was the mountain-top awakening of the Ódin-enchanted Valkyrie (perhaps the more specifically Scandinavian conception and therefore the later, since the story was not originally Scandinavian). There was also the proud princess tricked by her own stratagem (when Sigurd rode the fire but in the form of Gunnar) – the more southern one. That the lost poem that ends in the *Brot* represented this older 'more southern version' is probably borne out by the important point in which it does agree with the non-Scandinavian versions, namely that Sigurd was murdered out of doors in a wood and that Högni had a part in it (in the *Brot* itself Gudrún is shown standing at the doors of the hall as the brothers ride back).

It is significant that the compiler of the Codex Regius entered a note about this since it clearly puzzled him and his contemporaries (see p.238, note to stanzas 51–64). He notes that the Old Lay of Gudrún says the same – in this case, that Sigurd was slain at the Thing (the council place); and he is aware that this is the 'southern' version (*þýðvestur menn*, German men). The other story, the slaying of Sigurd in bed in Gudrún's arms, in keeping with the Norse tendency to the personal, and to the concentration of action in time and place, is represented in *Sigurðarkviða en skamma*, the extant Sigurd lay (see p.234), and this is the version followed (without comment) in the Saga, and in the Lay (see p.238).

My father did not discuss in these notes the development, in incompatible ways, seen in the *Völsunga Saga*, of the story of Sigurd and Brynhild in the Norse tradition. But his opinion on the cardinal question seems clear from a passing observation elsewhere that, in his view, the drink of forgetfulness given to Sigurd was 'invented by the author of the lost *Sigurðarkviða en meiri* [see p.234] to account for the difficulties raised by the previous betrothal of Sigurd and Brynhild.'

In conclusion, he wrote: There is nothing left for us now, therefore, but to express surprise that the author of the Saga, who could so decisively and unhesitatingly adopt one of the conflicting accounts of the murder, could not adopt a single view of Brynhild. Since the adoption of a single view of the murder must be due to artistic preference, one is perhaps only being just to the author of the Saga in assuming that the vagueness and uncertainty of Brynhild's position was not pure bungling on his part. He wanted a complex of conflicting motives and emotions for the central tragedy – to have these he was content to leave the previous relations of Brynhild and Sigurd confused. He had to, since each theory contributed to her motives.

In the Saga Brynhild's passion of rage and grief is in part due to pride – she has not wedded the supreme hero (and hates Gudrún on that account); but also, she has been wedded by a trick (and hates Gunnar and Sigurd on that account). Her oath has been broken and she hates herself. She really loves Sigurd alone: her heart's desire is frustrated, and she would kill what she loves rather than let a rival share it. Her betrothal to Sigurd has been broken by both of them – both by fate and by magic. She is wroth with Sigurd (and herself) on this account – and will not in any case endure her marriage to Gunnar longer. Behind all hangs Ódin, and his doom, and the vanity of her vows – he doomed her to wed. Inextricably interwoven is the curse on the gold.

Truly complicated! And though in building up largely a product of accident, its retention is due perhaps to taste. We may accept this, even if we are still on safe ground in affirming that a better artist could have retained all that was necessary of the two divergent Brynhild-heroines and not made them so obscure and indeed contradictory and unintelligible.

Earlier Workings of *Völsungakviða en nýja*

The earlier manuscript material of the *Upphaf* is not easy to interpret. There are two versions, which are readily placed in sequence: these I will call for ease of reference text A and text B. The first, or text A, with the title *Upphaf*, has almost as many stanzas as the final form, but not all in the same order, and the wording constantly differing, if for the most part only slightly. The opening stanza is among those that underwent the most change to reach the final form:

> Ere the years there yawned
> yearless ages,
> without sand or sea
> silent, empty;
> Earth was not moulded
> nor arched Heaven:
> an abyss gaping
> without blade of grass.

Stanza 4 ('Unmarred their mirth. . .') was not present. Stanza 13 (in text A stanza 12) reads:

> The wolf for Óðinn
> at the world's ending (> waits unsleeping),
> for Frey the fair
> flames of Surtur;

> the doom of Thór
> the Dragon beareth:
> all shall be ended
> and Earth perish.

Though not so marked in the manuscript, the words of the Sibyl clearly end here, and stanzas 14–15, in which the Sibyl speaks of the rôle of Sigurd at the Ragnarök, are here absent. Then follow in A stanzas 16–20 of the final text, the conclusion of the *Upphaf*, in which the Gods prepare for the Last Battle according to the prophecy, and ending with the words 'for one they waited, / the World's chosen'. In A at this point the meaning of those words is not explained. But in this version it is the stanzas 14–15 of the final form, absent here from the prophecy of the Sibyl, that form the conclusion of the *Upphaf*. The first reads:

> In Day of Doom
> he should deathless stand
> to die no more
> who had death tasted,
> the serpent-slayer.
> seed of Óðinn,
> the walls defending,
> the World's chosen.

And the concluding stanza in text A is virtually the same as stanza 15 in the final form. Thus the prophecy concerning Sigurd is present in A, but not as the words of the Sibyl.

The second text B is not titled *Upphaf* but *The Elder Edda* (the reason for this will appear in a moment). It is far closer to the final form in the detail of its wording, indeed it only differs here and there. That it was developed from text A is clear from the pencilled corrections made to A that appear in B as written. But it is much shorter than A. The opening stanza is absent (the poem begins 'The Great Gods once / began their toil') – but stanza 1 in the final form ('Of old was an age / when was emptiness . . .') is scribbled in pencil in the margin. Stanza 4 ('Unmarred their mirth. . .') is also absent, as it is in A; but most curiously, the whole of the prophecy of the Sibyl (stanzas 10–15) is missing. The B-text has thus only 12 stanzas. The last verse begins 'The guests are many'; and the last lines of the verse read, not 'for one they waited, / the World's chosen', as in A and the final text, but 'long awaiting / the last battle'. Thus the motive of Sigurd as (in Ódin's hope) the saviour at the Ragnarök is absent.

This truncated version of *Upphaf* is the opening of a paper read to, or perhaps more probably designed to be read to, a society, presumptively at Oxford. The first words following the poem were:

And that is, I think, all I have to say (of my own) concerning the *Elder Edda*. There is the ancient measure and strophe in which most of it is written – in which our own poetry was once composed, and in which it still can be if one will learn the craft (not an easy one) – there is the background of the imagination of its poets; and though this is not a translation of an Eddaic poem it is just like one, and all its elements

may be found in that book, most of them in the very first
poem of all which deals directly with this very theme.

Only the opening paragraphs of the paper are preserved,
either because they were written on the same page as the last
stanza of the poem and the rest was discarded, or because the
paper never went beyond this point, at any rate in this form.
There is no indication of date. There is also no way of
knowing for certain why my father reduced the poem in this
way; but a perhaps plausible explanation offers itself. The earlier
text A had introduced his very strange and distinctive conception of 'the special function of Sigurd', 'an invention of the
present poet', in his words (see Commentary, pp.183–85). He
now had the idea of introducing his paper with a brief recital of
a piece of his own 'Norse' poetry; but to use his *Upphaf* for this
purpose would require the omission of all the verses that bore
upon the idea of 'the World's chosen', the 'special function of
Sigurd' – the imposition of a new significance on the myth.

Did he see this brief work, when he wrote it, as the prelude
to a long poem on the legend of Sigurd? It seems impossible
to say (the title *Upphaf* does not necessarily imply this: it may
refer to the content of the poem, as I incline to suppose).

The other surviving earlier texts mentioned on p.40,
section I of *Völsungakviða en nýja*, 'Andvari's Gold', and
the first nine stanzas of section II, 'Signý', stand to the final
form as does text A of the *Upphaf*, in that there is constant
difference in detail of vocabulary and phrasing.

GUÐRÚNARKVIÐA EN NÝJA
eða
DRÁP NIFLUNGA

GUÐRÚNARKVIÐA EN NÝJA

1 Smoke had faded,
 sunk was burning;
 windblown ashes
 were wafted cold.
 As sun setting
 had Sigurd passed;
 and Brynhild burned
 as blazing fire.

2 Their bliss was over,
 their bale ended;
 but Gudrún's grief
 ever grew the more.
 Life she hated,
 but life took not,
 witless wandering
 in woods alone.

*

3   Atli ariseth
     armies wielding;
     on the marches of the East
     his might waxeth.
     Goths he tramples,
     gold despoiling,
     his horsemen countless
     hasten westward.

4   He, Budli's son,
     blades remembers
     that of Budli's brother
     were the bane of old;
     he, gold-greedy,
     grimhearted king,
     hath heard of the hoard
     on the Heath that lay.

5   Of Fáfnir's treasure
     fame was rumoured,
     that Niflungs held
     in Niflung-land;
     of Gudrún's beauty
     gleaming-lovely;
     of Gjúki aged
     to his grave passing.

*

6   From mighty Mirkwood
    came message darkly:
    'Atli ariseth
    armies mustering.
    Hate awakens,
    hosts are arming;
    under horses' hooves
    Hunland trembles!'

7   Gunnar spake then
    gloomy-hearted:

Gunnar   'Fierce will the feud be,
    fell the onslaught!
    With gold and silver
    shall his greed be stayed,
    with gold and silver
    or gleaming swords?'

8   Then spake Högni,
    haughty chieftain:

Högni   'The might of Sigurd
    we mourn at last!
    Victory rode ever
    with the Völsung lord;
    now alone will war
    our land defend.'

9 Then spake Grímhild
grey with wisdom:

Grímhild 'Gudrún is fair,
gleaming-lovely –
let us bind him in bonds
as brother wedded,
in Hunland's queen
our help seeking!'

10 Gudrún they sought,
grieving found her
in woodland house
weaving lonely;
weaving wondrous
webs bright-figured
with woe tangled
and with works of old.

*

11 Ódin she wrought
old, blue-mantled;
Loki lightfooted
with locks of flame;
the falls of Andvari
framed of silver,
the gold of Andvari
she gleaming wove.

12 The house of Völsung
  huge was timbered,
  the Tree there tossed
  tangled branches.
  There Grímnir's gift
  gleaming brandished
  Sigmund standing
  stern unbending.

13 The hall of Siggeir
  high was burning
  fire-encircled
  flame-devouréd.
  Signý stood there
  Sigmund greeting,
  fire about her,
  flame behind her.

14 Shields of silver
  had the ship of Sigmund;
  wild the waves were,
  wind them twisted.
  Sailed there slowly
  Sinfjötli's bier
  through stormy seas
  steered by Ódin.

15   There Regin wrought
by the red embers;
there Gram was hammered
amid gleaming sparks.
High loomed the head
of helméd dragon;
under black belly
there was blink of gold.

16   Long lay the shadow
of lone rider
golden-harnessed
Gram brandishing;
sun-bright Sigurd
seed of Völsung,
on Grani riding
into Gjúki's courts.

*

17   Golden weregild
Gunnar brought her,
haughty Högni
humbly bent him.
Gudrún they hailed,
Gunnar and Högni;
head she turned not,
hate still burned her.

18   In came Grímhild
       guileful-hearted:

Grímhild   'Dearest daughter
       droop no longer!
       Burnt is Brynhild,
       bale is ended;
       life yet shineth,
       thou art lovely still!'

19   Gudrún lifted
       her grieving eyes,
       dimmed with weeping,
       dark with mourning.
       Dark with wisdom,
       deep with purpose
       were Grímhild's eyes
       gazing through her.

Grímhild 20   'Atli ariseth,
       armies wieldeth,
       king of Eastland's
       countless peoples.
       His queen shall rule
       courts of splendour,
       over all women else
       on earth upraised.'

Gudrún 21 'Of gold were the days,
gold and silver,
silver and golden,
ere Sigurd came.
A maid among maids
in mirth walked I;
only dreams and shadows,
only dreams vexed me.

22 A hart I dreamed
high and golden:
now is sped the shaft
and spilled the blood.
A wolf thou gavest me
for woe's comfort,
in my brethren's blood
he bathed me red.

23 I love them little,
I believe them not,
but my brethren's blood
is no boot for me.
How shall husband heal me
of harm I bear
in hateful Hunland
who am hopeless now?'

Grímhild 24 'Thy brothers blame not!
　　　　　Brynhild wrought it,
　　　　　thy wrong and sorrow –
　　　　　it rues them sore.
　　　　　And dreams are but dreams,
　　　　　or else doom foretell;
　　　　　yet doom must be dreed,
　　　　　though dreams foreshow.

　　　　25 Hungold is bright,
　　　　　Hunland is wide,
　　　　　Atli mightiest
　　　　　of earthly kings.
　　　　　And gold is healing,
　　　　　though grieve the heart;
　　　　　a queen's bed better
　　　　　than one cold and bare!'

Gudrún 26 'Why drivest me on
　　　　　with daunting eyes
　　　　　dire of purpose,
　　　　　doom forestalling?
　　　　　To Sigurd thou gavest me,
　　　　　to sorrow it turned;
　　　　　now leave me to rest,
　　　　　leave thy daughter!'

Grímhild 27 'No rest for the living,
no room for tears,
who with pride and purpose
oppose their fate!
No rest I grant thee!
My redes hearken,
or rue for ever
thou wert wrought on earth!'

28 Dark hung her eyes
daunting Gudrún,
deep and dreadful,
dire with purpose.
For no word she waited,
wisdom knew she;
forth went Grímhild
from Gudrún's side.

*

29 Of Gudrún's beauty
glad was Atli;
of gold he dreamed him
guarded darkly;
of the serpent's hoard
that Sigurd left her,
of the wife of Sigurd
of women fairest.

30   Bridal drank he
blissful-hearted
to Gudrún pale
in gleaming robes.
Oaths he swore them,
to each her brothers,
and lasting truce,
league of kinship.

31   Dark and splendid,
dreadly builded,
and echoing vast
were Atli's halls.
Kings sat neath him,
countless chieftains,
and Hunnish horsemen
harnessed grimly.

32   High sat Gudrún
Hunland's mistress,
cold lay Gudrún
queen of Hunland.
Her lord loved her,
lovely was she;
laughter she knew not,
yet her limbs were white.

33   But longer him lasted
his lust of gold,
the gold he dreamed him
guarded darkly.
The serpent's treasure
they sent it never,
the Niflungs kept it
in Niflung-land.

34   Long he pondered,
till lust swayed him;
woes were wakened
and wars of old.
Long nights lying
he looked on her;
dark nights drowsing
he dreamed of gold.

35   Oaths he had uttered,
evil he pondered;
but his heart's purpose
was hidden under.
Yet words he muttered
in wandering sleep;
Gudrún guessed them,
gloom foreboding.

36   A feast he fashioned,
far proclaimed it;
to high-builded halls
his hosts were bidden;
all kith and kindred
called to greet him,
to dealing of rings,
drink and laughter.

*

37   On valiant horse
Vingi swiftly,
herald of Hunland,
hasted westward.
To Gunnar came he,
Gjúking mighty,
to halls of Rhineland
high and golden.

38   There drank they deep;
dark they eyed him,
Hun-speech hearing
in their hall ringing.
Cold fell his cry
calling loudly
under helm standing
hailing Gunnar.

Vingi 39   'Atli hath sent me
on errand speedy,
on horse hasting
through hoar forest.
Gunnar he greeteth,
Gunnar and Högni.
Be blithe he bids you,
to his boon hearken!

40   A feast he fashions,
fair he dights it,
all kith and kindred
calls to meet him.
Rings will he deal,
raiment costly,
saddles silverlaid,
and southern purple.

41   Shields shall ye choose there
and shirts of mail,
spears smooth-shafted
and splendid helms.
Gifts will he give you,
graven silver,
gold-hilted swords,
and goodly lands.'

42 His head bowed Gunnar
to Högni speaking:

Gunnar 'What saith Högni?
Doth he hear the summons?
Is not gold that glimmered
on Gnitaheiði
enough for Niflungs?
Need we bounty?

43 Is there sword in the East
that my sword matcheth?
Are there helms in Hunland
so high as ours?
Are we lieges of Atli,
lands receiving
from Hun master?
Högni answer!'

Högni 44 'Of Gudrún I think –
grim thoughts awake!
A ring she hath sent me,
a ring only.
Wolf's hair winds it,
woven round it,
wolves lie in wait
at the way's ending.'

Gunnar 45   'Yet runes she sends me,
    runes of healing,
    words well-graven
    on wood to read;
    fast bids us fare
    to feast gladly,
    old woes forgetting
    and ancient wrong.'

*

46   Gifts gave Gunnar,
    guerdon kingly;
    wine bade men bring
    to weary guest.
    Deep there drank they
    to day's ending,
    doom they recked not;
    din resounded.

47   In came Grímhild
    grey with wisdom,
    the runes she read,
    the written tokens.
    Her brows darkened
    boding evil;
    to Gunnar spake she
    grave and slowly.

Grímhild 48 'These runes I doubt:
they are writ with cunning,
strangely twisted,
stained and darkened.
There were others under,
now overlaid –
if I read them right
they were runes of ill.'

49 Gunnar had drunken,
to his guest turned he:

Gunnar 'Ye Huns have no wine
such as here runneth!
It irks us to ride
to your ale-quaffing;
guile fills your horns –
Gunnar comes not!'

50 Laughing said Vingi:

Vingi 'My lord shall I tell
that in courts of Gjúki
no kings are left?
There rules a queen,
a rune-conner;
his weighty words
a woman judgeth?

51   I must haste away,
so will hide it not,
that Atli is old,
but Erp is young.
Thy sister's son
is but seven winters –
strong hands he needs
to steer his realm.

52   In Gunnar hoped he
for guide and help,
of his sister's son
the safe keeper.
He weened ye might wield
his wide kingdom –
ye are fallen afraid,
and fear shadows.'

53   Högni him answered
hard and scornful:

Högni   'Daring speeches,
and drink-begotten!
Nor hoar nor weary
is here the king,
though queens in Rhineland
be counted wise.

54 Yet Atli I heard not
too old for guile,
war to ponder,
or wealth to covet.
And fey saith my thought:
"Far lies the day
ere Erp or Eitill
after Atli rule!"'

55 But loud cried Gunnar
laughing scornful,
deep had he drunken
darkly musing:

Gunnar 'Let wolves then wield
wealth of Niflungs!
Bears shall harbour
in barren courtyards.

56 Winds shall wander
where wine we drank,
but Gunnar will go
Gudrún seeking.
We fast shall follow
thy feet, Vingi!
Our horns shall be heard
Hunland rousing.'

57 (From heavy heart then
Högni answered:)

Högni   'I go with Gunnar,
though glad I am not.
Oft Grímhild's redes
we have grimly heard.
We took them ever,
though they turned awry;
truth now she teacheth,
and we trust her not.'

58 Then vowed Vingi
the venom-tonguéd –
oaths he recked not,
the oft forsworn:

Vingi   'May hell have me
and the high gallows,
may ravens rend me,
if the runes should lie!'

*

59 Niflungs rode forth
from Niflung-land;
fast their journey,
few went with them.
Grímhild stood there
grey and aged,
dark eyes were dimmed
death foreseeing.

60   Their word was spoken,
wills were hardened;
fate drove them on,
fey they parted.
None might hinder
near them thronging,
lords nor wisemen;
with a laugh they rode.

61   Steeds went striding,
stonefire glinted,
rocks were ringing,
roads resounding.
In hoar forests
harts were startled,
over hill and valley
hooves were beating.

62   Over river rowed they
roaring onward;
oars were bending
urged to breaking.
Foam flew from prow,
flashed and sparkled;
at bank unbound
the boats left they.

63   In the hoar forest
horns they sounded
Hunland rousing;
hooves were beating.
Golden harness
gleamed and sparkled;
steeds came striding
stung to madness.

*

64   From hill upon high
halls they looked on,
walls and watchtowers
wondrous-builded.
They were forest-girdled,
fenced with spearmen;
horses neighed there,
helms were glinting.

65   There was clamour in the courts,
cold rang the steel;
shafts were shaken,
shields them answered.
Gates found they barred,
grim doors of iron:
Högni smote them,
hewed them fiercely.

66 (Forth came Vingi
the venom-tonguéd:)

Vingi   'Ye need not to knock,
for known your coming!
The greeting is prepared –
the gallows waits you.
The hungry eagle,
the hoary wolf,
the ravens are ready
to rend your flesh!'

Högni 67 'Heralds were holy –
but unhallowed liar,
thou shalt hang the first,
and hell take thee!'
From the oak-branches
with arms corded
they hung him high
in the Huns' faces.

68 Huns loud clamoured,
hate was kindled;
forth rushed they fell,
fierce the onslaught.
In battle blended
Budlungs, Niflungs;
blades were brandished,
burst were helmets.

69   Back they beat them
     broken-harnessed;
     to the doors they drove them –
     din was in the gates.
     In leaped Högni,
     held the gateway,
     hewed two-handed,
     hurled them backward.

70   The few and fearless
     as a fire entered,
     as roaring flame,
     wrath devouring.
     Wolves sprang behind,
     the ways were reddened,
     the walls echoed,
     wailing filled them.

71   Steep, stone-builded,
     the stair arose
     to dark doorways
     dreadly timbered.
     There Högni halted,
     hailed them loudly:
Högni   'Forth, forth! O friends,
     the feast begins!'

72   Out came Atli,
anger-clouded:

Atli   'Welcome, my vassals!
Ye have well begun it.
Death the drink here,
doom the ending,
ropes here the rings –
if ransom fail.

73   That gold give me
that is Gudrún's right,
that Sigurd conquered,
the serpent's treasure!'
Högni laughed then,
on his hilts leaning;
Gunnar glowering
grimly answered.

Gunnar 74   'No gold from Gunnar
shalt thou get for ever!
Life canst thou take
at latest end.
Dear wilt thou buy it
in dread barter
of lords and lieges,
lives uncounted!'

Atli 75   'Fools the Niflungs,
feud-forgetful;
foul-stained their hands
with friend-murder.
Gudrún's husband
for Gudrún's wrong
a grim vengeance
will gladly wreak.'

Gunnar 76   'Here Gudrún spake not!
Golden weregild
she looks nor longs for –
the lust is thine!'

Högni   'For atonement now
time is over!
Words we need not,
war hath entered!'

77   Horns they sounded –
hall-walls echoed –
strode the stairway;
stern their onslaught.
The stones they stained
with streaming blood;
snaketonguéd arrows
sang about them.

78   Doors clanged backward,
din resounded:
Hunland's champions
hurled upon them.
Hard were handstrokes,
hewn were corslets,
as on hundred anvils
were hammers ringing.

*

79   In hall sat Gudrún
at heart weary,
from mood to mood
her mind wavered.
The din she hearkened,
deadly crying,
as back were beaten
the Borgund-lords.

Gudrún 80 'Little I love them,
long I hated!
A wolf they gave me
for woe's comfort.
Yet the wolf rends them,
and woe is me!
Woe worth the hour
that of womb I came!'

81 Her hands she wrung
on high standing,
loud called she clear
to lieges there:

Gudrún 'If any honour me
in these evil halls,
let them hold their hands
from this hell-labour!

82 Who would love requite,
who would lies disown,
who remember misery
by these masters wrought,
arm now! arm now!
aid the fearless
betrayed and trapped
by this troll-people!'

83 Atli sat there,
anger burned him;
yet murmurs mounted,
men were rising.
Goths were there many:
griefs they remembered,
wars in Mirkwood
and wars of old.

84   From the hall striding
high they shouted,
foes turned to friends
fiercely greeted:
'Goths and Niflungs
our gods helping
will hew the Huns
to hell's shadow!'

85   The few and fearless
fiercely answered
(their backs were driven
to the builded walls):
Niflungs   'Friends, come welcome!
The feast is high.
Now songs let us sing
of our sires of yore.'

86   Of the Goths' glory
Gunnar sang there;
of Iormunrek
earth-shadowing king;
of Angantýr
and old battles,
of Dylgja, Dúnheið,
and Danpar's walls.

87   Forth went Högni,
hate rekindled,
his son Snævar
at his side leaping.
Hewn was Högni
by a Hun chieftain;
his shield was shorn
in shards falling.

88   Snævar they slew there,
their swords stabbed him;
he left his life
laughing grimly.
Högni wept not;
from his hand the shield
stooping lifted;
strode then onward.

89   The stairs they strode
streaming redly;
at dark doorways
they dinned and hammered;
into halls of Atli
hewed a pathway;
rushed in roaring,
reeking-handed.

90 Gudrún they greeted,
   Gunnar and Högni:

Gunnar &   'This feast is fashioned
Högni   fair and seemly!
   Fell-shapen fates
   will force us ever
   as wife to give thee,
   and a widow make thee!'

Gudrún 91 'If for wrongs ye wrought
   ruth now moves you,
   doom forestall not!
   This deed forego!'

Gunnar &   'At our sister's prayer
Högni   let him slink away!
   Woman's robes ward him,
   not warrior's mail!'

92 Forth went Atli,
   anguish gnawed him;
   to Gudrún Högni
   said grim farewell:

Högni   'Thy price is paid,
   thy prayer granted!
   At life's forfeit
   we have loosed our foe.'

*

93 Forth sent Atli
his errand-riders;
Hunland hearkened,
hosts were arming.
Gallowsfowl to gladden
Goths and Niflungs
from the hall they hurled
the Hunnish corpses.

94 Daylight grew dim,
dark shadows walked
in echoing halls
that Atli loved.
In need most dire
the Niflung lords
doom awaited;
the doors were shut.

95 Night lapped the world
and noiseless town;
under ashen moonlight
the owls hooted.
At guarded doorways
Gunnar and Högni
silent sat they
sleepless waiting.

96 First spake Högni:

Högni   'Are these halls afire?
Of day untimely
doth the dawn smoulder?
Do dragons in Hunland
dreadly flaming
wind here their way?
Wake, O heroes!'

97 Gunnar answered:

Gunnar   'Guard the doorways!
Here dawn nor dragon
dreadly burneth;
the gabled houses
are gloom-shrouded,
under ailing moon
the earth is shadowed.

98 There is tramp of men
torches bearing,
clink of corslet,
clank of armour.
There is crying of ravens,
cold howls the wolf,
shields are shimmering,
shafts uplifted.'

Gunnar & 99 'Wake now, wake now!
Högni War is kindled.
Now helm to head,
to hand the sword.
Wake now, warriors,
wielding glory!
To wide Valhöll
ways lie open.'

*

100 At the dark doorways
they dinned and hammered;
there was clang of swords
and crash of axes.
The smiths of battle
smote the anvils;
sparked and splintered
spears and helmets.

101 In they hacked them,
out they hurled them,
bears assailing,
boars defending.
Stones and stairways
streamed and darkened;
day came dimly –
the doors were held.

102   Five days they fought
few and dauntless;
the doors were riven,
dashed asunder.
They barred them with bodies,
bulwarks piling
of Huns and Niflungs
hewn and cloven.

103   (Atli spoke then
anguish mourning:)

Atli   'My friends are fallen,
my foes living,
my kith and kindred
cloven-breasted.
I am wealth-bereaved
and wife-curséd,
of glory shorn
in the grey of years.

104   Woe and wailing
in my wide kingdom!
Where I feasted long
are fell serpents.
The proud pillars
are purple-stained
in the builded halls
that Budli reared.'

105   Then Beiti spake there
bale devising,
the king's counsellor –
he was cunning-hearted:

Beiti   'Accursed is become
thy carven house!
Better loss of little
than to lose thy all.

106   Fire still may tame
these fell serpents,
thy pillars be the pyre
of these proud robbers!'
For the ruin and wrack
wrath seized Atli;
that shame he shirked not,
shorn of glory.

107   Flame-encircled
fearless Niflungs
in riven harness
redly glinted.
Iron-bolted walls,
ancient timbers,
creaked and smouldered,
cracked and tumbled.

108 There hot and smoking
   fell hissing embers,
   and plashed and sputtered
   in the pools of gore.
   Reek was round them,
   a rolling smoke;
   dank dripped their sweat –
   the doors were held.

109 Their shields they raised
   over shattered helmets;
   they stamped the brands
   on streaming floors.
   Blacktongued with thirst
   blood there drank they;
   fell one by one
   on the ways to hell.

110 Out burst the brethren
   blackhued, grisly,
   boars bleeding-tusked
   at bay at last.
   The Huns grasped them
   helmless, shieldless,
   bare and bleeding,
   with broken swords.

111 As hounds affrighted
Huns were crying;
they were rent and riven
by reeking hands.
Necks were broken
and knees sundered,
ere the Borgund king
was bound and thrown.

112 Last fought Högni
alone hopeless;
his teeth tore them
as they tied him down.
The dust was bitten,
the doom fallen,
the Need of the Niflungs
and their night was come.

113 In dank prison
dark and evil
Högni hurled they;
Huns him guarded.
But Gunnar bound
in Gudrún's bower
was flung at the feet
of her frenzied lord.

Atli 114 'Too long have I looked
for this last meeting,
Budlung's vengeance
on Borgund lord.
Here lies at last
in lowly dust
lordly Gunnar!
Gudrún behold!

115 Sigurd remember,
and say me now,
is it sweet to see him
so sore avenged?
In my serpent-pit
snakes are waiting –
they bite more bitter
than blades of steel!'

116 Gunnar he trampled,
Gudrún saw him:

Gudrún 'Evil art thou, Atli.
May thy end be shame!
By Erp and Eitill
our own children
(sons of the sister
of these sad captives),
from the dust lift them!
Their death forego!'

Atli 117　'Let them give me the gold,
　　　　　the gleaming hoard,
　　　　　the serpent's treasure
　　　　　that Sigurd conquered!
　　　　　The gold, the gold
　　　　　that grieves my dreams –
　　　　　if Gunnar will grant it,
　　　　　I will grant him thee!'

Gunnar 118　'I will give thee the gold,
　　　　　goodly portion,
　　　　　the half yielding
　　　　　which I hold my own.
　　　　　Half hath Högni,
　　　　　my haughty brother;
　　　　　to his latest breath
　　　　　he will loose it not.

119　Let heart of Högni
　　　　　at my hand be laid
　　　　　from breast bleeding
　　　　　with blades severed;
　　　　　then gold will I give,
　　　　　gold of serpents –
　　　　　all shall Atli
　　　　　eager take it!'

Gudrún 120   'Yet Högni no less,
          mine hapless brother,
          I did beg from thee
          by those born of us!'

Atli   'Of his troll's temper
          yet true were the words!
          The gold will I gain,
          though Gudrún weep!'

121   Out went Atli,
          evil he purposed;
          but wisemen bade him
          wary counsel.
          The queen fearing
          of cunning thought they;
          a thrall they seized
          and thrust in prison.

*

Hjalli the 122   'Woe worth the wiles
thrall   and wars of kings,
          if my life I must lose
          in their luckless feud!
          The light of morning,
          labour daylong,
          fire at evening,
          too few my days!'

Huns 123   'Hjalli, swineherd,
        thy heart give us!'
        Shrilly shrieked he
        at the shining knife.
        They bared his breast,
        and bitter wailed he;
        ere the point pricked him
        he piercing cried.

    124   Högni heard him,
        to the Huns spake he:
Högni   'Noisome the shrieking!
        Knives were liever.
        If hearts ye wish
        here lies a better.
        It trembles not. Take it!
        Your toil were less.'

    125   The heart then cut they
        from Hjalli's bosom;
        to Gunnar bore it
        on golden dish:
Huns   'Here lies his heart!
        Högni is ended.'
        Loudly laughed he,
        lord of Niflungs.

Gunnar 126   'I hapless see here
              heart of craven.
              Högni hath not
              heart that trembles.
              Quivering lies it;
              quaked it swifter
              beating in baseborn
              breast ignoble.'

     127   Loudly laughed he
              at life's ending,
              when knife was come
              to Niflung lord.
              The heart they cut
              from Högni's bosom;
              to Gunnar bore it
              on golden dish.

Gunnar 128   'I haughty see here
              heart undaunted.
              Högni held it,
              heart untrembling.
              Unshaken lies it,
              so shook it seldom
              beating in boldest
              breast of princes.

129   Alone now living,
Lord of Niflungs,
the gold I hold
and guard for ever!
In hall nor heath
nor hidden dungeon
shall friend or foeman
find it gleaming.

130   Rhine shall rule it,
rings and goblets,
in weltering water
wanly shining.
In the deeps we cast it;
dark it rolleth,
as useless to man
as of yore it proved!

131   Cursed be Atli,
king of evil,
of glory naked,
gold-bereavéd;
gold-bereavéd,
gold-tormented,
murder-tainted,
murder-haunted!'

132   Fires of madness
           flamed and started
           from eyes of Atli;
           anguish gnawed him:

Atli   'Serpents seize him!
           snakes shall sting him.
           In the noisome pit
           naked cast him!'

*

133   There gleaming-eyed
           Gudrún waited;
           the heart within her
           hardened darkly.
           Grim mood took her,
           Grímhild's daughter,
           ruthless hatred,
           wrath consuming.

134   There grimly waited
           Gunnar naked;
           snakes were creeping
           silent round him.
           Teeth were poisoned,
           tongues were darting;
           in lidless eyes
           light was shining.

135 A harp she sent him;
   his hands seized it,
   strong he smote it;
   strings were ringing.
   Wondering heard men
   words of triumph,
   song up-soaring
   from the serpents' pit.

136 There coldly creeping
   coiling serpents
   as stones were staring
   stilled, enchanted.
   There slowly swayed they,
   slumber whelmed them,
   as Gunnar sang
   of Gunnar's pride.

137 As voice in Valhöll
   valiant ringing
   the golden Gods
   he glorious named;
   of Ódin sang he,
   Ódin's chosen,
   of Earth's most mighty,
   of ancient kings.

138   A huge adder
      hideous gleaming
      from stony hiding
      was stealing slow.
      Huns still heard him
      his harp thrilling,
      and doom of Hunland
      dreadly chanting.

139   An ancient adder
      evil-swollen,
      to breast it bent
      and bitter stung him.
      Loud cried Gunnar
      life forsaking;
      harp fell silent,
      and heart was still.

140   To the queen that cry came
      clear and piercing;
      aghast she sat
      in guarded bower.
      Erp and Eitill
      eager called she:
      dark their locks were,
      dark their glances.

*

141 Pyres they builded
proud and stately;
Hunland's champions
there high upraised.
A pyre they builded
on the plain standing;
there naked lay
the Niflung lords.

142 Flames were mounting,
fire was roaring,
reek was swirling
ringed with tumult.
Smoke was fading,
sunk was burning;
windblown ashes
were wafted cold.

143 A hall was thronging,
Huns were drinking
the funeral feast
of fallen men.
Foes were vanquished,
fire had burned them;
now Atli was lord
of East and West.

144 Wealth he dealt there,
  wounds requiting,
  worthy weregild
  of warriors slain.
  Loud they praised him;
  long the drinking,
  wild grew the words
  of the wine-bemused.

145 Gudrún came forth
  goblets bearing:

Gudrún 'Hail, O Hun-king,
  health I bring thee!'
  Deep drank Atli,
  drained them laughing:
  though gold he missed,
  yet was Gunnar dead.

Gudrún 146 'Hail, O Hun-king,
  hear me speaking:
  My brethren are slain
  that I begged of thee.
  Erp and Eitill
  dost thou ask to look on?
  Ask no longer –
  their end hath come!

147   Their hearts thou tastest
with honey mingled,
their blood was blent
in the bowls I gave;
those bowls their skulls
bound with silver,
their bones thy hounds
have burst with teeth.'

148   There awful cries
of anguish woke;
their heads men hid
their horror shrouding.
Pale grew Atli,
as one poison-sick,
on his face crashed he
fallen swooning.

149   To bed they brought him
in bower empty,
laid him and left him
to loathsome dream.
Women were wailing,
wolves were howling,
hounds were baying
the hornéd moon.

150 In came Gudrún
with ghastly eyes,
darkly mantled,
dire of purpose.

Gudrún 'Wake thou, woeful!
Wake from dreaming!'
In his breast the knife
she bitter drave it.

Atli 151 'Grímhild's daughter
ghastly-handed,
hounds should tear thee
and to hell send thee!
Stoned and branded
at the stake living
thou shouldst burn and wither
thou born of witch!'

152 Gudrún mocked him,
gasping left him.

Gudrún 'The doom of burning
is dight for thee!
On pyre the corpse is,
prepared the faggot!
so Atli passeth
earth forsaking.'

153 Fires she kindled,
     flames she brandished;
     the house was roaring,
     hounds were yelping.
     Timbers crumbled,
     trees and rafters;
     there sank and died
     slaves and maidens.

154 Smoke was swirling
     over sleeping town,
     light was lifted
     over land and tree.
     Women were weeping,
     wolves were yammering,
     hounds were howling
     in the Hun-kingdom.

155 Thus Atli ended
     earth forsaking,
     to the Niflungs' bane
     the night was come;
     of Völsung, Niflung,
     of vows broken,
     of woe and valour
     are the words ended.

*

156   While world lasteth
shall the words linger,
while men are mindful
of the mighty days.
The woe of Gudrún
while world lasteth
till end of days
all shall hearken.

157   Her mind wavered,
her mood grew cold;
her heart withered
and hate sickened.
Life she hated,
yet life took not,
witless wandering
in the woods alone.

158   Over wan rivers,
over woods and forests,
over rocks she roamed
to the roaring sea.
In the waves she cast her,
the waves spurned her;
by the waves sitting
she woe bemoaned.

Gudrún 159   'Of gold were the days,
gleaming silver,
silver gleaming
ere Sigurd came.
A maid was I then,
a maiden fair;
only dreams vexed me,
dreams of evil.

160   Fell sorrows five
hath fate sent me:
they slew Sigurd,
my sorrow greatest.
In evil loathing
to Atli me gave:
too long lasting
my life's disease.

161   The heart of Högni
they hewed living:
my heart it hardened,
my hardest woe.
Gunnar heard I
in the grave crying:
my grief most grim
was that ghastly voice.

162   My sons I slew
seared with madness:
keen it bites me
most clinging woe.
There sits beside me
son nor daughter;
the world is empty,
the waves are cold.

163   They slew Sigurd:
my sorrow deepest,
my life's loathing,
my life's disease.
Sigurd, Sigurd,
on swift Grani
lay saddle and bridle
and seek for me!

164   Rememberest thou
what on marriage-bed
in love we pledged,
as we laid us down? –
the light I would leave
to look for thee,
from hell thou wouldst ride
and haste to me!'

165 In the waves she cast her,
the waves took her;
in the wan water
her woe was drowned.
While the world lasteth
woe of Gudrún
till the end of days
all shall hearken.

*

166 Thus glory endeth,
and gold fadeth,
on noise and clamours
the night falleth.
Lift up your hearts,
lords and maidens
for the song of sorrow
that was sung of old.

COMMENTARY
on
GUÐRÚNARKVIÐA EN NÝJA

COMMENTARY
on
GUÐRÚNARKVIÐA EN NÝJA

In this commentary *Guðrúnarkviða en Nýja* is referred to as 'the Lay of Gudrún', or where no confusion is possible as 'the Lay', and *Völsungakviða en Nýja* as 'the Lay of the Völsungs'. As there are no sections in this poem, references are made simply by the numbers of the stanzas.

The subordinate title *Dráp Niflunga* means 'The Slaying of the Niflungs': on this name see the Lay of the Völsungs, VII.8 and note.

The relation of the Lay of Gudrún to its ancient sources is not essentially different from that of the Lay of the Völsungs, but in this case the sources are very largely extant in the poems of the Edda, and the *Völsunga Saga* is of far less importance. In its content the Lay of Gudrún is essentially a complex interweaving of the Eddaic poems *Atlakviða* and *Atlamál*, together with some wholly independent developments.

My father devoted much time and thought to *Atlakviða*, and prepared a very detailed commentary (the basis for lectures and seminars) on this extraordinarily difficult text. It is a poem that he much admired. Despite its condition, 'we are in the presence (he wrote) of great poetry that can still move us as poetry. Its style is universally and rightly praised: rapid, terse, vigorous – while maintaining, within its narrow limits, characterization. The poet who wrote it knew how to produce the grim and deadly atmosphere his theme demanded. It lives in the memory as one of the things in the Edda most instinct with that demonic energy and force which one finds in Old Norse verse.'

But the text as it stands in the Codex Regius, with its clearly corrupt, defective or unintelligible lines or stanzas, its incompatible additions, its strange variations in metre, has inevitably given rise over many years to a great deal of discordant critical analysis. Here I need say no more, however, than that my father tentatively interpreted the state of *Atlakviða* as the reworking of an earlier poem, a reworking that had then itself undergone 'improvements', additions, losses, and disarrangements.

Following *Atlakviða* in the Codex Regius is *Atlamál*, the longest of all the heroic poems of the Edda. Whether or not the author of this poem was familiar with *Atlakviða* (my father thought it improbable) it is decidedly later, and if it tells the same story and keeps the old names, it has nonetheless undergone an extraordinary imaginative transposition: it could be said that the story has been removed from the Heroic Age and re-established in a wholly different mode. Concerning this my father wrote: '*Atlakviða* seems to preserve a most primitive (unelaborated and unaltered) version of events. There is still a sense of the great kingdom of Atli, and the wide-flung conflicts of the ancient heroic days; the courts are courts of mighty kings – in *Atlamál* they have sunk to farmhouses. The geography, vague of course, is in keeping: the Niflungs ride fen and forest and plain to Atli (in *Atlamál* they seem only to row over a single fjord). We may notice also the old traditional *vin Borgunda* of Gunnar, and the *Myrkviðr* ('Mirkwood') specially associated with ancient Hun-stories' (see the notes to the Lay of the Völsungs VII.14 and 15). But in *Atlamál*, while the old 'plot' survives, the sense of an archaic and distant world, passed down through many generations, has altogether disappeared. And with it has gone altogether the hoard of the Niflungs and Atli's greed.

3–4, 6 These stanzas echo in their language the verses that Gunnar sang when he first came to the halls of Gjúki, and use several of the same phrases: see the Lay of the Völsungs, VII.14–15 and notes. Gunnar was recalling the earlier wars of Goths and Huns (14), and the battles in which 'the Borgund lords met Budli's host', and slew Budli's brother (15).

The compiler of the Codex Regius wrote a prose passage entitled *Dráp Niflunga* 'The Slaying of the Niflungs', evidently intended as an introduction to the poem that follows in the manuscript, which is *Guðrúnarkviða en forna*, the Old Lay of Gudrún. The passage begins thus:

Gunnar and Högni seized all the gold, the patrimony of Fáfnir. At that time there was strife between the sons of Gjúki and Atli: he charged them with the death of Brynhild. This was how they were reconciled: they were to give him Gudrún in marriage – and they gave her a draught of oblivion to drink, before she would consent to be married to Atli.

Here, as in the Old Lay of Gudrún itself, Brynhild is the daughter of Budli, and the sister of Atli. Since in my father's version of the story Brynhild was not associated with Atli this element is absent from his Lay of Gudrún. 'There is no trace in *Atlakviða* of Brynhild and all that complication,' he wrote, 'and in so far as the motive is apparent – it is not explicit – it is *the greed of Atli* and the cursed hoard that are at the bottom of the trouble.' On the drink of oblivion see the note to 17–28.

10–16   *Atlakviða* and *Atlamál* do not take up the story until the coming of Atli's messenger to the Gjúkings. The primary source for the story of Gudrún after the death of Sigurd is *Guðrúnarkviða en forna* (which has the story that Sigurd was not murdered in his bed but out of doors, see the note to IX.51–64 in the Lay of the Völsungs). In this poem Gudrún looks back in lamentation, and tells how she went and sat at night by the body of Sigurd where it lay in the forest; from there she wandered on and came at last to Denmark. It was in Denmark with Thora Hákon's daughter that the tapestry was woven, and it was there that Gunnar and Högni came to her, together with Grímhild.

In the Lay (stanza 2) Gudrún is said to have gone 'witless wandering in woods alone', and when Grímhild and her sons found her she was still living alone, and weaving her tapestry in a 'woodland house' (10).

In the brief text (iii) concerning this poem given on pp.52–53 my father wrote: 'Gudrún did not take her own life, but for grief was for a time half-witless. She would not look upon her kinsmen nor upon her mother, and dwelt apart in a house in the woods. There after a while she began to weave in a tapestry the history of the Dragon-hoard and of Sigurd.' Thus the introduction of the tapestry in the Eddaic poem became a device, having a wholly different content, to link *Guðrúnarkviða en nýja* to *Völsungakviða en nýja*.

17–28   An important element in *Guðrúnarkviða en forna* which is absent from the Lay of Gudrún is the draught of forgetfulness given to Gudrún by Grímhild, intent on making her forget her injuries and consent to be wedded to Atli. In the poem, followed by the Saga, several stanzas are devoted to Grímhild's potion, and its curious ingredients enumerated at length. But very strangely, the draught has no effect on Gudrún's mind: in the verses that follow she fiercely withstands Grímhild's persuasions; and it has been commonly supposed therefore that stanzas have been disordered, those referring to the potion being placed too early.

My father did not accept this explanation. The first draft of oblivion, administered by Grímhild to Sigurd, he believed to have been invented 'to account for the difficulties raised by the previous betrothal of Sigurd and

Brynhild' (see p.244). 'Here,' he wrote, 'we have the same mechanism again resorted to – and I think deplorably: for the mere repetition is distasteful, these drinks of Grímhild are too powerful or too powerless: why not give one to Atli too, and make him forget the Hoard!'

He thought it very probable that the stanzas relating to Grímhild's drink of forgetfulness was an interpolation by a later hand. In his Lay of Gudrún it is gone, and Gudrún (as is seen from stanza 28) submitted without sorcery to the strength of purpose of her formidable mother. In the Saga her last words to Grímhild were 'Then so it must be, but it is against my will; and no joy will come of it, but rather grief.'

22 Gudrún's dream is repeated from the Lay of the Völsungs, VII.2–4; lines 5–8 of the present stanza, referring to Atli, are repeated from VII.4, with change of 'A wolf they gave me' to 'A wolf thou gavest me'.

23 'boot' : remedy.

24 'dreed': endured (as in the Lay of the Völsungs, VIII.4).

29 'of gold he dreamed him': this is a relic, apparently, of an old impersonal construction of the verb 'dream': 'he dreamed of gold'. These lines reappear in stanza 33.

32–34 In *Atlamál* the life of Atli and Gudrún has been a horror of hatred and dissension; stanzas 32 and 34 of the Lay suggest rather the story glimpsed in *Atlakviða*, where when Gudrún stabs Atli in his bed it is said:

'Often had the ways of love been better, when those twain were wont many a time to embrace before their noble court.' In the Lay of Gudrún Atli is explicitly presented as torn between his love of Gudrún and his desire for the Niflung hoard.

35 In *Atlamál* (followed by the Saga) Gudrún overheard what Atli and his men said together in secret; in the Lay this is changed to her overhearing what Atli muttered in his sleep.

36 'kith': friends, neighbours, acquaintance (the original sense of the word in the phrase 'kith and kin'); again in stanza 40.

37–48 The narrative elements of the Hunnish messenger and the ring and runes sent by Gudrún are derived from both *Atlakviða* and *Atlamál*. The name Vingi is from *Atlamál*, but 'Cold fell his cry' (38) comes from *Atlakviða*, where Atli's messenger, there called Knefröðr, *kallaði kaldri röddu* 'cried with a cold voice', which as my father noted bore here a distinct sense, 'ill-boding, fateful'.

From *Atlakviða* come also the great gifts offered by Atli, and the words of Gunnar and Högni concerning Atli's invitation. In *Atlakviða* Gudrún's warning takes this form, in Högni's words:

> Hár fann ek heiðingja
> riðit í hring rauðum.
> Ylfskr er vegr okkar
> at ríða örindi.

317

(I found a hair of the heath-roamer / wound in the red ring./ Treacherous as a wolf is the road for you and me / if we ride on this errand.) But in *Atlamál* the wolf's hair is eliminated, and Gudrún sent a message in runes, which Vingi altered before he delivered it.

In the Lay of Gudrún both motives are combined (stanzas 44–5), and in this my father was following the Saga and the note entitled *Dráp Niflunga* in the Codex Regius. This latter adds that the ring was Andvaranaut (taken by Sigurd from Brynhild and given to Gudrún: but not so in the Lay of the Völsungs, see the note to IX.9–10).

39 'boon': request, entreaty.

40 'dights': prepares, makes ready.

42–58 I set out here the interweaving of sources in this passage in some detail, since it exhibits very clearly my father's narrative method in this poem.

In *Atlakviða*, Gunnar asks his brother why they should be tempted by Atli's bounty when they themselves own such wealth and such arms (see the Lay stanzas 42–3), and Högni, not replying directly, speaks of the wolf's hair twisted round Gudrún's ring. With no further direct indication of Gunnar's thoughts, he at once makes the decision to go, crying *Úlfr mun ráða arfi Niflunga*, the wolf shall possess the heritage of the Niflungs, if he does not return. In *Atlamál*, on the other hand, neither Gunnar nor Högni are shown to hesitate at all. The runic message that replaced the wolf's hair of

Atlakviða causes them no disquiet. It is only subsequently that Högni's wife Kostbera examines the runes and perceives that they have been overlaid on those originally cut; but Högni dismisses her warning, as he also dismisses her warning dreams. Gunnar's wife Glaumvör likewise has oppressive dreams, but they too are dismissed by Gunnar; and the brothers set out next morning. Kostbera and Glaumvör appear only in *Atlamál* and are not taken up into the Lay of Gudrún.

In the Saga a further element is introduced, in that Vingi, seeing that the brothers have become drunk, tells them that Atli, now aged, wishes them to become the rulers of his kingdom while his sons are so young (see stanzas 51–2 in the Lay). It is this that makes Gunnar decide to go, and Högni reluctantly to agree, before the closer examination of the runes and the telling of the dreams take place.

In the Lay my father has taken elements from both the Eddaic lays and from the Saga, but rearranged the context, so that the implications are somewhat altered. Gunnar's scorn for Atli's offer and Högni's warning about the wolf's hair are preserved, but Gunnar is now persuaded to accept the invitation by the ostensible meaning of Gudrún's runic message (45). It is Grímhild, not Kostbera, who warns that the runes have been tampered with, and that the underlying meaning was quite other – and this leads Gunnar to tell Vingi that he will not now come (49). This is the occasion of Vingi's final seduction (51–2); and though Högni remains scornfully unconvinced (53–4), Gunnar, who had 'deep drunken', cries out echoing the words of *Atlakviða*: 'Let wolves then wield wealth of Niflungs!'

The scene ends with a return to the runes: Högni observing heavily that when Grímhild's counsel ought to be attended to they dismiss her warning, and Vingi swearing, in an echo of his words in *Atlamál*, that the runes do not lie. Gunnar's character is maintained: see p.52(ii).

50 'rune-conner': one who pores over, closely examines, runes.

54 'fey saith my thought': I take, but doubtfully, the word 'fey' here to mean 'with presage of death'.

59 'few went with them': in *Atlakviða* there is no mention of any companions of Gunnar and Högni; in *Atlamál* they had three, Högni's sons Snævar (named in stanzas 87–8 of the Lay) and Sólar, and his wife's brother Orkning.

59–63 On their journey to the land of the Huns, as my father wrote of the passage in *Atlakviða* (see p.313), 'the Niflungs ride fen and forest and plain to Atli'. Stanza 62 is derived from *Atlamál*, where the furious rowing of Gunnar and Högni and their companions is described; but in the Lay the localized Scandinavian scene of *Atlamál* is not intended – they are crossing the Danube.

60 'fey': fated to die.

62 lines 7–8: this also is derived from *Atlamál*. My father remarked in a lecture that the abandoning of the boat by

the Niflungs, since they hoped for no return, seems to be a detail that belongs to the oldest form of the legend as it reached the North, since it is found also in the German *Nibelungenlied*.

65–67 While the great courts of Atli are obviously quite differently conceived from the farmstead of *Atlamál*, Högni's beating on the doors derives from it, as does the slaying of Vingi – though in *Atlamál* they struck him to death with axes.

68–92 In *Atlakviða* there is no fighting when Gunnar and Högni come to Atli's halls. Gudrún meets her brothers as they enter and tells them that they are betrayed. Gunnar is at once seized and bound (and it is here that he is called *vin Borgunda* 'lord of the Burgundians', the only surviving trace in Old Norse literature of the Burgundian origin of the Gjúkings: see p.228, note on VII.15). Högni slew eight men before he was taken.

In *Atlamál*, on the other hand, as in the German *Nibelungenlied*, there is fierce fighting on the arrival of Gunnar and Högni, and Gudrún, in this poem leaving the hall and coming to her brothers outside, takes part in it and herself strikes down two men. The fighting lasted through the morning, and eighteen of Atli's men were slain before Gunnar and Högni were taken. Then Atli speaks and laments his marriage and the loss of his men.

In the Lay this part of the narrative is greatly extended beyond what is told in either of the Eddaic lays or in the *Völsunga Saga*. The Saga introduces the idea of a lull in the fighting, not found in *Atlamál*, when Atli spoke of his loss and his evil lot, before the battle was rejoined and the brothers forced their way into the hall (cf. stanzas 71 ff. in the Lay). But after fierce fighting Gunnar and Högni were taken prisoner; whereas in the Lay the result of the assault is that they hold Atli at their mercy – and Gudrún persuades them to show it.

The Lay is far removed from *Atlamál* in the portrait of Gudrún, who is naturally not here presented as a fierce warrior-woman; and an entirely new element is introduced in the presence of Gothic warriors at Atli's court (83), on whom Gudrún calls for aid and who rise against their Hunnish masters (81–6); see the note to 86.

68 Budlungs: men of Budli (Atli's father).

80 'A wolf they gave me': see the note to stanza 22.

'Woe worth the hour': see the note to the Lay of the Völsungs, IX.29.

86 The introduction in the Lay of the Burgundians' new-found allies in the Goths at Atli's court leads to these references to ancient Gothic names remembered in old lays. This stanza is an innovation of my father's.

Iormunrek (*Jörmunrekkr*) was the Norse form of the name of Ermanaric, king of the Ostrogoths, the eastern branch of the Gothic people, who dwelt in the South Russian plains in the fourth century. The vast dominion of Ermanaric extended over many tribes and peoples from the Black Sea north towards the Baltic; but about the year 375, in his old age, he took his own life, in the face of the first overwhelming onset of the Asiatic steppe nomads, the Huns, who inspired widespread terror by their savagery and their appearance. To that distant time the song of Gunnar reached back, as did his minstrelsy at the feast held in honour of Sigurd in the halls of Gjúki (the Lay of the Völsungs, VII.14); the line 'earth-shadowing king' in the present stanza no doubt refers to the vastness of Ermanaric's empire.

In the centuries that followed Ermanaric became a mighty figure in the heroic legends of Germanic-speaking peoples, his name darkened by the evil deeds that attached to his fame. In the few traces of Old English heroic legend that survive he was remembered as *wrað wærloga*, 'fell and faithless', and in the little poem called *Deor* he appears in these lines:

> We geascodon Eormanrices
> wylfenne geþoht: ahte wide folc
> Gotena rices: þæt wæs grim cyning.

'We have heard of the wolfish mind of Eormanric: far and wide he ruled the people of the realm of the Goths: he was a cruel king.'

The names in lines 5–8 are derived from *The Battle of the Goths and the Huns*, a very ancient and ruinous Norse poem embedded in *Heiðreks Saga* (also called *Hervarar Saga*), which is to be seen as the bearer of remote memories of the first Hunnish attacks on the Goths, with ancient names preserved in a traditional poetry.

Of these names, Angantýr is a Gothic king; and *Dúnheiðr*, scene of a great battle, probably contains Norse *Dúna*, the Danube. 'Danpar-banks' in Gunnar's earlier song (Lay of the Völsungs VII.14) and 'Danpar's walls' in the present stanza derive from the Norse *Danparstaðir*, a survival of the Gothic name of the river Dnieper. Of its occurrence in *Atlakviða* my father noted in his lecture that it was 'a reminiscence probably of Gothic power and splendour in the old days before Ermanaric's downfall'.

87 Snævar is named in *Atlamál* as one of Högni's sons (note to 59).

91 'ruth': sorrow, regret.

93–112 This part of the narrative in the Lay is entirely independent of the Norse sources. Atli, being released, now sent for reinforcements (93), while the Niflungs held the doors of the hall (95) – and in this the German tradition of the legend appears, but strongly influenced by the Old English poetic fragment known as *The Fight at Finnsburg* (which is not in itself in any way connected with the Niflung legend). Beside stanzas 96–99 may be set the opening of *The Fight at Finnsburg* (translation by Alan Bliss, cited from J.R.R. Tolkien, *Finn and Hengest*, ed. Bliss, 1982, p.147):

> ' . . . gables are burning.'
>
> Hnæf spoke, the warlike young king: 'Neither is this the dawn from the east, nor is a dragon flying here, nor are the gables aflame; nay, mortal enemies approach in ready

armour. Birds are crying, wolf is yelping; spear clashes, shield answers shaft. Now that this moon shines, wandering behind the clouds, woeful deeds are beginning, that will bring to a bitter end this well-known enmity in the people. Awaken now, my warriors! Grasp your coats of mail, think of deeds of valour, bear yourselves proudly, be resolute!'

In the Lay the fighting is said to have lasted for five days (102); and in *The Fight at Finnsburg* the same is said.

It is interesting to see that in lecture notes on the *Nibelungenlied* my father wrote 'compare Finnsburg' against his reference to the scene when Hagen (Högni) and his mighty companion Volker the Minstrel guarded at night the doors of the sleeping-hall where the Burgundians were quartered, and saw in the darkness the gleam of helmets. So also he wrote of the Old English poem in *Finn and Hengest* (edition referred to above, p.27): 'The Fragment opens with the "young king" espying an onset – like the helmets gleaming when the sleeping hall is attacked in the *Nibelungenlied*.'

The German tradition is again present in the burning down of the hall in which the Niflungs were besieged. But in the *Nibelungenlied*, and in the thirteenth century Norwegian *Thiðrekssaga* based on North German tales and songs, this is altogether differently motivated, for it was Kriemhild (Gudrún in the Norse legend) who inspired the invitation to Hunland, in order to get vengeance on Gunther and Hagen (Gunnar and Högni) for the murder of Siegfried (Sigurd). It was Kriemhild who gave the order for the hall in which the Nibelungs slept to be set on fire; whereas in the Lay of Gudrún it is one Beiti, counsellor of Atli, who was the instigator of the burning (105). But the detail of the trapped warriors drinking blood from the corpses (109) is derived from the *Nibelungenlied*.

In *Atlakviða* Gudrún set the hall on fire at the end of the poem, after the murder of Atli and their children, and this appears at the end of the Lay of Gudrún (153).

105 The name Beiti is derived from *Atlamál*, where he is Atli's steward (see note to 118–131).

112 'the Need of the Niflungs'. 'Need' is written with a capital because the phrase echoes the last words of the *Nibelungenlied*: 'Here the story ends: this was *der Nibelunge nôt.*' The word *nôt*, which is in origin the same as English *need*, refers to the terrible extremity and end of the Nibelungs.

113–116 Atli's treatment of the bound Gunnar before Gudrún's eyes, while taunting her with the vengeance now achieved for Sigurd, is found neither in the Eddaic poems nor in the *Völsunga Saga*; but it is the spring of Gudrún's 'ruthless hatred' (133) and of her insanely savage action after her brothers have been killed: she makes her demand for her brothers' lives (116) in the form 'by Erp and Eitill our own children' (and in 120 'by those born of us!').

114 'Budlung's vengeance': the vengeance of Atli son of Budli.

118–131 In *Atlakviða* Gunnar, asked if would purchase his life with the gold, replied that 'The heart of Högni must lie in my hand.' They cut the heart from one 'Hjalli the craven' instead, and laid it before Gunnar, who knew that it was not Högni's heart, because it quivered; but it is not in any way explained why they did this. Then they cut out Högni's heart, and Gunnar knew that it was his, since it quivered scarcely at all. In *Atlamál* it is Atli who commanded the cutting out of Högni's heart, but Beiti Atli's steward suggested that they take Hjalli the cook and swineherd instead, and spare Högni; they seized the screaming Hjalli, but Högni interceded for him, saying that he could not endure the noise, and that he would 'rather play out this game myself'. Then Hjalli was released, and Högni was killed, and there is no mention of the story of the two hearts.

In the Saga the two are rather crudely combined: Atli commands that Högni's heart be cut out, a counsellor of Atli proposes the substitution of Hjalli, Högni intercedes for him; Atli then tells Gunnar that he can only purchase his life by revealing where the treasure lies, Gunnar replies that he must first see Högni's heart, and so Hjalli is seized again and his heart cut out, and the rest of the story is as in *Atlakviða*.

In the Lay of Gudrún the sources are interwoven more skilfully: it is Gunnar who demands to see Högni's heart, as in *Atlakviða*, but an explanation is provided (121) for the preliminary assault on Hjalli the swineherd: 'wisemen bade him / wary counsel' (they told Atli to beware), fearing the queen's wrath. Högni does not intercede for Hjalli, but merely expresses his distaste for the shrieking; and the swineherd is given no respite.

120 'Of his troll's temper / yet true were the words!' Atli refers, I believe, to Gunnar's words (118) concerning Högni and the gold: 'to his latest breath / he will loose it not.'

122 'Woe worth the wiles': A curse on the wiles; cf. 'Woe worth the while' in the Lay of the Völsungs IX.29 and note.

124 'liever': more acceptable.

128-130 In *Atlakviða*, when they brought the heart of Högni to Gunnar, he declared that 'Always I had a doubt, while two of us lived; but now I have none, since I alone am living. The Rhine shall possess the gold that stirs men to strife, the Niflungs' inheritance. In the rolling water shall the fatal rings gleam, rather than that gold should shine on the hands of the sons of the Huns.'

The actual casting of the gold into the Rhine is not referred to in *Atlakviða* (as it is in the Lay, 130, line 5, 'in the deeps we cast it'), and this led to the contention that Gunnar meant no more than that he would rather see the hoard drowned in the Rhine than adorning the Huns. My father strongly rejected this, on several grounds: the syntax of the passage; the statement by Snorri Sturluson in the Prose Edda that 'before they [Gunnar and Högni] departed from their land they concealed the gold, the heritage of Fáfnir, in the Rhine river, and that gold has never since been found'; and the references in the *Nibelungenlied* to the sinking of the treasure in the Rhine. He thought it probable that it was already part of the legend when it came North.

He noted also that the answer to the question, if the treasure was in the Rhine, what would it matter whether Högni were alive or dead, must be that Högni was the only party to the secret of where in the great river it lay; so in the *Völsunga Saga* Gunnar says: 'And now I alone know where the gold is, and Högni will not tell you', and Snorri's 'that gold has never since been found'. 'Doubtless it could have been fished up,' my father wrote, 'if you knew just where to look.' He believed nonetheless that the episode was a later elaboration (he called it 'theatrical-dramatic'), not perfectly fitting with the Rhine-gold motive: see further the note to 148–150.

130 lines 5–8: compare the lines from near the end of *Beowulf*, 3166–8:

> forleton eorla gestreon   eorðan healdan,
> gold on greote,   þær hit nu gen lifað
> ealdum swa unnyt,   swa hit æror wæs.

They gave the ancient wealth   to earth's keeping,
under stone the gold,   that there still dwelleth
as profitless to men   as it proved of yore.

(From an alliterative translation by my father of *Beowulf*
lines 3137–82.)

132–140   In *Atlamál* it is said, and it is repeated by Snorri,
that Gunnar in the snake-pit played the harp with his
feet, an idea that may have arisen from the observation
that he was bound, as is told in *Atlakviða* (and in the Lay,
113). In the Lay, following *Atlakviða*, Gunnar used his
hands. Other features of this episode in the Lay are
derived from the Saga: that Gudrún sent him the harp
(135), that his playing put the serpents to sleep (136), and
that he was finally stung to death by a huge adder (139).

141–147   The great funeral pyres are not in the Eddaic
poems, but Gudrún's revenge on Atli is told in both – the
same hideous motive as appears in the Greek legend, told
by Ovid in the *Metamorphoses*, of Procne, who for
vengeance killed her own son Itys and gave his flesh to
her husband, Tereus King of Thrace, to eat.

142   Lines 5–8 are repeated almost exactly from the first
stanza of the poem, where they are used of the pyre of
Sigurd and Brynhild.

148–50   I have said (p.312) that my father 'tentatively interpreted the state of *Atlakviða* as the reworking of an earlier

330

poem, a reworking that had then itself undergone "improvements", additions, losses, and disarrangements'. He believed that both the 'Högni-Hjalli episode' (see note to 118–131) and Gudrún's revenge on Atli through their own children were later elaborations by 'the *Atlakviða* poet' on the earlier poem that he was reworking.

This last section of *Atlakviða*, constantly difficult to interpret in the detail of its language, is not altogether intelligible at large, logically or psychologically. As it stands, Gudrún came to meet Atli when he returned from the murder of Gunnar in the snake-pit and welcomed him to the feast with a golden cup (cf. the Lay, stanza 145), brought drink and food to the assembled company, waited on Atli – and then declared with ghastly clarity what she had done and what they were doing. A great cry of horror and noise of weeping arose from the benches, but Gudrún did not weep: 'she scattered gold, with red rings enriched the men of her household. . . . Atli unsuspecting had drunk himself bemused; weapons he had not, he was not ware of Gudrún' (this last phrase is my father's translation of a Norse verb of uncertain meaning here). Then follows Gudrún's murder of Atli in his bed before she set the hall on fire.

'Why the distribution of gold,' my father wrote, 'when no help or favour was needed by Gudrún, or could be expected by a declared murderess of princes? Why the foolishness of Atli not suspecting Gudrún?'

His tentative solution was to suppose that while the perishing of Atli's son, or sons, may have been a very old part of the legend, it was not originally an essential part of Gudrún's revenge. The form in which we here find it interwoven (he wrote) is certainly mainly a Norse development, and the end of a long process. It is probable that it was not present in the 'original source' of *Atlakviða*, and that its introduction and interweaving with the main theme of revenge was the work of the *Atlakviða* poet.

He supposed that in an earlier form the story would have moved, after the funeral feast, to the verse describing Gudrún's gold-giving, which would in this case be naturally interpreted as her continuing the pretence of cheerfulness, and acceptance, distributing rich gifts to allay suspicion. Then Atli, 'unsuspecting' – because he had no reason for suspicion – went to his bed very drunk (this being one of the oldest elements in the whole story, see Appendix A, pp.345–46). But when the motive of the murdered children entered it had necessarily to be introduced in the course of the funeral feast. The stanzas referred to above were retained, but they were not successfully fitted to the insertion ('Why the distribution of gold? Why the foolishness of Atli?').

In his Lay of Gudrún my father devised a remedy for this in Atli's swoon of horror that caused the servants to carry him to his bed (148–149).

The author of *Atlamál* here suddenly turns to a tradition that Högni had a son who avenged him on Atli, and says (followed by the Saga, and by Snorri) that this son, who has not been previously mentioned in the poem, aided Gudrún in the murder. As is to be expected, this has no place in the Lay of Gudrún.

152–154   The burning of the hall by Gudrún is derived from *Atlakviða*: see note to 93–112.

156   Lines 5–8 are almost the same as the last lines of the Lay of the Völsungs (IX.82), and become also the last lines of the Lay of Gudrún (stanza 165) before the parting words of the poet to his audience.

157–165   In a pencilled note on the manuscript my father wrote that all the conclusion of the poem from stanza 157 should be omitted, only the final stanza 166 being retained. Rough lines drawn on the manuscript, however, show the omission as extending only to stanza 164, so that the last four lines of 156 are the same as the last four lines of 165 immediately following.

159–165   The verses given to Gudrún as she sits beside the sea are inspired by the late Eddaic poem *Guðrúnarhvöt*, but there is little close correspondence. The latter part of that brief lay is one of several 'Laments of Gudrún'; but it includes her grief over the final element in the Northern legend, which for his purposes in these poems my father excluded.

In *Guðrúnarhvöt* Gudrún tells that she attempted to drown herself in the sea, but the waves cast her up (as in the Lay of Gudrún 158), and her story was not ended. Early on, a wholly distinct and very ancient Gothic legend was threaded on to the acquisitive Niflung theme.

This legend concerned the death of the Ostrogothic king Ermanaric (see note to 86) at the hands of two brothers, in revenge for the murder of their sister; and the sister, Swanhild (*Svanhildr*), became the wife of Ermanaric and the daughter of Sigurd and Gudrún, her brothers (Hamðir and Sörli) the sons of Gudrún by her third and last marriage to a shadowy king named Iónakr.

Earlier in the Lay of Gudrún, when Gunnar sang of ancient Gothic deeds (86), he named Iormunrek (Ermanaric); and this of itself shows that my father was cutting away the Gothic legend from his Niflung poem, and setting Iormunrek in a historical context – for in history Ermanaric died some sixty years before Gundahari (Gunnar) king of the Burgundians.

Only in *Guðrúnarhvöt* is there any reference in Norse literature to the manner of Gudrún's death (self-destruction on a funeral pyre); but in the Lay of Gudrún she utters her lament, and again giving herself to the waves is this time taken.

APPENDICES

APPENDIX A

A short account of the
ORIGINS OF THE LEGEND

§I Attila and Gundahari

In both Lays my father used the expression 'Borgund lord(s)', chiefly in reference to Gunnar, or Gunnar and Högni (who are also called 'Gjúkings' and 'Niflungs'). In the commentary on the Lay of the Völsungs, VII.15, I have explained that he derived the name 'Borgund' from a single occurrence in *Atlakviða* of the title *vin Borgunda* 'lord of the Burgundians', applied to Gunnar, and that nowhere else in Norse literature was Gunnar remembered as a Burgundian. In this title appears one of the chief elements in the legend.

The Burgundians were in origin an East Germanic people who came out of Scandinavia; they left their name in Bornholm (Norse *Borgunda holm*), the island that rises from the Baltic south-east of the southern tip of Sweden. In the Old English poem *Widsith* they are named together with the eastern Goths (Ostrogoths) and the Huns: 'Attila ruled the Huns, Ermanaric the Goths, Gifica the Burgundians', which may be taken to be a memory of a time when the Burgundians still dwelt in 'East Germania'; but they moved westwards toward the Rhineland, and it was there that disaster overtook them.

Early in the fifth century they were settled in Gaul, in a kingdom on the west bank of the Rhine centred on Worms (south of Frankfurt). In the year 435, led by their king Gundahari, the Burgundians, impelled as it seems by the need for land, embarked on an expansion westwards; but they were crushed by the Roman general Aetius and forced to sue for peace. Two years later, in 437, they were overwhelmed by a massive onslaught of the Huns, in which Gundahari and a very large number of his people perished. It has been commonly supposed that the Roman Aetius, whose primary purpose was to defend Gaul from the encroachments of the barbarians, called in the Huns to destroy the Burgundian kingdom of Worms. There is no reason to suppose that Attila was the leader of the Huns in this battle.

But the Burgundians of the Rhineland were not wholly destroyed in 437, for it is recorded that in 443 the survivors were allowed to settle as colonists in the region of Savoy. A curious glimpse of them is found among the writings of Sidonius Apollinaris, a cultivated Gallo-Roman aristocrat, Imperial politician, and poet, born in Lyons about 430, and in his later years the bishop of Clermont, the chief city of the Auvergne. He left in his letters a portrait of the manners and mode of life in the strange society of southern Gaul in the fifth century.

But to the fastidious Sidonius the gross Burgundians were repellent and their culture wholly without interest. In a satirical poem he complained humorously of having to sit among the long-haired barbarians (who were excessively fond of him) and be forced to endure Germanic speech: to praise with a wry face the songs sung by the gluttonous, seven foot tall Burgundians, who greased their hair with rancid butter and reeked of onions. Thus we learn nothing from him of the songs which were sung by the contemporaries of Gundahari and Attila, but only that his own muse fled away from the noise.

That they preserved their traditions, however great the disaster of 437, is suggested by a Burgundian code of laws drawn up King Gundobad not later than the early sixth century, in which the names of ancestral kings are cited: Gibica, Gundomar, Gislahari, Gundahari. These names all appear in later legend, though it cannot be known what were the historical relationships between them. *Gundahari* is *Gunnarr (vin Borgunda)* in Norse. He appears in Old English in the very dissimilar but ultimately identical form *Guðhere*: in the poem *Widsith* the minstrel says that when he was 'among the Burgundians'

me þær Guðhere forgeaf   glædlicne maððum
songes to leane;   næs þæt sæne cyning.

('there Guðhere gave me a glorious jewel in reward for my song: he was no sluggish king.') In the German tradition he is *Gunther.*

Gibica, in the form *Gifica*, appears in the Old English *Widsith* as the ruler of the Burgundians together with the rulers of the Goths and the Huns, as I have mentioned above. In Norse the name became by regular phonetic change *Gjúki*, who is the father of Gunnar; in forms of the German tradition *Gibeche* is likewise the father of Gunther; but (especially in view of the placing of Gifica in *Widsith*) it may be that he was in history an illustrious ancestor of an older time.

'It is easy to understand,' wrote R.W. Chambers in his edition of *Widsith* (1912) 'why the story of the fall of Gundahari and his men in battle against the Huns was of interest not merely to the Burgundian, but to all his neighbours, till, as the centuries passed, it became known from end to end of Germania. Eight centuries after his fight Gundahari was still remembered from Iceland to Austria.'

With this view my father did not altogether concur. In notes for lectures primarily on the knowledge of the Völsung legend among Old English poets, he said: 'Guðhere's tale is one of downfall after glory – and sudden downfall, not slow decay – sudden and overwhelming disaster in a great battle. It is the downfall, too, of a people that had already had an adventurous career, and disturbed things in the west by their intrusion and by the rise of a considerable power at Worms. It is easy to see how their defeat by Aetius only two years previously would be telescoped in the dramatic manner of legend into the defeat by the Huns (if not actually connected in history, as it may have been).

'Guðhere, already valiant and a generous goldgiver as patron in *Widsith*, must have been *very renowned*. Mere downfall, without previous glory, did not excite minstrels to admiration and pity. However, we are probably not far wrong in guessing that there must – quite early – have been some other element than mere misfortune in this tale to give it the fire and vitality it clearly had: living as it did down the centuries. What this was we can hardly guess. Gold? It may well have been that gold, or the acquisition of some treasure (that later still became connected with some renowned legendary gold) was introduced to explain Attila's attack. Attila (when legend or history is not on his side) is represented as grasping and greedy. It may have been in this way that Guðhere ultimately got connected with the *most* renowned hoard, the dragon's hoard of Sigemund [in Old English], of Sigurd [in Old Norse].'

My father did not mean to imply that, in history, Attila was the leader in the attack on the Burgundians in 437, for which there is no evidence. He saw that 'Attila only appears in the story by an early legendary, or dramatic, simplification and heightening of the importance of the battle in which Guðhere perished. He became essential to it.' In the eighth century the Lombard historian Paul the Deacon (monk of Monte Cassino) knew Attila as the foe; and from his account it is seen that by then the tradition was that Gundahari was not slain in his own town of Worms, but marched eastwards to meet Attila: and this was an invariable feature of the legend in all its forms.

Profound as was the impression made in Germanic legend by the colossal figure of Attila, there is no occasion in this book to outline the history of the most renowned of all the barbarian kings, which necessarily involves the political and military complexities, often obscure, of his relations with the disrupted Empire; and indeed, in the development of the legend in Norse, it could be said that it was the manner of his death that counted for more than his life. At the same time there is no need, I think, to pass over altogether the extraordinarily clear glimpse of that fearful tyrant and destroyer that survives from more than fifteen centuries ago (in such contrast to Gundahari, of whose personal characteristics we know nothing at all).

This is owing to an accomplished and well-informed historian named Priscus of Panium (that being a town of Thrace), whose large work in Greek *Of Byzantium and the events connected with Attila* survives, lamentably, only in fragments; but one of those fragments contains the story of his journey into Hungary as a member of a small diplomatic deputation to Attila sent out from Constantinople, capital of the Eastern Empire, in the summer of the year 449. Attila received the Roman embassy in the village of wooden buildings that was his headquarters, standing in the midst of a vast plain without stone or tree; and Priscus not only narrowly observed the banquet at which Attila presided, and much else, but described it in such sharp detail as to suggest that he took notes at the time of all that he saw. In this unique account of a barbarian banquet in the Heroic Age Priscus described the elaborate and interminable ceremony in which Attila drank to the health of each guest in turn, and the fine feast served on looted silver dishes with looted drinking-cups of silver and gold – in contrast to the unadorned simplicity of

Attila, who drank from a wooden cup and ate only meat, on a wooden plate. He described the entertainment provided: there were singers who chanted songs in praise of the great deeds of Attila; there was a madman, and a buffooning dwarf, who aroused loud laughter, but not from Attila, who sat through all this in grim and rigid silence. But when his youngest son Ernac entered the hall Priscus saw that Attila looked at him 'with softened gaze' and stroked his face. He asked a Hun who sat beside him for an explanation of this, and he replied that the soothsayers had told Attila that the fortunes of his family would fail, but would be restored to greatness by this son. The carouse lasted far on into the night, but the Romans prudently withdrew long before it ended.

A description of the physical appearance of Attila is found in the work of a sixth-century historian of the Goths named Jordanes, and this description is directly derived from Priscus, though the original is lost. He was short in stature with a broad chest; his small beady eyes were set in a huge face; his nose was flat and his skin swarthy, his beard straggly and flecked with grey. His step was haughty, and he had a way of darting his glance hither and thither, 'so that the power of his great spirit appeared in the movement of his body'.

Most important for the large evolution of the legend was the great event of the year 451, the most famous battle of that age. In that year Attila moved with a huge army westwards towards the Rhine, mounting an attack on Gaul for which his motives are obscure. The Huns had destroyed the Ostrogothic power in the east in the fourth century, and Attila ruled over a great mixed dominion, as the Goths had done under Ermanaric (see the commentary on the Lay of Gudrún, stanza 86, pp.322–3). In his empire, and so also in his armies, were many East Germanic peoples; and now in his host came the Ostrogoths under their king Valamer, the Gepids under Ardaric, Rugians, Thuringians, and warriors of other nations beside. Against them came in uneasy alliance the Visigoths (the western Goths) of Tolosa (Toulouse) under their aged king Theodoric, Aetius the Roman general, Burgundians from their new lands in Savoy, Franks, even a contingent of Saxons. The battle is known as the Catalaunian plains (the plain of Champagne) and the Mauriac plain; it was fought in the region of Troyes (a hundred miles south-east of Paris).

Of the course of the battle very little is known. Jordanes, writing a century later, said that it was *bellum atrox, multiplex, immane, pertinax* (ferocious, confused, monstrous, unrelenting). Theodoric, king of the Visigoths, was among the vast numbers of the slain. The fighting continued into the night, and Attila retreated into his camp, which he had fortified with waggons. According to Jordanes, he had a great funeral pyre heaped up out of horses' saddles on which he intended to be burnt before final defeat should overtake him.

But the final assault was never made. The alliance against him broke up. Again according to Jordanes, the imminent prospect of the total destruction of the Huns filled Aetius with alarm. His deepest fear was the power of the Visigothic kingdom in the south of France, centred on Toulouse; and despite the eagerness of the young king of the Visigoths, Thurismund, to avenge on the Huns the death of his father in the battle, Aetius advised him to return to Toulouse, lest his brothers should seize the throne in his absence. This counsel Thurismund accepted ('without perceiving its duplicity'); the Visigoths departed from the battlefield, and Attila was allowed to escape from Gaul.

In the year 452, following the great battle, Attila crossed the Alps, and came down into Italy from the north-east. The cities of the north Italian plain were not only ravaged by the Huns but in some cases actually razed to the ground. Aquileia at the head of the Adriatic, which both as fortress and great trading centre was one of the foremost cities of northern Italy, was so utterly destroyed that when Jordanes wrote, a century later, there was scarcely a trace of it to be seen. Patavium suffered the same fate, and though unlike Aquileia it rose again, it is a striking fact that Padua has no Roman remains.

But Attila never crossed the Apennines, making for Rome. Whatever the reason, he returned to Hungary; and in the following year, 453, he died. The story of his death is known from Jordanes; but Jordanes expressly stated that he was following the authority of Priscus, and it can be taken to be precise history.

Attila in this year added one more to his many wives (*innumerabiles uxores* in Jordanes' words: the Huns were highly polygamous). His wife was a very beautiful girl named Ildico (it has been commonly thought probable that her name shows her to have been of Germanic origin – a diminutive form of *Hild*, or any name ending in *-hild*; perhaps a Burgundian). At the wedding feast Attila became hugely drunk and took to his bed, 'heavy with wine and sleep'; and there as he lay on his back he suffered a violent nose-bleeding, and was choked to death by the blood passing down his throat. Late on the following day his servants broke down the doors and found him lying dead and covered with blood 'without a wound', his bride weeping, covered by her veil.

Jordanes described the funeral of Attila, clearly still following the lost narrative of Priscus. His body was laid in a silken tent out on the plain, and the finest horsemen of the Huns rode round in circles, 'after the manner of the circus-games'; and they told of his deeds in a funeral song. After wild extremes of grief and joy his body was buried at night, covered in gold, and silver, and iron, with weapons taken from his enemies and many treasures; and then, 'in order that human curiosity should be kept away from such riches', those who performed the work of burial were killed. In the same way, after the death of Alaric king of the Visigoths in 410, the captives were made to divert the mountain-river Busento in Calabria from its bed, and then after the burial of the king and the returning of the river to its ordinary course they were all put to death.

But the figure of Attila rose from his tomb and took different shapes in the centuries that followed. Among Latin-speaking peoples he was taken up into what has been called 'ecclesiastical mythology', and became *Flagellum Dei*, the Scourge of God, divinely appointed to the devastation of a wicked world. In the lands of Germania there were two radically distinct traditions concerning him: he appears in a double light, generous patron and monstrous foe, and it is not difficult to see how this should have come about. On the

Catalaunian plains there was a colossal conflict between men of many Germanic nations. As I have said, in the hosts of Attila went men of many East Germanic peoples subject to the Huns, most notably the Ostrogoths, and for them Attila was the great King and overlord, to whom their own kings paid allegiance: indeed his very name *Attila* looks like a diminutive form of the Gothic word *atta*, 'father'. In South German (High German) tradition Attila, his name changed in the course of time through phonetic movement to *Etzel*, is a benevolent monarch, hospitable and ineffectual, far removed from the Attila of history.

But in more northerly lands his legendary image was derived from his enemies, and thence, by whatever route it came, the Scandinavians derived their grim and covetous king *Atli*, murderer of the Burgundians for the sake of the Nibelung hoard.

The story that Jordanes, following Priscus, told of the manner of Attila's death is beyond question the historical fact; and the knowledge that that was how he died was known to Chaucer more than nine hundred years later. His scoundrelly Pardoner finds in the death of Attila an anecdote to illustrate the evil of drunkenness:

> Looke, Attila, the gretë conqueróur,
> Deyde in his sleepe, with shame and dishonóur,
> Bledynge ay at his nose in dronkenesse;
> A capitayn sholde lyve in sobrenesse.

But a chronicler named Marcellinus Comes, writing in Constantinople at about the same time as Jordanes, knew a different story: Attila was stabbed in the night by a woman. It may well be that this story originated almost as soon as the true report – it was lying ready to hand.

In very brief remarks on this matter, my father sketched out his view of the further evolution of the Burgundian legend when the story that Attila was murdered by his bride had taken root. Such a deed must have a motive, and no motive is more likely than that it was vengeance for the murder of the bride's father, or kinsmen. Attila had come to be seen as the leader of the Huns in the massacre of the Burgundians in 437 (see p.341); now, the murder was done in vengeance for the destruction of Gundahari and his people. Whether or not Ildico was a Burgundian, her rôle in the evolving drama must make her so. And she avenges her brother, Gundahari.

The essential features of the Burgundian story are then present. Gundahari-Gunnar, *vin Borgunda*, was killed by Attila-Atli, and for this he was murdered, *in his bed*, by a woman. And the woman was Gudrún. But where the *gold* came from is of course a different question.

§ II Sigmund, Sigurd and the Nibelungs

As the story of the Burgundians evolved it became inter-twined with a legend (or legends) distinct in nature and origin: the dragon-slayer and his golden hoard, and the mys-terious Nibelungs (German *Nibelungen*, Norse *Niflungar*).

348

When that conjunction and combination took place cannot be said, but it seems plain that it was made in Germany, and not in Scandinavia.

This is a matter that raises many questions that cannot be certainly resolved, and its study has been marked by severe disagreements. My father took a deep interest in it; but in his lectures at Oxford he approached it primarily from his desire to convey an idea of the largely vanished heroic poetry of ancient England. Since in this book my object is to present his poems expressly in terms of his own beliefs and opinions, it seems best to introduce this sketch of the subject in the same way, with the same question: what can be learned of it from the scraps and fragmentary references of Old English poetry?

In fact, there is only one text from which to look for an answer to that question, namely, a passage in *Beowulf*. I give this passage here in my father's translation of the poem, which he made, I incline to think, at some time not far distant from that in which he wrote the Lay of the Völsungs and the Lay of Gudrún.

Returning from their riding from the hall of Heorot to see the mere into which Grendel had plunged dying, the knights were entertained by a minstrel of the king.

> At whiles a servant of the king, a man laden with proud memories who had lays in mind and recalled a host and multitude of tales of old – word followed word, each truly linked to each – this man in his turn began with skill to treat in poetry the quest of Beowulf and in flowing verse to utter his ready tale, interweaving words.

He recounted all that he had heard tell concerning Sigemund's works of prowess, many a strange tale, the arduous deeds of the Wælsing and his adventures far and wide, deeds of vengeance and of enmity, things that the children of men knew not fully, save only Fitela who was with him. In those days he was wont to tell something of such matters to his sister's child, even as they ever were comrades in need in every desperate strait – many and many of the giant race had they laid low with swords. For Sigemund was noised afar after his dying day no little fame, since he, staunch in battle, had slain the serpent, the guardian of the Hoard. Yea he, the son of noble house, beneath the hoar rock alone did dare the perilous deed. Fitela was not with him; nonetheless it was his fortune that the sword pierced through the serpent of strange shape and stood fixed in the wall, goodly blade of iron; the dragon died a cruel death. The fierce slayer had achieved by his valour that he might at his own will enjoy that hoard of rings; the boat upon the sea he laded and bore to the bosom of his ship the bright treasures, the offspring of Wæls was he. The serpent melted in its heat.

He was far and wide of adventurers the most renowned throughout the people of mankind for his works of prowess, that prince of warriors – thereby did he aforetime prosper – after the valour and might of Heremod, his might and prowess, had failed . . .

The remainder of the passage concerns the Danish king Heremod and does not bear on the question at issue here. In a lecture on the subject my father set down what he called 'preliminary points' – considerations arising from the Old

English evidences alone, without looking further afield. In what follows I give them in abbreviated form but almost entirely in his own words.

There cannot be any serious doubt that the reference in *Beowulf* is to a story related to the Völsung and Nibelung legends of other lands. The names Sigemund, Wælsing, Fitela (and his relation *nefa* to *eam* [nephew to uncle] of Sigemund), and the dragon with his hoard, must on grounds of philology and legend be ultimately the same as Old Norse *Sigmundr* son of *Völsung*, with his sister-son *Sin-fjötli*. This remains true in spite of the serious discrepancies: e.g. that Sigemund (not his son: no hint of whose existence is given) slew the dragon; or that a boat, not a horse, is the vehicle for the treasure.

The Burgundians are not referred to at all in *Beowulf*. Neither are many, certainly renowned, figures of Germanic story. The argument from silence is peculiarly perilous in dealing with remnants so haphazard and tattered as those we possess of Old English heroic traditions; and might seem absurd when applied to *Beowulf*, which is a poem, not a cat-alogue. Yet it actually has some point in this case. The Burgundian names *were* known to Old English, and the sub-jects of verse and tale. We cannot be certain that such a con-nexion was not present to the mind of the author of *Beowulf*. But it does not look like it.

The Burgundians are indeed known. But where we meet them in Old English, we find an exact reversal of the case in

Beowulf. No reference, at any rate, is made to their connexion with Sigemund Wælsing. The very early poem *Widsith* reveals a wide-flung interest in a huge nexus of legend: admittedly, specially devoted to the Goths or the northern sea-peoples, but it is not silent on more southern Germanic topics. It refers to Guðhere and to Gifica. It does not refer at all to Sigemund, or Wælsing, or Fitela, or the dragon. (*Widsith* has indeed a specially historical tendency.)

Certain reference to the 'Wælsingas' is indeed in Old English literature confined to *Beowulf*. [My father added 'literature' on account of the place-name *Walsingham* in Norfolk.] If we add to this the absence in nomenclature of the special names peculiar to this story in its full-grown form (Guðrún, Grímhild, Brynhild) we shall be forced at the outset to conclude that it is probable:

that Sigemund Wælsing had no pre-eminent place in Old English traditions, in spite of the words *wreccena mærost* used of him in *Beowulf* [in the translation given above 'of adventurers the most renowned'], which may be no more than poetic for 'a famous adventurer';

that his tale from the earliest times was of the more mythical-legendary kind – not one of the historical-legendary traditions;

that it was not concerned with Burgundians, who certainly were originally figures of history, but with the dark background of the story that in High German had practically faded out of memory: the part that in Old Norse (though remodelled and drastically altered) concerns the mysterious Odinic Völsungs before the advent of Sigurd. The names are

Sigemund, Fitela, Wælsing: these we can find trace of (even outside *Beowulf*). The names – women's names especially – which mark the vital connexion with the Burgundians and their fall cannot be discovered in Old English times in Old English form.

These are only *probable* considerations. But they are important even so. For the tone, manner, and details of the Old English references are peculiarly important. In general we are likely to get in Old English allusions to an earlier state in legendary development, before the confusion or combinations of later days in other lands. It is therefore vital to note that the most reasonable interpretation of Old English material is that the Sigemund story was originally of an older more mythical type; that it co-existed with the Burgundian legend, *but was not yet connected with it.*

The major problem raised by the passage in *Beowulf* in its relation to the Norse story as it appears in the *Völsunga Saga* is of course the fact that in *Beowulf* Sigemund is famed for his slaying of a dragon and the gaining of its treasure hoard, whereas in Norse Sigmund has nothing to do with any dragon, and it is Sigmund's son Sigurd who is the famous dragon-slayer. Some scholars have held that Sigemund's dragon in *Beowulf* originally belonged to Sigurd, but was transferred to Sigemund when the two came to be linked as father and son. Others have said that there is no reason to suppose that the author of the Old English poem had ever heard of Sigurd. Some have said that Sigemund and Sigurd were originally wholly independent heroes; others, that one hero became divided into two.

My father accepted that his view was necessarily speculative, but nonetheless favoured it strongly.

'We cannot tell if Old English knew of a famous son of Sigemund. But in favour of the highly probable answer "it did not" are these considerations.

'In the first place, great heroes (*wreccena maerost*), especially if untrammelled by history, are apt to generate sons who carry on or duplicate their father's deeds, to satisfy the desire for more, or to introduce new elements, or to link with other tales.

'In the second place, no such son is anywhere mentioned in Old English.

'And in the third place, when such a son appears, his function is solely to connect with and become a chief character in the Burgundian story, *to bring the gold into it* – and where he exists he has his father's dragon and gold exploits attached to him. But in Old English these are not yet detached from Sigemund.'

My father did not discuss in his lecture notes other and strongly divergent opinions on this subject, apart from some remarks on the view that Sigemund's dragon in *Beowulf* is a dragon of a very different sort from Sigurd's, and that in fact they were unconnected. 'But it is a dragon,' he wrote. 'And dragons are not common as essential actors in Germanic stories – in spite of the impression given by their being prominent in the Völsung stories and *Beowulf*. It is highly unlikely – however different in detail – that there should be no connexion between Sigemund's *wyrm* and Fáfnir.

'This of course is immeasurably strengthened if we believe that in order to connect with the Guðhere (Gundahari, Gunnar) stories a son was given to Sigemund (naturally his name begins with *Sige-*), but that this stage, presumably reached in Low or High Germany first, was not reached in Old English (which probably drew from archaic sources, and did not reflect the state of the legend contemporarily in Scandinavia and Germany about the year 800 or later).'

He thought also that the origin of the *re-forging* of the great sword Gram (*Gramr*) – carried by both father and son – is to be found here. The fact that the second element in the son's name is not constant seemed to be significant. In Old Norse he is *Sigurðr,* derived from a deduced earlier form *Sigi-warð,* in Old English *Sigeweard,* later *Siward;* whereas the German name is quite distinct: *Siegfried (Sîfrit)* corresponds to an Old English *Sigefriþ.* That the element *mund* in the father's name is constant points, he thought, to its being the older form.

His belief that, as he said, we are in the presence of the *duplication* of a hero and his marvellous sword of strange origin – as opposed to the view that the father and the son were once entirely distinct and unconnected beings – leads to the conception, in his words, of a legendary hero of supreme valour and beauty, whose name began with the element *Sige-* 'victory'. The gleaming eyes of Sigurd (the Lay of the Völsungs VIII.29, IX.26,59) are probably an original trait. In all probability his most renowned exploits concerned a dragon and a hoard, and – possibly – a mysterious, half-supernatural bride.

Questions fundamental to the genesis of the legend are how it came about that the 'Dragon-hero' intruded into the story of Attila and the Burgundians, why the treasure-hoard of this hero was called the Hoard of the Nibelungs, and why the Burgundians themselves came to be called the Nibelungs. In the only lecture-notes of my father's on these matters, or at any rate in the only ones that survive, he indicated his own views very briefly (and not at all points in a way easy to interpret), no doubt because his primary concern was with the Sigemund passage in *Beowulf*. I shall not therefore enter into any close account of the numerous attempts to solve these baffling and tantalizing questions, but do no more than sketch out some essential aspects. I have also of necessity avoided reference to the German tradition, represented primarily by the *Nibelungenlied*, except where its evidence is essential even within these limits.

A widely held but by no means unchallenged theory rests upon the interpretation of the name *Nibelung (Niflung)* as etymologically related to a group of Germanic words meaning 'darkness' or 'mist' (modern German retains the word *Nebel* 'mist'). This is brought into connection with certain things said about the Nibelungs. Snorri Sturluson said of the grandsons of King Gjúki that they were 'black as a raven in the colour of their hair, like Gunnar and Högni and the other Niflungar'; and in a much earlier (ninth century) poem they are called *hrafnbláir* 'raven-black': in the Lay of the Völsungs (VII.10) it is said: 'As ravens dark were those raven-friends'.

An essential element in this theory is the figure of Högni, as he appears in German tradition. In the *Nibelungenlied* his name is Hagen, and he is not the brother of the Burgundians but their kinsman and vassal. Ferocious and cruel, hating Siegfried and indeed his murderer, he is very unlike the Norse Högni. In the *Thiðrekssaga*, a large compilation made in Norway, in Bergen, about the middle of the 13th century, but based on stories then current in North Germany, Högni, as he is named in this work, is the half-brother of the Burgundians, for a fairy or incubus slept with his mother, and the offspring of the union was Högni. In the *Thiðrekssaga* his appearance is troll-like, and he is said to have been all over dark, with black hair and black beard. Especially notable is the fact that the name Hagen/ Högni does not alliterate on G, showing that he did not originally belong to the Burgundian clan at all.

An important evidence appears at the beginning of the *Nibelungenlied.* When Siegfried arrived at the Burgundian court at Worms Hagen looked down from a window at the magnificent knight who had ridden in with a fine company; and guessing who it was he told King Gunther a story concerning a great exploit of Sigurd. With the air of a casual insertion, Hagen's story is briefly reported in the poem in a very obscure fashion, and I will refer here only to features essential for this purpose.

Siegfried was one day riding alone past a mountain, and he came upon many men gathered round a huge treasure which they had carried out of a cavern. For reasons that are not clearly explained Siegfried came into conflict with 'the bold Nibelungs', the two princes named Nibelung and Schilbung, and slew them, and their friends. He fought also with a dwarf named Alberich, and subdued him, but did not kill him: he had the hoard taken back into the cavern whence it had come, and made Alberich the guardian of the treasure. He was now the lord of 'Nibelungeland', the possessor of the great hoard, and for the rest of the first part of the *Nibelungenlied* he has the support of warriors from Nibelungeland, who are called Nibelungs. But in the second part of the German poem, which is held to rest on a quite different poetic source, the name 'Nibelungs' is applied, very strangely and on a first reading of the poem most disturbingly, in a totally different sense: it now means the Burgundians, just as it does in Norse.

Hagen also knew, and told this to Gunther, that Siegfried had slain a dragon and bathed in its blood, from which his skin grew so horny that no weapon would bite it. But this is in no way associated with the Nibelung hoard.

In the *Nibelungenlied* the hoard is associated with a dwarf, and a cavern in a mountain. What is the significance of the Dwarves?

In Norse mythology we are confronted, in the mythological poems of the Edda and also in Snorri Sturluson's treatise, with a great many scattered hints and observations about the minor beings of the immensely rich and many-peopled heathen supernatural world. Taken all together it is baffling; and beyond question there was once a whole world of thought and belief concerning these beings which is now almost totally lost. However, bearing in mind that Snorri was writing in the thirteenth century and that behind him stretch century upon century of unrecorded, various and shifting beliefs, we may notice what he says: which is, that there are the Light Elves, *Ljósálfar*, and the Dark Elves, *Dökkálfar*. The Light Elves dwell in a glorious place called *Álfheimr* (Elf-home, Elf-world), but the Dark Elves 'live down in the earth, and they are unlike the Light Elves in appearance, but much more unlike in nature. The Light Elves are fairer to look upon than the sun, but the Dark Elves are blacker than pitch.'

So far as we can now tell, there seems little difference between the Scandinavian Dark Elves, black as pitch and living underground, and the *Dvergar*, Dwarves; in fact Snorri more than once refers to Dwarves as inhabitants of *Svartálfaheimr*, the Land of the Dark Elves. The Dwarf Andvari, original owner of Fáfnir's treasure, dwelt, according to Snorri, in the Land of the Dark Elves (see the commentary on the Lay of the Völsungs, p.189): there he kept his hoard within a rock, and there Loki caught him.

Characteristics of the Dwarves in Old Norse literature may be briefly mentioned. They are above all master-craftsmen, the makers of marvellous treasures and wonderful weapons. The most renowned objects in the Norse myths were made by Dwarves: Ódin's spear Gungnir, Thór's hammer Mjöllnir, and Skíðblaðnir, the ship of the God Freyr, which could carry all the Gods, yet was made so intricately that it could be folded up like a napkin and put in a pouch.

Dwarves lived always underground or inside rocks (an echo was called *dverg-mál,* 'dwarf-talk'); and they possessed vast knowledge. If caught in the open after sunrise they were turned to stone. There is a poem in the Edda, the *Alvíssmál,* in which the God Thór asks many questions of a Dwarf named Allvíss ('All-wise'); and Thór kept him answering his questions so long that the sun came up. The poem ends with Thór crying: 'Dwarf, you are *uppi dagaðr*', you are 'dayed up', the sun has caught you.

The train of thought that emerges from all this will be clear, and the conclusion. Dark Elves, black as pitch, and Dwarves, closely related in Norse mythology if not identical, guardians of treasure in caverns and rocks; Alberich and Andvari; the origin of the Nibelung name in connection with 'darkness' words; Hagen's 'elvish' birth, his dark and troll-like appearance in *Thiðrekssaga.* On this theory, this is what the Nibelungs originally were: they were beings of darkness, Dark Elves or Dwarves, and Siegfried/Sigurd stole their great treasure from them.

This 'mythological' theory, or some form of it, is radically challenged by other scholars. From place-names and personal names in the region of Burgundian settlement there is evidence that is interpreted to mean that *Nibelung* was the name of a powerful Burgundian family or clan. Putting the matter in its simplest form, it is supposed on this basis that the (purely human) Nibelung clan of Burgundia either possessed very great wealth in historical fact, or else very early had it attributed to them; and 'the hoard of the Nibelungs' was the family treasure of the Burgundian kings.

That my father subscribed to the 'mythological' theory in some form is plain; but his view of the process by which the Burgundians became Nibelungs is nowhere clearly or fully expressed in his writings. He had suggested (see this Appendix p.341) that the connection of the 'Dragon-hero' with the Burgundian king Gundahari began with 'gold' as a motive to explain Attila's attack (when Attila had become the leader of the Huns in the destruction of the Burgundian kingdom of Worms). As Gundahari faded back into the past (he wrote), old legends of fairy-hoards localized on the Rhine naturally became attached to the famous king in Worms: 'this treasure probably had demon or dwarvish guardians already, but need not originally have been the same as Sigemund's gold, though it may well have been.'

'It would certainly seem', he said, 'that the gold-hero who intrudes into the Burgundians had already gathered round him *enemy Niflungar*, who robbed him of life, bride, and treasure. The historical Burgundians partly take their place, and though there is never complete fusion they are darkened.' He also saw it as virtually certain that the *Nibelungenlied* is the more original 'in making the demonic and cruel Hagen not a brother, but an associate vaguely connected with the Burgundians. Very likely Hagen/Högni is a relic of some old mythical figure connected originally with the gold, or at any rate with the mythical pre-Burgundian part of the "Sigurd" story.'

From observations such as these in his notes one can perhaps surmise that my father saw the genesis of the central part of the legend after this fashion. The Dragon-hero was already the robber of the Hoard of the dark, demonic Nibelungs (whom my father expressly saw as 'the original owners'), and he brought with him into the Burgundian legend the story of how the Nibelungs in revenge slew him, and took the treasure.

With the fusion of the two legends, the Burgundian princes necessarily became his enemies: he must be killed in order that they should become the possessors of the gold, and they drew into themselves, so to speak, something of the dark Nibelung nature. It was from the 'Nibelung' side of the composite legend that the 'demonic and cruel' Hagen ultimately came, with (in the *Nibelungenlied*) his lust for the gold and his guarding it to the death, his relentless hatred of Siegfried leading to his murder. Hagen became more or less assimilated to the Burgundians, and in the Norse (as Högni) wholly so; but the Burgundians on their side became Nibelungs, or Niflungar.

My father also surmised that the demonic bride was part of the complex of legend that was brought in with the Dragon-hero into the Burgundian story; and that when he brought with him his enemies the Nibelungs, they came not only as the robbers of his life and the treasure, but also of his betrothed. 'It seems probable,' he said, 'that the robbing of Sigurd of his bride by the *Niflungar* is part of the old legendary plot that was handed over to the Burgundians. And the Valkyrie-bride has all along retained too much that is fierce and inhuman about her for completely successful treatment.'

Thus, finally, the hoard of which Sigurd was robbed became (by a curious irony) the Hoard of the Nibelungs (as it had always been); for the Burgundians were now the Nibelungs. And Gunnar acquired the Valkyrie.

APPENDIX B

THE PROPHECY OF THE SIBYL

I include this poem by my father in rhyming couplets as a companion to the altogether distinct *Upphaf* to the Lay of the Völsungs, since it also was inspired by the Eddaic poem *Völuspá* (see the commentary on the Lay, pp.183–84).

It is found in a single very fine decorated manuscript; of earlier work there is now no trace. There is no evidence of any kind for its date, but on general grounds I would be inclined to ascribe it to the 1930s.

The Prophecy of the Sibyl

From the East shall come the Giant of old
and shield of stone before him hold;
the Serpent that the world doth bind
in towering wrath shall him unwind
and move the Outer Sea profound,
till all is loosed that once was bound.

Unloosed at last shall then set forth
the ship of shadow from the North;
the host of Hel shall cross the sea
and Loki shall from chain be free,
and with the wolf shall monsters all
upon the world then ravening fall.

Then Surtur from the South shall fare
and tree-devouring fire shall bear
that bright as sun on swords shall shine
in battle of the hosts divine;
the hills of stone shall bend their head;
all men the paths of death shall tread.

Then darkened shall the sunlight be,
and Earth shall founder under sea,
and from the cloven heavens all
the gleaming stars shall flee and fall;
the steam shall rise in roaring spires
and heaven's roof be licked with fires.

*

A house there is that sees no sun,
dark-builded on the beaches dun
where cold waves wash the Deadly Shore,
and northward looks its shadowy door;
the louver poisoned rain lets fall,
of woven serpents in the wall.

Laden in heavy streams there wade
men perjured, men who have betrayed
the trust of friend; and there the coward
and wolvish murderer is devoured:
the dragon who yet Yggdrasil
gnaws at the roots there takes his fill.

Dim-flying shall that dragon haste
over the beaches dark and waste,
up from the Nether-fells shall spring
bearing those corpses under wing,
then plunge, and sea close o'er his head
for ever, o'er the doomed and dead.

*

At last once more uprising slow
the Earth from Ocean green shall grow,
and falls of water shimmering pour
from her high shoulders to the shore;
the eagle there with lonely cry
shall hunt the fish on mountains high.

The younger gods again shall meet
in Idavellir's pastures sweet,
and tales shall tell of ancient doom,
the Serpent and the fire and gloom,
and that old king of Gods recall
his might and wisdom ere the fall.

There marvellous shall again be found
cast in the grass upon the ground
the golden chess wherewith they played
when Ásgard long ago was made,
when all their courts were filled with gold
in the first merriment of old.

A house I see that standeth there
bright-builded, than the Sun more fair:
o'er Gimlé shine its tiles of gold,
its halls no grief nor evil hold,
and there shall worthy men and true
in living days delight pursue.

Unsown shall fields of wheat grow white
when Baldur cometh after night;
the ruined halls of Ódin's host,
the windy towers on heaven's coast,
shall golden be rebuilt again,
all ills be healed in Baldur's reign.

APPENDIX C

FRAGMENTS OF A HEROIC POEM
OF ATTILA IN OLD ENGLISH

These verses in the old English alliterative metre were composed at some date unknown, but I think it at least very probable that they belong to the same period as all the writings in this book, my father's earlier years at Oxford after his departure from Leeds.

In content and internal sequence both pieces are closely based on the Old Norse *Atlakviða*. There is more than one copy of each, with minor progressive improvement. In each case I have appended a translation and a few explanatory notes.

I

This text corresponds to the first eight stanzas of *Atlakviða*. It is a part of the Norse poem that poses many difficulties and doubts; and it seems conceivable that my father selected it precisely because it is the beginning of the poem, as if at one time he thought to transform it in this way in its entirety. For the corresponding passage in the Lay of Gudrún see pp.265–67, stanzas 37–44.

Ætla Guðhere   ar onsende
cenne ridend – Cneofrið hatte – :
com to geardum Gifecan,   Guðheres healle;
beornas ymb heorðe   beore gefægon.
Druncon dryhtguman   on dreorsele,   5
mod miðende   meldan sæton;
Huna heteþanc   hæleþ ondreordon.
Secg suðlendisc   sliþan reorde,
Cneofrið ciegde   cuma on healle:
'Hider on ærende   Ætla mec sende   10
geond Wistlawudu   wegas uncuðe
mearh ridendne   midlbætedne;
het inc gretan wel,   Guðhere, beodan
þæt git helmum þeahte   to his ham cwomen.
Þær git sceld sculon agan   ond sceaft smeðne,   15
helm goldhrodene,   Huna mænigo,
sadol seolforweredne,   serc scynestan,
blancan betstan   bitolhæbbendne,
wæde wealhbeaswe,   ond wacne gar.
Cwæþ þæt he giefan wolde   inc Gnitanhæðe,   20
weald þone widan   on geweald sellan,
ofer giellendne gar   ond gylden stefn,
maðmas micle,   mearce Dænepes,
ond þæt mære holt – Myrcwudu hatte.'

Ða heafod hylde   helm Burgenda,   25
Hagenan sægde: 'Þa wit hyraþ swelc,
hwæt rædeþ unc se rinc,   runbora geonga?
On Gnitanhæðe   ic gold ne gefrægn

369

þæt wit oþres ne ahten   efnmicle sped.
Wit seld agon seofon   sweordum gefylled,   30
þára sint hiltu gehwilces   heawen of golde;
mearh is mín mærest,   mece betsta,
helm hwitesta   ond hilderand
ahyþed of horde   hean Caseres –
þonne ealra Huna   an is min betera.'   35

Hagena 'Hwæt biecnede seo bryd   þa heo unc beag
            sende,
weargloccum wand?   wearnunge geteah!
Þy ic wriðen fæste   þær wulfes hær
hares hæþstapan   on hringe fand,
wylfen, þæs ic wene,   bið uncer waþ heonan.'   40

Ætla sent to Guðhere a bold messenger
riding – Cnéofrið was his name:
he came to the courts of Gifeca, to the hall of
        Guðhere;
about the hearth warriors rejoiced in the ale.
The men of that company drank in the gloomy hall,   5
the *meldan* sat hiding their thoughts;
the warriors feared the hatred of the Huns.
The man from the south cried out with a fell voice,
Cnéofrið, the stranger in the hall:
'Hither upon an errand Ætla sent me   10
on unknown ways through the Vistula forest
riding the bit-bridled steed;
he bade me greet well you twain, Guðhere, and ask

that you come covered by your helms to his abode.
There you shall have shield and smooth-shaven lance 15
gold-adorned helmet, a great company of Huns,
silvered saddle, coat of mail most shining,
the finest horse that bears a bridle,
clothes of foreign scarlet, and slender spear.
He said that he would give to you Gnitanheath,   20
give into your power the wide woodland,
shrieking spear and golden prow,
great treasures, the abodes of the Dnieper,
and that forest renowned that is called Mirkwood.'

Then the lord of the Burgundians turned his head,   25
to Hagena he spoke: 'When we hear such things
what does he advise us, the young counsellor?
I have not heard of a gold hoard on Gnitanheath
that we twain did not possess another of as great
        abundance.
We have seven halls filled with swords,   30
the hilts of each of them hewn of gold;
my horse is the most renowned, my sword the best,
my helm the brightest, my battle-shield
plundered from the treasure of the high emperor –
mine alone is better than [those] of all the Huns.' 35

Hagena 'What did the bride signify when she sent us a ring,
wound it with wolf-hair? She offered us warning!
Fast bound on the ring I found the hair of a wolf,
of the grey heath-roamer:
wolvish, as I think, will be our journey hence.'   40

Notes

1 *Ætla, Guðhere*: the Old English forms of the Norse names Atli and Gunnar.

2 *Cnéofrið*: the name of Atli's messenger in *Atlakviða* is Knefröðr: see the commentary on the Lay of Gudrún, stanzas 37–48.

3 *Gifeca*: the Old English form of the Norse name Gjúki, father of Gunnar: see Appendix A, p.340.

5–6 In a lecture on the text of *Atlakviða* my father took the meaning of the verse at this point to be that there was merriment in the hall among Gunnar's folk, but the Hunnish envoys sat silent, hiding their thoughts. But his Old English verses may not proceed from this interpretation.

The Old English word *melda* means one who declares, tells, informs, or betrays. The man in *Beowulf* who stole the goblet from the dragon's hoard and led Beowulf and his companions to the lair is called a *melda*. But I do not know what significance my father gave to the word in this verse.

11 *Wistlawudu*. This name occurs in the poem *Widsith*:

> ful oft þær wig ne alæg,
> þonne Hræda here   heardum sweordum
> ymb Wistlawudu   wergan sceoldon
> ealdne eþelstol   Ætlan leodum.

'Seldom was warfare stilled, when the host of the Hrædas [Goths] about the Vistula forest had to defend with their swords their ancient dwelling-place from the people of Attila.'

The reference to *Wistlawudu* is a vestige of very ancient tradition; for it was about the end of the second century that the Goths departed on a vast south-easterly migration from the Baltic coast and the Vistula valley, and at length settled in the plains to the north of the Black Sea. But in *Widsith* 'the Vistula forest' is thought of as the primeval forest separating the territories of the Goths and the Huns, and is to be equated with *Myrkviðr* (see the commentary on the Lay of the Völsungs, VII.14 (pp.227–28): in *Atlakviða* Knefröðr says that he had ridden through *Myrkvið inn ókunna*, Mirkwood unexplored.

20 Ætla's offer (following *Atlakviða*) of 'Gnitanheath', where Fáfnir had his lair, as if it were a part of his dominion constitutes a problem to which a number of solutions have been proposed. My father thought it probable that there was an ancient association of Gnitaheiðr with a gold hoard, of which we know nothing, and that this caused it to be attracted to Fáfnir, that is, became later the name of the region where he had his lair and his treasure. I cannot account for the form *Gnitanheath*.

27 The word *runbora* seems not to be recorded in Old English, but I take it to mean 'one who bears *run*' in the sense of '(secret) counsel', hence 'counsellor', equivalent to the recorded word *rædbora* of the same meaning.

36 *Hagena*: Högni.

37 *weargloccum* 'wolf's hair': in Old English the word *wearg* was used exclusively of an outlaw or hunted criminal but Norse *vargr* retained in addition the sense 'wolf'. From this was derived the name of the *Wargs* of Middle-earth.

39 The word *hæðstapa* 'heath-roamer' occurs in *Beowulf*, where it is used of a stag. In *Atlakviða* the word used is *heiðingi*, of similar meaning: see the commentary on the Lay of Gudrún, stanzas 37–48, where the verse in the Norse poem is cited.

II

This second text corresponds to verses much further on in *Atlakviða*, beginning at stanza 24, *Hló þá Högni* . . . 'Then Högni laughed. . .' The passage in the Lay of Gudrún is stanzas 127–130.

After line 19 my father evidently rejected a passage from his poem, since it is not repeated in the finished copy. The Old English poem takes up again, and concludes, with *Atlakviða* stanza 32, *Lifanda gram* . . ., 'the living prince. . .'

Þa hlog Hagena   þe man heortan scear
of cwican cumbolwigan – cwanode lyt;
blodge on beode   to his breðer gæf.
Þa se gar-niflung   Guðhere spræc:
'Her is me heorte   Hagenan frecnan,   5
ungelic heortan   eargan Hellan;
bifaþ heo lythwon   nu on beode liþ,
efne swa lyt bifode   þa on breoste læg.
   Swa scealtu, Ætla,   ealdum maðmum,
leohte life samod   beloren weorðan!   10
Her æt anum me   is eal gelang
hord Niflunga,   nu Hagena ne leofað:
a me twegra wæs   tweo on mode;
untweo is me,   nu ic ana beom.
Rin sceal rædan   readum golde   15
wrohtweccendum,   wealcende flod
entiscum yrfe   Ealdniflunga;
blican on burnan   beagas wundene,
nealles on handum   Huna bearna!'

                    *

Leod lifigendne   on locan setton   20
Huna mænigo.   Hringbogan snicon,
wyrmas gewriðene   wagum on innan.
Slog þa Guðhere   gramhycgende
hearpan on heolstre.   Hringde, dynede,
streng wið fingre.   Stefn ut becwom   25
heaðotorht hlynnan   þurh harne stan

374

feondum on andan.   Swa sceal folccyning
gold guðfrea   wið gramum healdan.

Then Hagena laughed when they cut out the heart
from the living warrior – little did he wail;
on a dish, bleeding, to his brother they gave it.
Then spoke Guðhere, the spear-Niflung:
'Here I have the heart of Hagena the brave,   5
unlike the heart of the craven Hella;
little does it quake now it lies on the dish,
even so little did it quake when it lay in the breast.
    So shall you, Ætla, be deprived
of the old treasures, of light and life together;   10
to me alone belongs
all the hoard of the Niflungs, now Hagena lives not.
One of twain, ever was there doubt in my mind;
no doubt have I, now I am alone.
The Rhine shall rule the red gold   15
that stirs men to strife, the rolling flood [shall rule]
the heritage of the old Niflungs, come from giants.
The twisted rings shall gleam in the river
and by no means adorn the hands of the
children of the Huns.'

*

The living king they set in a fenced place,   20
the host of the Huns. Serpents were creeping,
coiled snakes within the walls,

but Guðhere wrathful-hearted struck
the harp in his hiding-place. Rang, resounded,
string against finger. His voice came   25
clear as a war-cry through the grey rock
in rage against his enemies. So shall a king of the people,
a warlike lord, guard his gold against foes.

Notes

2   The element *cumbol* in the compound word *cumbolwiga* meant an ensign, a banner.

4   *gar-niflung.* In earlier forms of this passage my father wrote *gimneoflung* here, at line 12 *hord Neoflunga*, and at line 17 *Ealdneoflunga.* I cannot account for these forms of the name, but in any case in the final text he returned to *Niflung, Niflunga.* In the earlier forms (only) he wrote the word *gar* 'spear' against *gim* 'jewel' in *gimneoflung*; but since the verse in *Atlakviða* has *Mærr kvað þat Gunnarr, geir-Niflungr* ('Glorious Gunnar spoke, the spear-Niflung') I have adopted this.

6   *Hella*: in *Atlakviða* and in the Lay of Gudrún the name of the thrall is Hjalli.

17 *entiscum yrfe.* This puzzling line depends on a very debatable verse in *Atlakviða*, in which the word *áskunna* 'of divine race' precedes *arfi Niflunga* 'the heritage of the Niflungs'. In his comments on this my father seems to have favoured *áskunna Niflunga* 'the Niflungs of divine race', while admitting that it is not clear what was meant by this, rather than taking it with *arfi*, saying that 'it is very dubious if one can speak of a hoard as being "of divine race".'

    In his Old English version he wrote first here *óscund yrfe* (where *óscund* means 'of divine race, divine', the word *ós* being the etymological equivalent of Norse *áss*, plural *æsir*), then changed it to the adjective *entisc* (and subsequently *entiscum*) 'giant, of giants' from the noun *ent* (from which was derived the name of the Ents of Middle-earth). In a subsequent copy he wrote *óscund* in the margin against *entisc*, as if still uncertain.

25–26   It is notable that almost exactly the same words

stefn in becom

heaðotorht hlynnan   under harne stan

appear in *Beowulf* lines 2552–3, where they are used of Beowulf's great cry of challenge at the approach of the dragon.